FROM
Too Young to Die

Or maybe she should explore her feelings about her family and friends. About how much she cared about them, and how precious they'd become during her illness. And what about life once she got out of the hospital? Would she be normal again? Who would ask her for a date? Who would ever kiss her or want her? Melissa sighed and thumbed through the blank pages. *Sixteen is too young to die,* she thought. She tossed the book aside, knowing that she had a lot to say and no earthly idea of how to say it.

FROM
Goodbye Doesn't Mean Forever

"People don't get what they deserve—good or bad. Life isn't always so logical."

"The rain falling on the just and unjust?" Jory asked.

"Yes, but regardless, we still have one very real thing going for us. We have hope, and I think that's what separates us from the rest of creation. We get to hold on to hope . . . hope for things not seen."

Jory was moved by Mrs. Austin's faith and she wondered if she'd ever feel that way herself. Would she ever come to accept gracefully what she couldn't understand or change?

ALSO AVAILABLE FROM DELL LAUREL-LEAF BOOKS

DAUGHTER OF VENICE, *Donna Jo Napoli*

SHABANU: DAUGHTER OF THE WIND
Suzanne Fisher Staples

DR. FRANKLIN'S ISLAND, *Ann Halam*

COUNTING STARS, *David Almond*

GODDESS OF YESTERDAY, *Caroline B. Cooney*

ISLAND BOYZ: SHORT STORIES, *Graham Salisbury*

SHATTERED: STORIES OF CHILDREN AND WAR
Edited by Jennifer Armstrong

THE LEGEND OF LADY ILENA, *Patricia Malone*

MIDNIGHT PREDATOR, *Amelia Atwater-Rhodes*

Lurlene McDaniel

ALWAYS
AND
FOREVER

Two Novels

LAUREL-LEAF BOOKS

Published by
Dell Laurel-Leaf
an imprint of
Random House Children's Books
a division of Random House, Inc.
New York

This edition contains the complete and unabridged texts of the original editions. This omnibus was originally published in separate volumes under the titles:
Too Young to Die copyright © 1989 by Lurlene McDaniel
Goodbye Doesn't Mean Forever copyright © 1989
by Lurlene McDaniel

Visit us on the Web! www.randomhouse.com/teens
Educators and librarians, for a variety of teaching tools, visit us at www.randomhouse.com/teachers

ISBN: 0-553-49419-8

Printed in the United States of America
First Laurel-Leaf Edition May 2004
OPM   10 9 8 7 6 5 4

CONTENTS

Too Young to Die

———

*Goodbye
Doesn't Mean Forever*

Too Young to Die

For my sons, Sean and Erik

———

"Not only so, but we also rejoice in our sufferings, because we know that suffering produces perseverance; perseverance, character; and character, hope. And hope does not disappoint us . . ."

ROMANS 5:3–5a (NIV)

Chapter One

~~~

"Melissa. Melissa Austin, are you awake?"

Melissa groaned at the sound of her name being whispered with repeated pokes in her side. She opened her eyes wide enough to see that her bedroom was still shrouded in darkness—pitch black darkness. What could Jory possibly want at this hour of the morning?

"Go away . . ." she muttered. Her arms and legs felt like lead weights, her brain foggy and disoriented. Every joint in her body ached.

Jory persevered. "But it's four A.M. Aren't we going with Michael as his spotters?"

It came back to Melissa in tiny spurts. Michael, her brother. Hot-air ballooning, his favorite sport. Jory Delaney, spending the night in order to drive Michael's pickup truck as his chase vehicle while he maneuvered his balloon into the Florida sunrise above. "It can't be four o'clock already. We only just went to sleep!"

"Correction," Jory said. "*You* fell asleep the minute you hit the bed. *I've* been up all night waiting for this."

Naturally Jory would be anxious, Melissa thought as she struggled again to clear her head from the cobwebs of sleep. She wished she felt better. "You've got to get over this fixation on my brother," she grumbled,

1

more annoyed at having to get up so early than with Jory. "He's twenty and you're sixteen—just like me. He's a sophomore at the junior college. You're a junior in high school—just like me. He's . . ."

". . . waiting for us in the kitchen. So get a move on," Jory directed, ignoring the facts that Melissa pointed out. "If Michael asked me to push peanuts with my nose on the streets of downtown Tampa, I'd do it. Remember Romeo and Juliet. Princess Di and Prince Charles. We're only talking four years here."

Jory flipped on the overhead light, and Melissa felt as if her eyeballs had been pricked with pins. She swung her legs over the side of her bed, stood, and almost fell over.

"Whoa. You okay?" Jory asked, already tugging on her jeans.

"Of course I'm okay," Melissa lied, feeling light-headed. "Just a little wobbly from lack of sleep." She ambled to her dresser and rummaged for jeans and a T-shirt, dragging her thick, straight, black hair out of her eyes. She had one leg in her jeans when Jory said, "Melissa, you're bleeding."

Sure enough, blood trickled down her tanned leg from below the knee. "Oh, I must've cut it when I shaved my legs last night."

"And it's still bleeding? You'd have thought it would have clotted by now."

"Could you hand me a tissue and that roll of tape? I don't think there are any more gauze bandages left."

Melissa wiped off the trail of blood and secured the tissue over the cut. It did seem odd that it was still bleeding hours later. She forgot the cut as she dabbed on blusher and lipstick and decided she should buy a concealer stick for the dark circles under her eyes.

"Are you coming?" Jory asked impatiently from

the doorway. "In lieu of a toothbrush, how about a mint? We've got to go!"

Melissa clasped her waist-length hair back and followed Jory into the kitchen where Michael was already waiting. "I thought I was going to have to wake you two myself," he muttered. "I've made coffee for the thermos and there's granola bars in the cupboard. Let's get going." He was dressed in well-worn jeans, and his black hair was still damp from a shower, all five foot ten of him smelling of clean, fresh soap.

"Sorry," Melissa said, catching the keys that he tossed for his pickup truck.

"I'll ride in the back with the balloon. We've got twenty minutes to get to the field and meet the others."

Melissa sensed Jory's disappointment. "Why don't you drive?" she suggested to Michael. "We can all crowd into the cab."

Michael turned his sapphire-blue eyes toward her. Sometimes looking at him was like looking into a mirror. He had the same square face, high, angular cheekbones, and dark eyebrows as she. "All right," he said. "At least I drive faster than you." Jory flashed Melissa a glance that screamed *thank you!*

Outside the dark morning was humid and heavy. Melissa walked around Jory's new white convertible, running her hands along the gleaming paint covetously. The three of them squeezed into the cab of Michael's beat-up truck, and Melissa waved Jory in first, making certain she was wedged in the middle.

Michael sipped coffee from a Styrofoam cup, driving with one wrist draped over the steering wheel. "Are you meeting in the usual place?" Melissa asked.

"The usual." It was a cow pasture in the northwest corner of the county.

"Is ballooning fun?" Jory asked.

"There's absolutely nothing like it," Michael told her. "It's hard to describe. There's nothing but sky and wind and the whoosh of the gas jets. I suppose it's as close to heaven as some of us will ever get."

"Maybe you could take Jory up sometime," Melissa ventured.

Michael laughed. "I took you up, and how did you repay my gesture?"

"So I'm afraid of heights and got sick to my stomach." Melissa defended herself indignantly. "It could have happened to anyone."

"I've been skiing in Aspen and water-jetting in the Bahamas, but I've never been ballooning," Jory offered. "I've got a stomach like a rock, and heights don't bother me."

Melissa smiled at Jory's hints, but she wished Jory hadn't mentioned her many adventures. Rich girls put Michael off, and he probably thought she was boasting. Not that Jory was snobby. It wasn't her fault she'd been blessed with a wealthy family.

"I think you're better off staying on the ground," Michael said evasively.

He turned the truck off the road and it bounced through pasture land. Suddenly the headlights glared on a group of people clustered in the field. Several wore shirts stamped "Blue Sky Balloon Club." Michael halted, pulled on the hand brake, and stepped out onto the spongy sod while Melissa and Jory tagged behind. Someone said, "We almost started without you, Austin. Sun's due to rise in half an hour."

"My spotters overslept," he said, dragging his balloon off the truckbed. The lightweight nylon fluttered while Melissa helped him spread it out on the ground apart from the other balloons. Propane tanks hissed hot air into the necks of the dormant balloons, and they rose slowly like giant mushrooms. As each one filled, a person climbed into the dangling basket while others released ropes and the balloons drifted upward, like colorful bubbles in the sky. Michael leaped into his basket, and Melissa watched as the ropes were loosened and the mammoth balloon floated up through the gray morning mist.

"I'd have given my eyeteeth if he'd taken me," Jory said with a sigh.

"Maybe some other time." Melissa consoled her gently. Why couldn't Michael be sensitive to Jory's feelings for him? "Come on." She took Jory's arm. "Now *our* job starts."

In the truck, Melissa drove across the bumpy terrain toward the road. "Don't let him out of your sight. When he sets it down, we have to be there to help him pack it up."

"Seems like a lot of hassle for such a short ride to watch the sunrise."

"He loves it. And I'm glad he got into it. If Michael isn't working either of his jobs, he's going to school. Mom worries about him—she thinks he works too hard for his own good. But my brother's *very* determined to succeed."

"He isn't the only one," Jory said, pouring a cup of coffee and shooting Melissa a sidelong glance. "You've had your nose in a book ever since school started two weeks ago. You haven't even taken time to do anything fun with me lately."

"Don't be selfish, Jory. The PSATs are coming up in October and I've got to score big if I'm going to be eligible for a National Merit Scholarship next year."

"Do you still have your hopes set on Princeton?"

"If it's good enough for Brooke Shields . . ." Jory

giggled. But Melissa added, "Seriously, I don't want to be stuck at a junior college like Michael. I want to go somewhere new, do something productive and meaningful with my life."

"Does that mean law?"

"Probably. But I'm keeping an open mind." She glanced over at Jory. Her auburn bangs hung shaggy over her carefully plucked eyebrows. Her pert, turned-up nose gave her a sassy look brightened by almond-shaped sea-green eyes. Jory appeared to wear a perpetual pout, but her frequent dimpled smiles softened her face. Melissa considered her best friend seriously. She was pretty, rich, and smart to boot. "You could come to Princeton, too, if you concentrated on studying instead of boys and partying."

"Ugh." Jory wrinkled her nose. "One genius in this friendship is enough. I'll be your manager."

"Lawyers don't need managers."

"All right, your social director. Surely you plan to *date* between spurts of studying."

"There's really no one I'm interested in." Melissa felt color creep up her neck, and her conscience nagged, *except Brad Kessing.* Blond. Athletic. Bright. A senior. And absolutely unobtainable. Melissa knew what the most popular kids at Lincoln High thought of her—she was "bookish" and "pretty but intellectual."

"And why not? Gosh, Melissa, have a little self-confidence. Look at yourself: gorgeous black hair down your back, huge blue eyes, legs that start at your neckline, and brains coming out of your ears. You could have any guy at Lincoln you set your mind on."

"My mind's on college, Jory. That's my number-one priority. Are you watching Michael's balloon?" Melissa deftly changed the subject.

The sky was streaked with color, melting from indigo into pale lavender, laced with fingers of pink. Jory rose up on her knees and stretched the upper half of her body out of the window of the cab. "I see him! He's pretty high up and heading east." The wind caught her words and flung them back.

"Drat!" Melissa eased over into the traffic, looking for the first road that turned left. "If he's high up, that means there are power lines. Don't lose sight of him." She found a road and turned, caught sight of the balloon in her windshield, and accelerated. A sharp pain shot through her knee and she winced.

"Are you all right?" Jory asked, sliding back into her seat.

"Just my rheumatism acting up," she joked. "Now tell me why you won't come to Princeton with me? Your grandfather will send you anywhere you want to go."

"You said it yourself, Melissa—I'm a party girl. Princeton's too staid and proper for me. Besides, someone has to stay behind and keep an eye on your brother."

Melissa rolled her eyes. "You're impossible! Stick with guys our own age."

"They're absolute children."

By now the sun was up and the light through the windshield pierced Melissa's eyes.

"I think he's coming down," Jory said, pointing to the red-and-yellow balloon drifting down toward an empty field.

"Terrific," Melissa grumbled. "How am I going to get through the barbed wire?"

"There's a gate." Jory pointed excitedly.

Melissa drove the truck through the gate and then headed across the vast green pasture, where

Michael's balloon squatted, already deflating and fluttering in the breeze like a sailboat.

"God, that was great!" Michael shouted as the girls climbed out of the truck to help him fold the giant arch of nylon and put it back on the truck. His blue eyes shone and his face was flushed.

"He's high," Melissa teased, her words doubled with meaning.

"It's incredible—high above the earth, seeing the world like a bird does. Man, it's almost better than—" He caught himself, glancing self-consciously at Jory.

"Better than sex?" Melissa finished drolly, quoting one of his frequently used descriptive phrases. "I wouldn't know."

"You better not." He grinned. "Now let's get moving and I'll treat everybody to breakfast."

Melissa laughed and reached to unlatch the back of the truck. She stared down at an ugly purple bruise on her arm. Now how in the world had she gotten that, she wondered. She ignored it and dropped the tailgate with a bang.

"Don't break it," Michael chided. "It's not much, but it's paid for."

"Sorry. I lost my grip."

They crowded into the cab and Michael headed back across the field toward town. Jory chattered in a stream of quick, witty observations about ballooning and Michael's passion for it. Melissa dropped her head against the seat and watched the cloudless blue sky shoot past, her eyelids growing heavy. She wished she weren't so tired. But it was good to be alive. Good to breathe in the fresh, warm September air.

Lulled by the movement of the truck and the

warm sun, Melissa felt content. Her junior year of high school would be her best, and her grades would be her highest. She'd make sure of it. The course of her future depended on it.

Chapter Two

"You didn't have to be so rude to Jory, Michael," Melissa said testily the minute they walked into the kitchen of their house and Jory had driven off in her convertible.

"Rude? What are you talking about?" Michael lowered himself into a chair, stretched out his long legs, and clasped his hands behind his head. "I thought I was very tolerant under the circumstances."

"What circumstances?"

"She's a bubblehead."

Melissa felt her anger rise. "She's my best friend and has been since the fifth grade."

"She's also rich and spoiled. Why does she hang around here anyway? And why does she go to Lincoln High when she could go to any private school in the city?"

Melissa answered his second question first. "She goes to Lincoln because she likes public school. A lot of kids prefer Lincoln to private schools." *Like Brad Kessing*, she reminded herself. For although he traveled in Jory's charmed circle of monied elite, he too preferred Lincoln. "And she hangs around here because she has a crummy home life."

"And ours is perfect?" There was an undertone of bitterness in his question that made Melissa sigh.

She sat across from him at the table and fiddled

with the salt shaker. "I didn't say it was perfect. Face it, Michael, Dad's been gone six years and he's not coming back. *I* think Mom's done a terrific job of keeping us together, don't you?"

He nodded. "Mom's a great lady. But she works too hard."

"That's what she says about you."

A small smile started at the corners of his mouth. "That's because I'm going to be rich someday, just like Miss Delaney. Then Mom won't ever have to go downtown to the office again. And she won't have to worry about paying bills and trying to make ends meet."

"You know it's not that bad since she's gotten her promotion. And besides, you're missing the point. Jory has money and two parents but she's not particularly happy, and that's why she likes to come over here. We may not have much money, but at least we're a family. I think Jory senses the closeness between us and wants to be a part of it." Melissa paused, remembering the times over the years that Jory had come home from school with her. She'd stay as late as she could, until Mom had to drive her home to an often dark and empty house in the exclusive neighborhood of mansions where she lived.

"Her parents are always off chasing real estate deals, and Jory's left alone. Her older brothers and sisters all live in other states, and none of them are close to her anyway. I mean, not like you and I are."

"She's not always alone," Michael said with a twinkle in his eye. "She's usually over here."

"Oh you!" Melissa flung the salt shaker at him, exasperated.

"Now don't tell me you aren't just a tiny bit envious of her," Michael said. "I see the way you look at her car. Wouldn't you like to have someone hand you the keys to a machine like that, absolutely free?"

"I didn't say money isn't important. I said it doesn't buy happiness."

Michael leaned across the table and tugged affectionately on her hair. "Ah, the idealism of a sixteen-year-old! What I'd give to have it again."

Melissa lunged at him and he laughed, catching her wrist. She grimaced as his fingers closed around her bruise. He dropped her arm and eyed the ugly purple mark in surprise. "What's that? And how did you get it?"

"Just a bruise, and I don't know." She was curious about her bruises too, but couldn't figure out how she got them. "Probably stumbling around in the dark at four A.M.," she said, poking Michael lightly in the arm.

"Does it hurt?"

"It's a little sore, but it'll go away." Unable to divert his look of concern, she teased, "You know how we princesses are. Just a pea under our mattress and we turn black and blue."

Michael stood and stretched, his physique rippling with muscle. "I think I'm gonna crash for a couple of hours before I go to work. Tell Mom not to count on me for supper. I'm working overtime at the warehouse shelving stock. We get paid double time on Saturdays you know."

"You don't *have* to work so hard for your money," Melissa said, the light of mischief in her eyes.

"How's that?"

"You could always marry it."

Michael shook his head in amusement. "And I'll bet you can fix me up with just the right rich girl."

"In a few years." Melissa smiled. "She's much too young for you now."

"You're a hopeless romantic, Sis."

"And you're a hopeless pragmatic."

"I tell you what, when you get that law degree, I'll hire you to run my empire."

She stuck out her tongue, and he bounded out of the kitchen with a laugh.

On Monday, Jory picked Melissa up for school. Melissa decided it wasn't a bad way to arrive each day—in a sporty white convertible with plush red interior. After Jory's second tour of the parking lot, Melissa asked, "Is there some reason we're cruising and not parking?"

"Absolutely. We want to be seen, don't we? How can we march straight into the building without first making sure that everyone at Lincoln is totally aware of our arrival?" To emphasize her point, Jory waved at a group of students congregated in the lot. Behind them, Lincoln High rose, an ultramodern glass and concrete structure, only two years old and already nearly filled to capacity. Yellow buses unloaded at the far end of the parking lot, and Melissa was glad she didn't have to be on one.

"When you're finished cruising, could you please park? I need to get to homeroom early," Melissa said. "On Friday, Mr. Marshall said he wanted to see me first thing today."

"Ugh." Jory wrinkled her nose. "What a way to start the week. Well, it can't be anything you've done wrong—everyone knows Melissa Austin is the model student."

Jory slowed and honked. Melissa glanced in the

direction her friend waved, and her heart suddenly somersaulted into her throat. Brad Kessing stood next to his bronze Firebird, dressed in khaki slacks and a sky-blue cotton shirt that accentuated his athletic build. The sunlight highlighted his golden blond hair. "Hey, Brad," Jory called.

Melissa started fidgeting around in her purse for her hairbrush, and her nervousness must have caught Jory's attention. "What's the matter?" she asked.

"I just noticed that I look a mess. My hair's got a mind of its own today and—"

"Melissa, do you have a thing for Brad?"

"Oh, he's all right."

"All right?" Jory mused. "Then how come you're turning three shades of red?"

"I am not!"

"Are too!"

Melissa settled pleading eyes on her friend. "Just keep it to yourself, okay?"

"Why? I can introduce you two. Brad and I go way back. Our parents play doubles at the country club all the time."

"Just drop it," Melissa demanded, speaking under her breath, even as Brad sauntered over to Jory's car and leaned his elbows against the door frame. "Hi, Jory. What's up?"

"Nothing much. Do you know my friend, Melissa Austin?"

Brad's cool blue eyes took her in, and Melissa's mouth went dry. The strong lines of his jaw and chin etched themselves into her brain. "Hey, Melissa."

She managed a nod before Jory blurted, "Are you playing in the club tournament next Saturday?"

"Not this time. The soccer coach wants us to take

it easy so we don't get injured before practice starts for the season. How about you?"

"Me—tennis?" Jory wrinkled her nose. "That *is* the game with the racket and the little fuzzy ball, isn't it?"

Brad laughed. "You're some athlete, Delaney." His attention turned to Melissa. "Do you know any more about sports than she does?"

"I play racquetball with my brother every now and then, but that's about as athletic as I get."

Brad scrutinized her, studying her features one by one while her stomach fluttered. "Maybe Jory could bring you out to the club sometime and we could knock a few balls around."

"Maybe."

"Just name a time," Jory said. Melissa could have killed her. From far away, a bell sounded. The spell was broken and Brad straightened, breaking his hold on Melissa's gaze. He tapped the side of the car. "Maybe I'll see you two around later."

As he ambled across the parking lot, Jory called, "Count on it!"

"That was *so* embarrassing, Jory," Melissa hissed. "Why didn't you just ask him to take me out on a date?"

Jory snapped her fingers. "Why didn't I think of that?" She maneuvered her car into a space that was too small. "I told you I wanted to be your social director."

"Well, I don't need a social director. I want to keep my mind on studying, because I'm going to get a scholarship. I haven't got time for guys this year." She opened the door and banged the side of the car next to Jory's. "Now how am I supposed to get out?"

"Simple," Jory said with a smile. "Climb over." She had already stood on the seat and swung her legs to the asphalt below. Melissa followed, and as she sat on the edge of the door she caught Jory staring wide-eyed at her legs, which were blotched with large purple bruises. "What happened to you?" Jory asked.

Melissa felt a sharp pain in her knees and ankle joints when she hit the pavement. "Nothing. And don't try to change the subject. You practically threw me at Brad. He must think I'm a real jerk."

"Oh, honestly, Melissa. You know what your problem is?"

"No. But I'm sure you're going to tell me."

"You're too serious. These are supposed to be the best years of our lives. You should be dating, partying, having fun . . ."

"I know exactly what I want. And a boyfriend is low priority." She limped slightly as she caught up with Jory.

"Well, I *do* want a boyfriend," Jory said. "And if I can't have the one I really want—"

"Michael?"

Jory cut her a sideways look. "—then I'll become experienced enough to appeal to him in the future. In the meantime, though, it's the party life for me. Do yourself a favor, Melissa, and go after Brad before he gets snatched up by some ditzy sophomore."

Melissa shook her head. Jory would never understand. Melissa wanted to take the world head-on. Like Michael, she wanted things from life, things that college and hard work could bring her. Life was more than an endless round of parties and days spent at the country club. Romanticism aside, Melissa knew she had a pragmatic streak, too.

She said goodbye to Jory and promised to meet

her at the car after school. Late for her meeting with Mr. Marshall, she rushed toward homeroom shrugging off a nagging fatigue, and when she swung into the doorway Mr. Marshall smiled at her.

"Good to see you, Melissa. Come closer. I want to ask you something." She approached his desk and he tossed aside his pencil.

"You're a very bright girl and doing far above average work. How would you like to come out for Brain Bowl this year?"

Chapter Three

"Brain Bowl?"

"Surely you're aware of the countywide Brain Bowl competition. It's a chance for the brightest students from each high school to come together and test their knowledge against each other in a team setting."

Melissa did know about Brain Bowl. She'd watched some of the finalist matches the previous spring on Tampa's educational TV channel. "I know it's a tough game."

"True. After county competitions, there are state. Even nationals."

Melissa shifted her notebook to her hip, her interest piqued by Mr. Marshall's words. "There're prizes, aren't there?"

The teacher pushed his glasses higher on his nose and smiled. "Big prizes. For the county winners, a trip to Washington, D.C., a thousand dollars in savings bonds to each panelist, and two thousand for the school. But for the state winners, it's a trip to Europe and a four-year scholarship."

Melissa's eyes narrowed. "But I thought only seniors were allowed to participate."

"Usually. But we need to have juniors primed for next year's competition. Since Lincoln High is so new, we didn't do very well in our last two outings. But this year, it's going to be different."

"How?"

His grin was broad and reminded Melissa of a little boy's. "Mrs. Watson and I are in charge. The preliminary rounds don't start until March, but we believe that if we start working now, we'll have a shot at putting the best possible team out there. Interested?"

Melissa nodded emphatically. She was very interested. "What Mrs. Watson and I did was to go through all the achievement scores for every one of Lincoln's juniors and seniors. We've based our selections on IQ and grade point average. You're high on both."

She felt deep satisfaction from knowing her hard work was paying off. She'd have to tell Jory the next time they got into a discussion about her studious habits. Mr. Marshall picked up a file folder and flipped through it. "However, being smart isn't enough in Brain Bowl. You also need a certain aggressiveness—" he gestured with a fist, "—a special presence when the heat's on you to come up with an answer."

"How do I try out for the team?"

"It's a multistage process," Mr. Marshall told her. "Next week we're testing all the kids whom we've already weeded out as having the academic potential. There will be a battery of tests after school for two days. They'll be academic, of course, with some psychological testing. We'll need parental consent for you to take the tests." He reached into the folder and handed her a form. "If you score in the range we need, you'll begin Brain Bowl drills three days a week during sixth-period study hall, and then probably every day after school until the competition begins.

"We won't choose the final team—four panelists and two alternates—until a month before the competitions. Then we'll *really* hit the drilling hard. Probably every day, so there won't be much time for anything else. Especially a social life." His eyes drifted. "My wife threatened divorce if I got involved in Brain Bowl again this year, but there's something about the event. You get sort of swept up in it." He grinned with satisfaction. "Anyway, you should realize that you may work for months and still not be selected for the final team. But we're not restricting the panel to seniors. We're going after the right chemistry, the right mix of talent. We want to win!" He paused. "For the Green and Gold, of course."

Lincoln's colors. "Of course." By now, homeroom was filled, and Melissa had to take her seat. "I'll get my mother to sign the form, Mr. Marshall. I'd like to be eligible for the selection."

He flashed her another smile. "I thought you might. You're a good student. And Mrs. Watson thinks you're team material."

Melissa had had Mrs. Watson the year before for advanced English and had earned an *A*. She walked to her seat with her head spinning. Brain Bowl. A four-year scholarship. At the least, a savings bond. She wanted to make it. Inwardly she smiled, feeling a rush of confidence mingled with joy. *Princeton*. Maybe it wasn't such a pipe dream after all.

That night she helped her mother make a salad. It was just the two of them since Michael had classes. Melissa related every word of her conversation with Mr. Marshall to her mother. "I've got the form in my room," she said. "You will sign it, won't you?"

Mrs. Austin, a tall, slim woman with dark hair, listened intently. Melissa felt her mother's eyes on her. "Is that the way you want to spend your junior year? Studying after school almost every day? Without any guarantees you'll make the team?"

"I want to go to college."

Her mother sighed. "How did I ever raise such success-oriented kids? All I wanted to do when I was your age was get married."

"I want it all, Mom. Lots of women have careers and families. Why can't I do both? *You* do."

"I *had* to," her mother reminded her. "I would have been perfectly content to stay at home and raise babies. But, when I did have to go to work, it would have been much easier if I'd had an education to fall back on. As it was, I started at the bottom."

Melissa remembered. After her husband had walked out, Janelle Austin had started with the phone company as an operator on the night shift, even though it meant leaving fourteen-year-old Michael in charge at home. Melissa had learned to rely on Michael and to feel safe with him guarding the doors—Michael and his baseball bat would fight off any intruder! For a while they had been strapped financially, but they'd made it. And they'd made it with enough style that Jory Delaney, the cute little rich girl in Melissa's fifth-grade class, spent every available moment at the Austin household.

"Michael wants to be wealthy enough so that you'll never have to work again," Melissa said over the sound of running water as she washed vegetables.

"That's very kind and noble of him. But I'd probably work now even if I didn't have to. Once the two of you are out on your own I'll have little else to do."

Melissa felt a certain sense of pity for her mother. *Alone*. That's how she was facing the rest of her life. Sometimes Melissa wondered why she had never remarried. She was still pretty. Perhaps her clothes were a bit dated. . . . Melissa shot her mother a glance. Did she still miss their father? Still long for him? The image of Brad's clear blue eyes floated into Melissa's memory. A girl could easily lose her perspective and allow herself to get lost in them. She jerked herself away from the seductive daydream. No. She'd made up her mind. Studies came first from now on. The Brad Kessings in her life would simply have to wait. She refused to travel the same road her mother had.

A sudden, sharp pain in her fingers caused her to drop the vegetable peeler with a noisy clank.

"Goodness. What happened?" her mother asked.

Gingerly Melissa flexed her fingers. "Just a cramp," she said. But it had been more than that—more like a deep aching inside her joints. Maybe her crack to Jory about rheumatism wasn't so far off the mark.

A rap sounded on the back door. "Well, hello, Jory," Mrs. Austin said, smiling.

"Am I interrupting supper?"

"We haven't started yet."

"Then I'll come back later."

"I wouldn't think of it. Come in."

Jory shrugged at Melissa self-consciously. Her auburn curls were streaked with hair paint, and her outfit was straight out of a fashion magazine. Melissa was sure it had cost a fortune. "I—uh—was just driving by." Melissa waved her over to the sink.

"You know you don't need an excuse to stop in, Jory," Melissa's mother said, taking salad plates out of the cupboard.

"It's just that my parents are at the club tonight. Some sort of charity auction. The house felt lonesome . . ." Her sentence trailed and she shifted from foot to foot.

"Have you eaten?"

"Uh—sort of."

"For Jory, 'sort of' means a Coke and a bag of chips."

"Coke and chocolate chip cookies," Jory corrected with a smile that crinkled her eyes and revealed her dimples.

"We're only having chef's salad, but you're welcome to join us."

"Michael's at school tonight," Melissa added, conveying information in a way that only Jory would understand.

"I'd love to stay," Jory said, acknowledging Melissa's message and Mrs. Austin's invitation with gratitude. "I've always *loved* your chef's salad."

"Here." Melissa handed Jory three glasses. "There's ice tea in the fridge. You'll have to work for your supper."

"Small price," Jory said while opening the freezer door to get ice.

They sat at the kitchen table eating and talking. It often amazed Melissa how much Jory could talk. Afterward Jory shooed Mrs. Austin out while she and Melissa cleared the table and stacked dishes in the dishwasher. "So you're going out for Brain Bowl?"

"Sure am."

"Guess I'll have to find something to get involved with then," Jory said.

"You could test," Melissa urged. "I know you're very smart."

Jory rolled her eyes. "Pul-eez. I couldn't walk in the door with my grade point average. No, you go on without me. You're the one who wants to go to Princeton."

Melissa nodded. Although she hated to admit it, Jory had brains, but no initiative. "I haven't made it yet," she said.

"You will. Hey! Why don't you plan on spending next Friday night with me?" Jory asked with a quick turn of her body. "The testing will be over by then, and my folks will be on a cruise to the Bahamas. We can rent a ton of VCR movies, stay up all night, and pig out on pizza."

Melissa considered the offer. "You won't make me sit through *Aliens* again, will you?"

"You mean that touching story about monsters wrapping humans in cocoons for future meals? Naw."

"Some comedies this time, all right?"

"We'll go to the rental store together, and you can pick out any ones you want. I'll put it on Daddy's tab." Her smile was impish. "Then we'll take off Saturday morning for the country club—go swimming, have lunch, do the sauna. I'll put that on Daddy's tab too."

Melissa flicked water in Jory's face. "You're impossible!"

"What else are rich parents good for?"

To help send you to college, Melissa thought. How could Jory be so casual about her future?

Melissa hung back in the girls' room until the very last minute on the afternoon of the test. She nervously dropped her hairbrush while running it through her hair for the umpteenth time. She noticed her face in the mirror looked gaunt, and dark circles smudged the skin beneath her eyes. She needed to get more rest, she thought, so she wouldn't look like a raccoon.

Melissa adjusted her blouse and noticed another purplish blotch on her arm. "Oh, good grief," she said to her reflection. Not another bruise. Melissa didn't know what was causing them, but she did know she had to do something about them. Why, just the other day she'd caught her phys ed teacher staring at the bruises on her legs. "Leg makeup," she mumbled in a sudden flash of inspiration. She'd buy leg makeup to hide them. Dancers used that trick all the time.

Pushing the bruise problem to the back of her mind, Melissa tried to focus on the situation at hand. *The test*. At the testing room she paused, wondering how many people would be inside. Would she know anyone else? It's probably a roomful of nerds with IQs in the extraterrestrial range, she told herself. *What chance have I got?*

The room was surprisingly crowded, and she did recognize many faces. *Shocking to find out who's really smart*, she mused. Melissa looked around for an empty chair. Suddenly, her gaze stopped short and her stomach lurched as Brad Kessing flashed her a dazzling, heart-thudding grin.

Chapter Four

～

Melissa felt herself blush. She nodded briskly at Brad's smile and hurried past him to an open desk in the very back of the room. Of all the kids at Lincoln, Brad Kessing was the last she had expected to see sitting in the room. *Well, why not?* her mind argued. She'd heard that he was smart. She only wished that seeing him hadn't rattled her so. Why had it? Why, when she'd vowed not to be distracted by boys this year in pursuit of her academic goals?

You're being ridiculous, she told herself with annoyance. *You don't have time for infatuations.*

For that's all it was. Brad simply had the right blend of looks and charm that appealed to her.

Melissa's thoughts were interrupted as Mr. Marshall came in and tried to quiet the restless group of students assembled in the room. "Good afternoon," he began, dropping a stack of papers on the desk in front of him. "Mrs. Watson will be here shortly, but I want to get you started." He surveyed the room with a broad grin. "Do you realize that your cumulative IQs rank up in the same numerical category as the national debt?"

Giggles twittered and feet shuffled. "As Mrs. Watson and I have told each of you during the past few days, it is our goal that Lincoln put together the best combination of talent and skill for the countywide

Brain Bowl competitions. It's not just brains we're looking for, but self-confidence, openness, an ability to think quickly on your feet . . ."

Mr. Marshall's voice trailed off as Mrs. Watson, a small-boned woman who moved with economical, determined purpose, entered the room. She had black hair, and features that were sharp and angular. Her brown eyes were studious, seeming to miss nothing. As she surveyed the room, kids sat up straighter and became subdued. She said, "I'm glad to see so many of you here. Today's test is a quest for knowledge. We've compiled the questions from actual Brain Bowl questionnaires. Tomorrow's test will gauge emotional and psychological factors."

A student quipped, "You mean, it'll tell you if any of us are crazy geniuses?"

"We already know *that*," Mr. Marshall joked. "The tests will tell us who's able to sit under the interrogator's eye without flinching." He rolled his hands together like a mad-scientist and caused another ripple of giggles through the audience.

Melissa listened intently, determined to score high in every area. Mrs. Watson continued. "From these tests, we'll whittle the group down to twenty-five people whom we'll interview and pare down to ten finalists. The group of finalists will be decided quickly—I'd say within two weeks. That panel of ten will drill together, study together, and work side by side until April, when we'll choose six final panelists to begin the preliminary rounds of Brain Bowl. After that initial round-robin—since I *know* Lincoln will still be in it"—a smattering of applause broke out— "we will advance to All-County—which will be televised, I might add—and from there to State finals."

A hush fell over the room as the meaning of Brain

Bowl suddenly became real to each student. Then Mr. Marshall asked, "Any questions?" There were none, so he passed through the rows and lay the tests face-down on each desk. Mr. Marshall returned to the front of the room and announced, "Let the games begin."

Melissa took a deep breath, mumbled a quick prayer, and began.

"Did you ace it?" Jory asked through a mouthful of pizza as she sat on her living room floor the following Friday night.

Melissa shrugged but offered a satisfied grin. "I didn't flunk. Actually, I knew more than I thought I would. And the psychological part was a breeze. I gather from the questionnaire that I'm socially well adjusted."

Jory gave Melissa a teasing look. "But how can that be when you had every opportunity to linger and talk with Brad Kessing after the tests and instead chose to zip away the minute they were over?"

Melissa gasped. "Who told you that?"

"Brad, of course. He asked me if you were attached or if you just didn't like him."

Flustered and embarrassed, Melissa was at a momentary loss for words. The truth was, she'd been too much of a coward to talk to Brad. He made her feel off balance and out of sorts. She was attracted to him but resisted it. "What's not to like?" Melissa asked nonchalantly. "I knew I was coming over here to spend the night and had a million things to do before I could come."

Jory rolled her eyes in feigned tolerance. "Well, I defended you staunchly, so you still have a shot at him. I told him you were probably preoccupied, since you had your heart set on making that brainy team. He understood."

Melissa wished Jory wouldn't be so helpful. What did she have to say to make her friend understand that she was committed to matters of the mind and not the heart? She scanned the living room with its Louis XIV heirloom furniture, plush lemon-yellow carpet, porcelain knickknacks, and cut-crystal vases of silk flowers. It crossed her mind that maybe Jory recognized something that Melissa could not see—that she probably could focus on school and have a social life, too. And that maybe it was unreasonable for her to deny her feelings about Brad.

Her gaze returned to where Jory had set the pizza box on a gleaming fruitwood coffee table. A grease stain streaked the dull shine of the wood. "You're ruining your mother's table," she noted irritably.

Jory shrugged. "The maid will clean it tomorrow. Are we going to watch movies or blabber?"

"Which TV? The one in your room, the den, or the family room?" Melissa asked, knowing that the irony of the question would be lost on Jory. Didn't *every* house have three TVs?

Jory jumped up. "Family room. Come see how I've fixed us up."

Melissa tagged after her to a cavernous room with beamed ceilings. The carpet had been covered with down comforters and mounds of pillows. Bowls of fruit nestled amid the folds of satin softness. "What's this?" Melissa asked with genuine delight.

"A Turkish harem room, dummy. Like it?"

"It's dynamite."

"Thanks." Jory's pixie grin highlighted her dimples and made her green eyes shine. *Why wasn't*

Michael nuts for her? Melissa wondered. "I've even rounded up some sexy negligees." Jory held up two wisps of flowing nylon. "Siren Red or Ice Princess Blue?" She asked.

"I feel red," Melissa giggled, taking the scarlet fabric from her friend. In minutes, both girls had shed their clothing and wrapped themselves in the sheer lingerie. Melissa whirled, her hair rippling loose and free down her back. "This is positively sinful."

"Yeah. But isn't it fun?" Jory spun around too. "You know, you need to eat more pizza. You're losing weight."

"You know what they say: 'You can't be too rich or too thin,'" Melissa joked.

"I'm not kidding," Jory answered seriously. "You really have lost weight."

Melissa smoothed the filmy material over her flat stomach. "Do you think so?"

"I know so."

"Well, it's probably just the cut of the gown."

"No, I don't think so . . ."

Melissa grew flustered and a little self-conscious over Jory's comments. "Don't make such a big deal about it, Jory. Are we going to blabber or watch movies?"

Jory shrugged and began sorting through the pile of videocassettes they'd chosen earlier that afternoon from the video store. "What'll it be?"

Melissa flopped provocatively onto the sea of cushions and nibbled daintily on a cluster of grapes. "How about *Casablanca*? I feel romantic."

Jory shook her head and shuffled through the stack. "You're weird, girl. You want romance, but not with a real live willing and able guy!"

"Dreams take less energy than the real thing,"

Melissa said, as a sudden tiredness rushed through her. She stifled a yawn.

"You're not going to fall asleep on me like the last time you stayed over, are you?" Jory demanded with a cry.

"Absolutely not," Melissa said, even as her eyelids struggled to stay open. "Well, I may doze off, but nudge me for the scene in the fog, when Bogart and Bergman say goodbye."

Jory gave an exasperated sigh and stretched out next to Melissa on the fluffy floor coverings. "Some concubine you'd make," she grumbled. "Asleep before the sheik arrived."

Melissa managed a smile and drifted into a hazy world of lethargy. "When the prince comes, have him give me a kiss."

"What if he's a frog and gives you warts?"

"Then I'll defend him. He has a right to an attorney." The last thing she remembered was Jory's squeal of exaggerated distress as sleep overcame her.

The next morning, Melissa buried her face in the downy coverings, too tired to move, feeling as if she'd been drugged.

"Rise and shine," Jory directed from the far side of the room, balancing an ornate silver tray laden with doughnuts and Cokes. "Time for breakfast."

Melissa groaned. "What time is it?"

"Nine on the nose, and we have a full day ahead of us."

Melissa struggled up, raking her tousled hair from her eyes. She felt tired and achy. She hoped she wasn't coming down with the flu—not with so many great things going on in her life. She reached for a glazed doughnut. It tasted warm and sweet. "Delicious."

"I drove over to the bakery myself because I couldn't blast you awake. You missed some good movies," Jory added with a hint of accusation.

Sheepishly, Melissa shrugged. "Sorry. My eyes just refused to stay open. This past week must have been more strenuous than I thought."

"Yes. Deep thinking can be hazardous to your health."

Melissa pelted Jory with a fluffy pillow. "Well, I'm awake now. What's the game plan?"

"The country club, of course."

Melissa glanced toward the bank of high windows in the room. Sunlight slanted inward, in taut ribbons. "We can swim in your pool," she suggested, still feeling sluggish.

"Forget it! Get your suit on. We're leaving in thirty minutes. There's a certain lifeguard who's come to my attention . . ." She let the sentence trail suggestively.

"I told you to stick to guys at Lincoln."

"And I told you they're all children. I prefer older, more experienced men. Come on, let's move it."

In the bathroom, Melissa tugged on her bathing suit, then stepped into crisp white shorts and a gauzy blue cover-up. She twisted her thick black hair into a braid and secured it with a gold clip at the end. Finally, she smoothed on some waterproof leg makeup she'd bought. It had cost a fortune, but it did an excellent job of concealing those ugly bruises. The makeup had become a regular part of her dressing routine, though she'd forgotten to use it after gym class Friday, and she'd caught her teacher staring at her legs again. It was so embarrassing, she vowed to be more careful.

She daubed on lipstick and blusher and met Jory at the car.

Melissa lolled against the upholstery of Jory's convertible, watching the intense blue sky slip past overhead. Hot Florida sun beat down despite the early morning hour as the car wound its way through the wrought iron gates of the country club and along a winding driveway lined with oleander.

Jory stopped in the circular driveway before a massive stone-and-cypress building, where a valet opened their car doors. Melissa grabbed her duffel bag and followed Jory up the steps into the cool interior. Tropical flowers and pools of water graced a giant lobby domed by soaring ceilings and skylights. Tinted glass walls allowed sunlight to filter through to palm trees growing in cultivated garden boxes and hibiscus blooming in thick profusion. Jory elbowed Melissa. "Let's hit the pool first. We'll do the sauna and game rooms later."

Melissa needed no further urging. She longed to stretch out on a chaise lounge and drift lazily in a netherworld of near sleep while the sun browned her body.

The pool area wasn't crowded. Red striped umbrellas dipped over redwood tables on the deck. Melissa blinked against the reflection of bright sun on the calm water. "That's him," Jory whispered, pointing to a bronzed lifeguard perched in a special chair on the far side of the pool. "You'll excuse me while I go check out his availability?"

Melissa nodded, depositing her towel on a lounge and lying down on her stomach. "Don't let me cramp your style."

Jory paused and remarked wistfully, "I wish it were Michael."

"Maybe someday . . ." Melissa said consolingly and closed her eyes. The sun soaked through her. She barely heard the sounds of the splashing and laughing surrounding her. She might have gone to sleep, but a voice said, "Hello, Melissa."

She sat up, startled, and found herself face to face with Brad Kessing.

Chapter Five

❧

"Hi," she said, as a surge of adrenaline chased away her sun-induced stupor.

"It's good to see you. Jory mentioned that you two might come out here today."

Jory. No wonder she'd insisted on coming to the country club. "You're not swimming?" she asked. Brad wore yellow jams and a tank top that showed off his tanned and powerful upper body. Mirrored sunglasses dangled from a cord around his neck.

"Just finished," he said. "I was thinking about playing racquetball, but I need a partner."

His look was an invitation. "I'd like to, but I'm a little low on energy," she told him, knowing she had neither the stamina nor the presence of mind to get through a game with him.

His blue eyes traveled the length of her, and she felt a tingling sensation that she associated with romance novels. "Want to go through the gardens in the back? There are ponds with goldfish a foot long."

She'd walked the gardens often with Jory, but to go there now with Brad. . . . She glanced at Jory, who was engrossed in conversation with two guys at the lifeguard station. She'd never miss her. "Sure. You lead the way."

As she slipped on her cover-up and sandals, Brad flipped her heavy braid, the tips of his fingers brushing lightly over her shoulder. She followed him down a flagstone path, and in minutes the pool area had disappeared. Silence settled around them in thickets of green as they stepped into a tropical forest. Ficus trees, crotons, and exotic shrubs were intertwined with purple and fuchsia bougainvillea flowers. Brad broke the intimate silence by asking, "How do you think you did on the Brain Bowl testing?"

"I think I did all right. And you?"

His grin was lopsided. "I'm a Kessing. Kessings always do all right. It's in the family rule book."

His comment was puzzling, but she didn't question it. "And I thought you were only interested in soccer."

They stopped on a wooden bridge arched over a winding stream where the water was green and still. "Jocks aren't supposed to be smart. Is that what you mean?" His question made her feel foolish.

"I didn't mean it the way it came out. I guess I was just surprised when I walked into the room and saw you in the front row." Her palms grew sweaty. Nothing she was saying was coming out right.

"We jocks have reputations to maintain. I try not to let on that I can think as well as I can kick a ball." There was a hint of amusement in his words. "But I do intend to make the Brain Bowl team."

She met his intense blue-eyed gaze steadily. "So do I."

"Deep down I have a secret desire. I want to be a Rhodes Scholar. Do you know what that is?"

He toyed with her braid, and her thoughts scattered. "It has something to do with athletics and academic achievements, doesn't it?" she said.

"Actually, it's a scholarship to Oxford University in England. My grandfather was a Rhodes Scholar, and I guess I've always wanted to follow in his footsteps."

Brad intrigued her. She'd never really known a guy who was interested in anything so profound and serious. Most boys she'd dated were only concerned with the latest football scores—or their own scores when it came to girls. But Brad was someone who really thought about his future. "I hope you get it," Melissa said with sincerity.

His smile was intimate as he said, "I always get what I go after." Melissa's heart hammered and her mouth went dry.

Brad rested his elbows on the rough wood of the bridge and leaned over, pointing toward the water. "Look, there's a fish." She caught a flash of gold as a fat, lazy fish ventured from beneath an overhanging rock. "Actually, they're carp, not goldfish."

Brad touched the nape of her neck and stroked her soft skin with his thumb. Melissa's knees turned weak and she leaned against the bridge railing for support. "Maybe that will be a Brain Bowl question," she said lamely, then told herself that it was a stupid thing to say.

"If we're on the team together, we'll be seeing a lot of each other."

His observation made blood pound in her temples. She didn't want this to be happening to her. "The team! I'm aiming for the first cut right now. I can't think beyond that."

"You'll make the first cut."

"How do you know?"

His smile was slow, confident. "Because *I'm* going to make the first cut. And I want you to come with me."

His sense of confidence momentarily overwhelmed her. He straightened and turned her to face him. "Melissa." His voice went low and quiet. "Can I unbraid your hair?"

Flustered by his request and change of subject she stammered. "Y-Yes. If you want."

He reached over her shoulder and pulled the tightly wound braid forward, unclasping the gold clip. She couldn't tear her eyes from his face, couldn't stop the emotions and sensations pouring through her body. Brad unwound the plait slowly, dragging his fingers through the thick, dark masses of her hair until the strands fell loose and free. He sifted it through his fingers like sand, gathering it into handfuls. A breeze spun wispy strands across her face. "God, you have beautiful hair." His whisper sounded worshipful.

Time stood still for her, in a rain forest of green and yellow, in eyes the color of the sky. Her breath pressed against her lungs, unable to escape. She managed to mumble, "Thank you."

Brad lifted a fistful of the dark tresses and let it fall, bit by bit, in a feathery cascade. When the last strands settled, he rested his hands on her shoulders. The thin, gauzy cloth of her shirt seemed nonexistent. He cleared his throat. "I'd like to get to know you better, Melissa. Maybe after the team's chosen . . ."

"Yes. Maybe."

He looked at the water below and a gathering of orange-and-white flecked fish. As he rambled on about the carp, she noticed that his arm never left her shoulder. And his fingers, long and gentle, never stopped stroking the dark veil of her satin, waist-length hair.

"You're awfully quiet. Didn't you have a good time?" Jory's words intruded into Melissa's brooding silence as they drove through the familiar streets of Melissa's neighborhood in the dusk.

"Of course I had a good time. The whirlpool and sauna were great."

Jory switched on her headlights. "But you're not telling me what happened in that hour you disappeared into the gardens with Brad."

If Melissa hadn't been so tired, she might have been irritated with Jory's probing. "Nothing happened. We went for a walk. We looked at the fish."

"You rebraided your hair when you came back to the pool area."

Melissa was relieved that Jory couldn't see the flush on her face because of the darkness. "It came undone."

Jory blew through her teeth skeptically, drove the car into Melissa's driveway, and shut off the engine. "It's okay to like Brad, you know," she said. "There's nothing wrong with balancing a social life with your studies."

"It seems that I don't have much choice," she admitted grudgingly. "He's very hard *not* to like."

Jory's smile was so obvious, Melissa could feel it in the dark interior of the car. "It's nice to know you're still human and that blue eyes and blond hair can still affect you."

"I'd have to be a corpse not to be affected."

Jory chuckled. "Well, under the circumstances, I'd say you were in for a banner year, Melissa Austin."

"*If* I make Brain Bowl," she cautioned. "I told you, studies come first with me this year."

"Okay. *If* you make Brain Bowl, and *if* you date Brad, will you confess that this could possibly be the best school year of your life?"

Melissa released an exasperated sigh. "I confess, Your Honor."

"Good," Jory said, opening the car door and jumping out. "Now let's go inside, where I can catch a glimpse of your gorgeous brother and make a fool of myself over him."

"You're impossible," Melissa laughed, climbing out of the car and heading to the door.

"True. But if I weren't, what would you do for comic relief?"

Melissa hugged her friend impetuously. "Study!" She entered the warm glow of her kitchen, where her mother had left a plate of homemade chocolate chip cookies on the table with a note saying, "Ran to the store. Be back in an hour."

Jory eyed the plate longingly, and Melissa read her thoughts just as surely as if she'd spoken them aloud. There would be no one back at her house. Her parents were still on their cruise. Nothing but a dark, lonely house that people passed through but rarely lived in. "Why don't you help me eat these?"

"You wouldn't mind? I mean, since there's no one home at my house, I could stay for a little while . . ."

Melissa pulled out a chair and shoved her friend into it. "Sit and eat. What kind of a friend would leave me alone to devour an entire plate of cookies just when I'm being noticed by the best-looking guy at Lincoln High? Do you want me to have to waddle up to the Brain Bowl podium?"

Jory reached for a cookie and munched it thoughtfully. "You *are* going to make the team, Melissa. I meant it when I said this is your year. Nothing can stand in your way."

Partly because of Jory's and Brad's enthusiasm, Melissa floated through the next several school days, and when Mr. Marshall told her of her selection to the initial group of twenty-five, she wasn't surprised. Three afternoons of playing the game convinced her that she was a good contestant. Brad was sensational, and by the following Friday, when Mr. Marshall and Mrs. Watson chose the ten finalists, Melissa's confidence buoyed her through morning until the list was posted on Mr. Marshall's bulletin board at noon. Melissa's name topped the list; Brad's was second. She barely read the others.

"I told you so," Brad said after stopping her in the hall between classes.

The fluttery sensation that she felt whenever she glimpsed him in the corridors churned in her stomach. "I never doubted it for a moment," she said.

His laugh was quick. *It certainly is going to be a banner year,* she reminded herself when he touched the heavy length of her hair with a casual, offhanded purpose. "I'll see you later."

Melissa was still floating on a cloud of happiness when, during seventh-period study hall, she was summoned to the dean of women's office. Curiosity dogged her down the hall to Mrs. Crane's cubicle.

The dean of women was friendly, blond, and stylishly dressed. "Have a seat, Melissa." She motioned to the chair beside her neat and orderly desk. "Congratulations on your selection to the Brain Bowl team. It's certainly the best one Lincoln's had to date."

"Thank you, Mrs. Crane." A slight case of jitters set in while the dean studied her for a few thoughtful moments, sweeping her with questioning, intelligent eyes.

"Have I done something wrong, Mrs. Crane?"

"Not at all."

Melissa began to grow wary, even apprehensive,

as the dean focused her attention on Melissa's long, graceful legs. Self-consciously, Melissa tucked one ankle behind the other and wished she'd worn jeans instead of a skirt. "I give up. What's wrong?"

"That's what I want you to tell me, Melissa."

Confusion blanketed Melissa's mind. "I don't understand. What do you want me to say?"

Mrs. Crane reached over and patted Melissa's hand as one might stroke a frightened child. "My dear, there are laws protecting children from parental abuse."

Melissa was dumbfounded. "E-Excuse me . . . ?"

The dean offered an indulgent, all-knowing half-smile. "The bruises on your legs have been reported, Melissa. You can tell me the truth. Is anyone hurting you at home?"

Chapter Six

Horrified, Melissa stared openmouthed at Mrs. Crane.

"Now, dear," the dean said, with a patronizing pat. "Please understand me. As a minor, you are protected by certain laws, and we school personnel only want to make sure that no one harms you. It's for your own good that I'm asking you to be honest with me."

Melissa's thoughts whirled and tumbled. *She thinks my mother beats me!* The impact of the thought sent blind rage coursing through her. A mental picture of her mother—bent over the kitchen table writing checks to pay a mountain of bills—flashed through her mind. In an instant, Melissa was on her feet. "Are you asking me if my mother hits me? No one in my house has ever struck me! No one!"

"Now, now, Melissa. Calm down. We can't ignore those bruises on your legs."

"I don't know how I got these stupid bruises. But they didn't come from my mother." Her anger was so intense that her teeth chattered. "There's some other reason for them."

"What other reason?"

Caught off guard, Melissa sputtered. "Maybe it's gym class. I don't know!"

Mrs. Crane refused to abandon her tack. "I can't let this go unreported, Melissa. I must call your

43

mother in for a consultation. I would be negligent in my duties if I didn't."

"Don't you dare! My mother is wonderful. She'd never, *never*, strike me! You leave her alone."

"Melissa, please . . ."

Melissa didn't wait to hear what else the dean had to say. She bolted from the office and ran outside into the bright morning light. She shut her eyes in pain and felt dizzy as she ran through the parking lot, clutching her purse tightly. At the city bus stop she leaned against the bench for support.

Finally home, Melissa collapsed on her bed in tears and exhaustion. She knew she was skipping school and didn't care. She was so angry, she swore she'd never set foot in that school again.

Melissa snuggled into her covers, and when she woke the phone was ringing. Her mother's voice was anxious. "Melissa. Honey, are you all right?"

It took her a minute to clear her head and remember why she was home. "I'm all right, Mom."

"The school called. They said you ran away. I took the chance that you'd have the good sense to go home."

"I'm home. I'm okay . . ."

"Melissa, wait there for me. I'm leaving the office right now. I'll be there in twenty minutes."

"But . . . You don't have to leave. Everything's all right."

"Twenty minutes," her mother said urgently and hung up. Melissa washed her face, trying to pull herself together. She did feel lousy. What's wrong with me? she asked herself. She touched the glands in her neck and realized they were swollen. She couldn't get sick now—not with the start of school and Brain Bowl and . . .

When her mother arrived, Melissa slipped quietly into her arms, deeply comforted by the familiar hug. "Mrs. Crane told me what happened. We'll deal with her later. But now, let me see your legs."

Obediently, Melissa allowed her mother to examine her. "There really are a lot of bruises, honey. Are you sure you don't know how you got them?"

"No." Her body felt heavy, and all she wanted to do was lie in her mother's arms and go to sleep. "But let's not get so worked up over this, Mom. I've probably got the flu."

"I think you have a fever too. I'm calling Dr. Pace. I want him to check you over."

"I don't need to go see him, Mom. I'll take some aspirin and go to bed, and by tomorrow I'll be fine."

"This isn't a voting issue, Melissa. We're going to the doctor's." She smoothed Melissa's hair and forced a small smile. "Besides, I need vindication for the school. I can't let them think I beat my children into submission, now can I?"

Melissa shrugged. "I guess not," she said.

Dr. Pace's examination was routine. He checked Melissa with sure, confident fingers, feeling her swollen glands and bruises, then taking blood. She squeezed her eyes shut as the needle pricked her arm. "It's just the flu, isn't it, Dr. Pace?" she asked as he secured a bandage over the puncture in her vein. "I told Mom it's nothing but some flu that's going around."

His smile was professional, noncommittal. "It's something. We're just not sure what, yet."

"What do you *think* it is?" her mother asked uneasily. "I don't like the looks of all those bruises."

Melissa rolled her eyes, wishing her mother would ease off and that Dr. Pace would just send her home. "It could be as simple as anemia—that's common in girls Melissa's age," he said.

"Then I'll take iron pills," Melissa said, relieved.

"Or, it could be mononucleosis." Dr. Pace peered at her over his glasses. "Which means you'll have to give up kissing."

She smiled at his attempt to cheer her. "No problem there. I've dedicated myself to studying this year. Boys are out."

"Melissa made the Brain Bowl team," her mother said, as if that might influence the doctor in some way.

"I can go back to school, can't I?"

"I want to check a blood smear under my microscope. I'll be right back."

Melissa turned to her mother, who was sitting stiffly in her chair. "It's going to be all right, Mom," she said. Frankly, she was glad her mother had insisted on the checkup. She had been feeling bad for a long time, and deep within she had been concerned about it. If she was going to give Brain Bowl, and Brad, her best shot, she'd have to get better.

"Of course, you're going to be all right, honey. But I wish you'd told me about the bruises when they first appeared."

Dr. Pace returned, his expression unreadable. He positioned himself in front of her. "Your red blood count is low . . ."

Her smile was quick with relief. "Then just write me a prescription for iron pills and I'll take them faithfully. I promise."

He held up his hand. "Whoa. It's not that simple, Melissa. Your white cell count, on the other hand, is rather high."

"So?"

"So I'd like to check you into the hospital for a few days of testing."

Melissa's heart almost stopped beating with the shock of his request. "The hospital!" Her mother echoed her words.

"Just for testing," he emphasized hastily.

"Why? I have school. I can't go to the hospital."

Dr. Pace took her hand. His was warm. Hers was cold. "Think of it as a vacation. You can bring your books. You'll even have a phone and a TV in your room—first-class accommodations at Hotel Tampa General."

"Is this absolutely necessary, Dr. Pace?" Her mother's voice sounded taut.

"Yes. It's important that we find out exactly what's ailing Melissa."

Melissa wanted to ask him what he was testing for, but she sensed he would not say. "When do I have to go, Dr. Pace?"

"The sooner the better. My receptionist will call and have your admitting papers prepared by this afternoon."

"So soon?"

"The sooner we get started, the sooner we'll know what we're fighting." Dr. Pace squeezed her hand. "Now, don't look so frightened. It's for your own good." He helped her off the examining table. She wanted to run out of the room screaming, but instead she offered a brave smile that in no way reflected the terror she was really feeling.

"Not bad, Melissa. Private room and everything." Jory toured her hospital room with an appraising eye. From the bed, Melissa watched her step carefully around Michael, who was sitting in a chair near the window, a worried scowl on his face. Through the blinds, Tampa's evening sky glowed with the aura of city lights.

"Want to take my place? All you can eat for only a pint of blood a day."

Jory shivered at Melissa's ghoulish humor. It comforted Melissa to have her friend pacing the room, for her visit lent a sort of normalcy to an otherwise terrible day. Ever since Melissa had phoned her and Jory had exploded with phrases such as "Nosy Mrs. Crane" and "Are you all right?" and "I'll be there as soon as visiting hours start," she had felt less alien in her antiseptic surroundings.

Only Michael's brooding countenance could penetrate the pretense of well-being Melissa had tried hard to create. He hadn't been at all understanding about her admission to the hospital for tests. Was he just as afraid for her as Melissa was for herself?

"Brad asked about you today," Jory said. "I told him you'd gone home sick. He says he hopes you get well quick. The first full-fledged Brain Bowl drill starts next week."

"Oh, they said these tests won't take more than a few days." She propped herself against the pillow, allowing her dark hair to spread out in a fan on the crisp, white, starched linen. "Tomorrow they're doing a bone marrow aspiration."

"Ugh!" Jory blurted. "Sounds yucky."

Melissa saw Jory's face redden as Michael shot her a disgusted look. Instantly, Melissa felt sorry for her, knowing firsthand the feeling of saying something stupid in front of someone you want desperately to impress. "Dr. Pace says it's not so bad if I get a good technician."

"What are they going to do to you?" Michael asked.

"They take a sample of my bone marrow from inside my hip with a special syringe."

"They stick a needle into your bone?" Jory turned pale as Michael asked the question.

Melissa chewed her lip, anxious not to let on to Michael how scared she really felt. "It only takes a few seconds."

Through clenched teeth he said, "These guys had better not hurt you."

"Yeah, or I'll have my uncle in New Jersey fly down and break their legs," Jory announced.

Melissa tried to calm them both with a smile. "Hey, come on. I'm a big girl—I can take whatever they dish out. Besides, I'm too old to cry."

When visiting hours were over and Melissa was left alone, she plucked at the bed sheets, her bravado drowned in the hospital's night sounds that echoed around her. She *was* scared. And she *did* want to cry. Melissa felt overwhelmed with self-pity and helplessness. *Why is this happening to me?* Yesterday she'd been a normal sixteen-year-old girl on the verge of everything wonderful. Now she was hospitalized, and she was being poked and prodded, bled and taped.

She fought back the urge to weep, picking up her brush from the nightstand and absently running it through her hair. She remembered Brad's fingers, and she longed to savor his touch one more time.

"I'd heard from the nurses that there was a fox on the floor. They didn't lie." The male voice coming from her doorway startled Melissa so completely that the brush fell from her grip and clattered to the floor. In the doorway stood a stranger, surveying her with an insolent, wolfish grin.

Chapter Seven

～❧～

Her surprise turned to anger as she stared at a tall, thin boy on crutches braced against the door frame. "Who are you, and what are you doing in my room?"

"My name's Ricter Davis. You can call me Ric. I have a room down the hall. What are you in for?"

Still startled, Melissa appraised him through angry eyes. He was at least her age, maybe older. His brown hair brushed his shoulders and his piercing brown eyes and lean, raw-boned features appeared arrogant. "Weren't you taught to knock before barging into somebody's room?"

"Hey, it's a free country, and besides, your door was open. I was watching you brush your hair, but you were in the twilight zone and didn't see me."

It annoyed her to think he'd been studying her without her knowing. She wanted to say something curt, to make him go away, but before she could he hobbled toward her on his crutches. Suddenly, she noticed that his left leg was severed below the knee. She tried not to stare, but her eyes seemed glued to the void where his leg should be.

"It's been amputated," he told her frankly, allowing shame and shock to collide inside her. Reaching the side of her bed, he added, "It's all right to stare. Everybody does."

"I . . . I didn't mean to. You just startled me."

"What's your name?"

"Melissa Austin." Did he have to stare so openly, so steadily at her?

"Why are you here?"

"Just tests. I'm having a bone marrow aspiration in the morning."

His expression never changed. "Too bad."

"Why? Why is it too bad? Does it hurt?"

"The test doesn't hurt as much as the results."

She sat up straighter against the pillows, uneasiness gripping her stomach. "What is that supposed to mean?"

He hesitated. "I'm sorry. I shouldn't have said that . . . I'm not sure what I meant . . . I really should get back to my room," he said faltering. "I'll stop by tomorrow, and we can talk."

Melissa searched for a tart answer, wanting to let him know that she wasn't interested in seeing him again. "Don't bother," was all she could manage.

Ric arched an eyebrow, turned on his crutches, and hobbled to the door. "Tomorrow," he said, and he disappeared. She listened to the squeak of the crutches' rubber tips fade in the darkness.

The technicians came for her early the next morning. Melissa forgot about her surprise visitor in her preoccupation with the tests. First, they did an electrocardiogram. "To rule out rheumatic fever," a man in a green lab coat told her, exposing her chest and sticking small metal disks to her skin. Wires from the disks led to a machine that scribbled on graph paper. "This gives us a picture of your heart's working condition."

"Rheumatic fever causes heart damage, doesn't

it?" As soon as she voiced the question, the thought frightened her. "What causes it?"

"Untreated strep."

Melissa swallowed against a scratchy throat. Could she have had strep throat and ignored it long enough to have caused rheumatic fever to develop?

The bone marrow aspiration was not so pleasant as the electrocardiogram. The nurse and technician were friendly, almost cheerful, making Melissa wary. They placed her on an examining table on her stomach, a pillow tucked under her pelvis. The nurse cleaned her hip area with iodine. The brown liquid felt cool and stained her creamy, white skin. Next she applied a cooling spray. "This is a local anesthetic, Melissa," the woman explained. "It will numb the site so you won't feel the needle going in. We'll insert it into the spongy part of the bone where your marrow is manufactured, and it won't take but a few seconds to withdraw the cells we need for lab analysis."

Melissa clutched the metal edge of the table, determined to focus her attention on the white tiled wall in front of her and not on the syringe that looked a foot long. She gritted her teeth as pressure, then pain, overcame her. It felt as if a vacuum cleaner were sucking out some of her insides. When it was over, the nurse gave her a perfunctory pat. "There. Now that wasn't so bad, was it?"

Yes, it was horrible. "No problem," she said as she blinked back tears.

"You'll be tender in that spot for a little while, but you can get up and walk around once you get back to your floor." The nurse settled Melissa in a wheelchair for the ride back to her room. "There's a video game machine up there if you're into Space Invaders."

But Melissa didn't want to socialize. She just

wanted to return to her room and study. Regardless of her hospital visit, she was determined to make a good showing in the Brain Bowl drill next week. Besides, studying let her escape from worrying about her mysterious illness.

Jory called at lunchtime. "Where are you?" Melissa asked.

"Drove over to McDonald's for lunch. I'm at the pay phone next door at the Seven-Eleven."

The familiar image of that corner, a hangout for Lincoln students, sprang so sharply into Melissa's mind that a lump came to her throat. "What'd you have to eat?" she asked, clearing her throat.

"The usual—Big Mac and large fries. You know my weakness for grease. Hold on—I have someone here who wants to say hi."

Sounds of the phone being fumbled and passed came through the receiver. "Hi, Melissa."

"Hi, Brad." Her voice went soft when she heard his.

"Jory tells me you're skipping school for a few days."

"Jory exaggerates. I'll be home in another day. I thought I'd experience firsthand the life of a laboratory rat. So far, it's not much fun, but it's given me a whole new respect for people who march for animal rights."

Brad chuckled. "Hey, did I ever tell you I'm glad you made the Brain Bowl team?"

"Yes, but not nearly in enough detail. I left school a bit suddenly the other day." She allowed the sarcasm to bleed into her inflection. "But you did predict at the country club we'd both make it. Are you psychic?"

"Just confident. And besides, didn't I say I wanted you on the team with me?"

Her pulse quickened. "Yes, you did."

"So hurry up and get out of that hospital. I wouldn't mind a few private study sessions between the two of us."

"I'll tell my doctor to put a rush on my case."

The phone passed back to Jory. "Well, I've gotta run. Chemistry lab next period, you know. Ugh. I hate it."

"Don't blow anything up."

"Ha-ha! I'll stop by to see you tonight. Do—uh—do you want me to bring a visitor?" Jory asked the question in a conspiratorial whisper.

"Don't you dare drag Brad up here, Jory Delaney! Do you hear me?"

"Just asking . . ." Jory huffed in mock innocence. "It's not every day you can legitimately have a guy ogle you while you're lying around in your nightgown. It could be kind of sexy."

"Forget it."

"I could bring the red harem gown . . ."

"*Jory!*"

"Suit yourself. See ya later."

Melissa hung up with an amused shake of her head. Jory was incorrigible. Maybe that's why I like her so much, Melissa thought. Lucky, carefree, Jory. With nothing more serious on her mind than a chemistry lab.

Michael popped his head around her door frame. "Up for some company?"

Delighted to see him, she lifted her arms for a hug. "I thought you were working this afternoon."

"I'm between jobs. Also, I have class tonight, and I didn't want to go an entire day without seeing you. Mom says she'll be up this evening. How are they treating you?" The lightness left his voice.

She rubbed her hip gingerly. "I've had better times in my life. But the sooner I get all this testing done, the sooner I can get back to a normal life."

He tugged affectionately on a hank of her hair. "You look pale."

"Michael, there is something I want to talk to you about."

"Name it."

Melissa fidgeted with her covers. "The money for all these tests. How's Mom gonna pay for all this? It isn't exactly built into our budget."

She saw his blue eyes, so like her own, take on a look of concern. "Mom has a good insurance policy. It'll pay for most of this."

"But we're talking about major bills. Even the balance after insurance pays its share will be hard to afford."

Michael tipped his head and smiled. "Why don't you read these fashion magazines Jory brought and stop worrying your pretty head about hospital bills?"

"Look, Michael, if I'm going to get that National Merit Scholarship I can't numb my brain with fluff about designer labels and the latest hairstyles."

"And you can't afford designer labels either," Michael teased.

"You're making fun of me," she snapped.

Michael hugged her and kissed her forehead. "Not at all, Melissa. I think you're beautiful. And brave, too. I'd kick somebody's face in if he tried to stick needles in *my* bones."

The blatant admiration in his voice made her own voice stick in her throat. "Don't be such a baby," she said, attempting to hide her embarrassment.

He laughed and kissed her goodbye.

Later that night, after her visitors had left, she

caught a glimpse of the boy Ric walking past her room. She quickly averted her eyes and held her breath, hoping he wouldn't follow through on his promise to visit her a second time. She didn't like him and she didn't want to know him. Luckily, he passed by without even glancing inside. She sighed and scooted down under her covers, wearied by the rounds of testing and the gaiety she felt compelled to show her visitors.

She hated to have her mother worry. Melissa was worried enough herself. She wanted out, wanted to go home and resume her regular schedule. They'd have some of the test results back by the morning, according to Dr. Pace. Until then, there was nothing for her to do but wait.

Two doctors came midmorning, while she was engrossed in her history book—Dr. Pace and Dr. Rowan, a bear-size man with bushy brown hair and large, strong hands. Behind them stood her mother and Michael. Melissa's surprise at seeing her family gave way to apprehension immediately. Her mother's face was pasty white.

"So many of you?" She gave a nervous twitter of a laugh. "Will it take two of you to hold me down for today's tests?"

Dr. Rowan said, "No more tests, Melissa."

"Mom? Why aren't you at work?"

"I wanted to be here when they talked to you, so I took the day off."

Fear tasted metallic in Melissa's dry mouth. She dipped her head, struggling to catch Michael's eyes, but he refused to meet hers. "Okay. So it's more than anemia." Why was her voice so high-pitched?

"Melissa, it isn't a common anemia. Or mono."

Dr. Rowan grasped her small hands, and she could feel the strength of his.

"Or rheumatic fever," she pronounced insightfully. Her gaze fastened onto the front of his lab coat, spotlessly white except for a faint brown stain on the pocket. She wondered if he knew that the pristine whiteness was marred by that single spot. "All right. I give up," she said, a bit too brightly. "What do I have?"

Dr. Rowan's unswerving gaze trapped hers and held it. "The diagnosis is lymphocytic leukemia, Melissa." His voice sounded clinical and very far away. "It's a form of cancer."

Chapter Eight

❡

Melissa laughed. Dr. Rowan sounded absurd, and her family, hovering around her bed with stricken expressions, reminded Melissa of a silent movie. She quickly sobered and said, "I don't believe you. You must have made some mistake. I'm sixteen years old. How can I possibly have leukemia?"

Dr. Rowan gave her hands a slight squeeze. "The bone marrow aspiration confirmed it, Melissa. Leukemia is a blood disorder. It occurs when young white blood cells formed in the bone marrow reproduce abnormally and crowd out the normal ones. They take up the space of the red blood cells and the platelets. Platelets cause your blood to clot normally, and because your supply is low you've been bruising easily. Without enough red blood cells to carry oxygen, you become anemic. That's why you've been so tired all the time, and why you look pale."

Melissa only half heard him. She didn't care how many facts he produced to back up his diagnosis. She didn't believe him. "Maybe the tests were wrong." She withdrew her hands from his and folded them primly in her lap. "Tests can be wrong, can't they?"

"Sometimes. But not in your case."

Melissa glanced around him to her mother's face, where she saw the truth. "Oh Mom . . ."

Her mother wrapped her in her arms and held

her tightly. "We'll fight it, Melissa. You've got the best medical help available. And we'll fight it."

Dr. Rowan cleared his throat. "Medicine has made great advancements over the past few years in the treatment of different kinds of leukemia. Although we have no cure for the disease, we do have very sophisticated ways of dealing with it. The important thing now is to begin treatment as soon as possible."

"What kind of treatment?" Melissa's voice quavered as she asked the question.

"Traditional treatments include chemotherapy. That's when we bombard the leukemic cells with large doses of powerful cancer-fighting chemicals . . ."

"I know what chemo is," she snapped. "I read. I'm not stupid."

Dr. Rowan continued patiently. "Once we initiate chemo, we'll expect an improvement. It will take several days to establish the right combination of drugs, but our goal is to get you into remission as quickly as possible. Remission is a decrease, sometimes a reversal, of your symptoms. After we achieve remission, you'll go on to maintenance."

"Maintenance?"

"Yes. Once initial treatments do their job and healthy blood-forming tissue begins to regrow, you'll take oral medication. You'll only have to come to the clinic every few weeks for testing and possible further IV chemotherapy. The longer you remain in remission, the better your chances for a complete recovery."

"And if there is no complete recovery?" Melissa's mind was spinning, but the question popped out. Somehow, his words sounded ominous.

Dr. Rowan's expression grew somber, and he touched her arm; his eyes were filled with deep compassion. "I believe in being honest with my patients,

Melissa. I believe in being truthful because it's necessary for them to actively participate in the treatment of their disease. I'm not going to lie to you, but I won't leave you without hope either. People *do* survive leukemia. If you remain in a continuous first remission for five years, we consider you cured."

"And if I don't?"

"We try for a second remission. We also consider a bone marrow transplant. That's the grafting of healthy marrow from a biologically compatible donor into your marrow."

Suddenly, Melissa felt overwhelmed by too much information that threatened to split her head open. She couldn't stand to hear any more that Dr. Rowan had to say.

Mercifully, her mother interrupted. "What are you going to be doing for Melissa right now?"

"Today we'll do a lumbar puncture. We'll take fluid from around Melissa's spinal cord and examine it to determine if the leukemic cells have invaded your central nervous system. That test will also help us decide on the best combination of drugs to begin fighting your leukemia."

Melissa understood that suddenly her body had become a war zone. Her internal defenses no longer controlled what was happening inside of her. "When will you start the drugs?"

"Tomorrow."

"So soon?"

"Clinically, the disease progresses rapidly. We must begin treatment immediately." The pressure of his large, warm hand on her arm made her nod almost imperceptibly.

"Do it," she said, gazing toward her mother and Michael. "Hurry and get started. I want to go home."

* * *

Melissa lay curled in a fetal position on her hospital bed. She felt empty. How long had she cried? An hour? Two? After the lumbar procedure, she'd been returned to her room. Someone brought a supper tray, but it sat untouched on her bedstand.

"You should eat, Melissa. You have to keep your strength up." Her mother's voice caused her to stiffen.

"For what?" Melissa asked, her own voice quivering. "So they can bleed me again? Stick me with more needles?"

"I'm sorry, honey . . ."

"Sorry!" Melissa flopped over and glared straight at her mother's face. "Is that all you can say? That you're sorry?"

"What do you want me to say?"

Melissa ignored the pinched look around her mother's mouth and the strained expression in her eyes. She wanted someone to hurt as much as she was hurting. "It's probably *your* fault, you know. You had me! You must have caused it."

"That's not true! The doctor assured me that cancer is not necessarily inherited and it's not contagious. It's a disease that can strike anyone."

"Why did it have to happen to me?" The sobs started again, but when her mother reached over to comfort her, Melissa pushed her away. "Go away. Just go away and leave me alone."

"Melissa, please . . ."

Melissa refused to listen. All she wanted was to be left alone. She turned to face the blank wall, twisting the bed sheet into a ball under her chin. She wasn't sure when her mother left, but she sensed she was alone again. She'd hurt her mother. She knew that, but it was too late to change it now. *So what?* she thought. *Life is full of pain.*

"Hello, Melissa."

Ricter Davis. Why wouldn't everybody leave her alone? "Go away," she mumbled.

"It's Ric."

"I know who it is. I don't want to talk to anybody."

"Because you have cancer?"

The word seemed dirty, unclean. She rolled over to face him, enraged and ready to lash out at him. "What I have is none of your business."

Ric lifted himself onto her bed and laid the metal crutches across the end of her mattress. "Let's talk about it."

"I don't want to talk."

"Sometimes talking helps."

His eyes were empathetic, and for the first time Melissa's hostility wavered. "You knew what they were testing me for the other night. Why didn't you tell me?" Her words were accusing.

"Why didn't you ask?"

"I didn't *know* enough to ask."

"They do bone marrow studies to rule out leukemia. You should have asked your doctor if you were curious."

It was as if he'd told her it was her fault she hadn't been forewarned about her diagnosis. Her anger flared again. "Drop dead."

His smile was sardonic. "I might just do that."

"Meaning?"

"Meaning I know where you're at. I have cancer, too."

His revelation left her groping for words. "I . . . I didn't know . . ."

"It's not leukemia, like yours. It's osteogenic sar-

coma—bone cancer. That's why they cut off my leg."
He motioned to the void below his thigh. She shuddered in spite of herself. "Repulsive, isn't it? Not to
mention the crimp it's put in my track career."

"Track?"

"I was a marathoner for the University of South
Florida. Had a scholarship and everything." He
slapped the stump of his leg. "Not much of an Olympic future for a one-legged runner."

"I'm sorry . . ."

"I went through the chemo part, too." His eyes
held hers without mercy, without pity. "It's no picnic,
but you *can* do it."

Melissa swallowed hard and wished she could escape her nightmare. *This can't be happening to me.
Not me.* She sat up and hugged her knees to her chest,
suddenly self-conscious that she wore nothing beneath
the thin cotton gown. "Why are you in the hospital
now?"

"More tests. Just to see if it's spread to other parts
of my body."

"And?"

"And so far, I'm clean."

"That's good, isn't it?"

"Real good." His voice had dropped so low, she
had to lean forward to catch it. "The physical therapist
is trying out a new prosthesis on me. That's an artificial
limb. The last one caused skin ulcers because it didn't
fit right."

Melissa shut her eyes and sighed. She didn't
want to be hearing about this. There was a horror in it
all that nauseated her. Ric was only a few years older
than she was—too young for cancer. She raked her
hand through her hair, shaking it out of her face. It
billowed, comfortingly, against her back. She re-

flected on an earlier part of their conversation. "The chemo," she asked. "What's it really like?"

His gaze went guarded. "It doesn't matter what it's like. It's something you have to do."

His evasive answer frightened her. "Tell me, Ric. Please."

"You'll be sick."

"I understand."

"No, you don't. You'll be so sick, you'll wish you could die."

Tears welled inside her but she fought them down. She refused to cry in front of him. "Does anything help?"

"Try to eat, even when you know it won't stay down. Don't be a stoic—get mad, cry if you want to. And don't go through it alone. If your family can't be with you when you're heaving up your guts, get a nurse."

Coldness crept up her spine and she sat motionless. The one small, weak light over her hospital bed could not dispel the gloom. She felt Ric shift off of her mattress.

"Where are you going?" Momentary panic set in as she realized she didn't want to be alone. Her feelings for Ric had done a 180-degree turn. Now she didn't want him to leave.

"Back to my room."

"Do you have to? I'm scared."

Unexpectedly, his hand reached out, caught her chin, and lifted it. His eyes locked onto hers. "Jesus, you're pretty."

There was a sadness in his whispered words she didn't understand. "So what? What do my looks have to do with anything?"

"Just an observation." Ric shrugged, but she felt

baffled, as if his remark had a deeper meaning she couldn't quite grasp. "Your doctors will send someone in to teach you about positive imaging, Melissa. It's sort of a mind-over-matter approach to healing. Listen to her and do exactly what she tells you. No matter how bad it gets, don't give up."

"Will you come back?"

A mysterious smile twisted the corner of his mouth. "Of course. We're alike, you know. Pretty soon you won't have a whole lot in common with your former world."

Images flashed through her mind: home, school, Jory, Brad. A gulf separated them from her and the sterile, bleak walls of the hospital. "I won't let that happen," she said.

"We'll see." At the doorway he paused and looked at her with a long, soul-searching stare. "Too bad about your hair."

"What about it?"

"The chemo will take it. It'll take it all."

Chapter Nine

❧

"You heard me, Jory. Cut it." Melissa eyed the scissors in her friend's hand, ignoring Jory's startled look.

"When you asked me to sneak a pair of scissors up to your room, I didn't know you were planning on cutting off your hair. Come on, Melissa . . . What gives?"

Sitting cross-legged on her bed, Melissa pressed her lips together in steely determination. Her testing had been completed, and just an hour ago Dr. Rowan had informed her and her mother of the course of treatment he had prescribed for her case.

"I've written down the names of the drugs, their frequency of administration, and their side effects." He had given Melissa a piece of paper with neatly typed columns, but she had resisted reading it. "You'll be taking pills, getting injections, and taking some medications intravenously so we can regulate their entrance into your bloodstream more easily. Blood work will be done daily, bone marrow exams once every two weeks during induction. These drugs are very powerful, and by killing off the leukemic cells, they threaten the healthy ones, too."

"In short," Melissa had interrupted. "You're killing me softly with the medicine."

Dr. Rowan had crossed his arms over his broad, barrel-shaped chest. "We're saving you slowly from your disease," he had corrected. "You'll be given your first doses immediately, and you'll go down to the special chemo room in a little while."

Once he'd left, Melissa had taken her pills and endured a stinging shot that instantly nauseated her. She had urged her mother to go to work and stop back later in the afternoon, and then called Jory, catching her before she'd gone off to school. "Come by the hospital first," she had said. "And bring your scissors."

Now, as Jory clutched the scissors tightly, Melissa told her, "They'll be coming to take me down for my first round of chemo real soon. I want my hair cut before they walk in the door. Are you going to do it for me, or do I have to do it myself?"

"But, Melissa," Jory argued, "you've had long hair all your life. And it's so gorgeous. Why chop it off now? It doesn't make any sense."

"It's got to come off," Melissa said woodenly, fighting fiercely to hold back her tears. "I'd rather take it off myself than have the chemotherapy do it for me."

"I don't understand."

"Oh, Jory, stop acting so dumb! The chemo will make it all fall out. It's a side effect. It's the price I have to pay for a cure. Now do you get it?"

"I . . . I didn't realize . . . I'm sorry, Melissa. Really sorry."

"Yeah—well, so am I. But being sorry won't change it. By the time they finish giving me the drugs to make me well, I'll be bald. If I cut it now, myself, maybe that won't be so horrible."

Jory hesitated, studying the scissors. "I'm not a beautician, you know."

Melissa punched her friend's arm playfully. "I've seen you take scissors to your own hair plenty of times. Like in freshman year, when you were in your punk phase and you spiked your hair. . . . Remember?"

Jory cringed. "That was the only time my parents ever noticed me. My father yelled for a week. It reflected on his image at the country club to have such a spaced-out daughter, you know."

Melissa heard the bitterness in Jory's voice. She closed her hand around Jory's and whispered, "Let's get started, okay?"

Jory flashed an impish smile. "If this works out, maybe I'll move to Australia and take up sheep shearing." She combed the dark, thick hair, slipped the scissors into the shining mass next to Melissa's ear and cut.

In minutes, the bed was covered with hair. Melissa closed her eyes and sat perfectly straight, feeling her head grow lighter as the hair fell away. Cool air fanned the exposed nape of her neck and she shivered. The silence in the room was broken only by the steady snip of the metal blades. Even Jory, usually bubbling with chatter, was quiet.

"What the hell is going on!" The roar of Michael's voice made Melissa jump, and Jory squealed as the scissors clattered to the floor.

Michael grabbed Jory roughly by the shoulders, his face pinched and angry. "What are you doing to my sister?"

Jory gaped numbly, her eyes round and wide and her hands clenched behind her.

Melissa reached out and grasped Michael's arm. "Stop it, Michael! Let go of her. It's not her fault—I asked her to cut my hair."

"You what?" He turned his fury on her. "Why the hell did you do a stupid thing like that?"

Melissa squared her chin and mustered a steely

look. "Because the chemotherapy will make me go
bald, and I refuse to let it have my hair. *I'm* taking it
off before the medicine does, and I asked Jory to help
me. Now tell her you're sorry."

Jory had turned stiff and ghostly white, obviously
shaken by Michael's outrage. Michael clenched his
fists and worked his jaw, clearly trying to control his
emotions. "I'm sorry, Jory." He faced his sister and
lifted what was left of her newly cut hair off her forehead. "Are you sure about the chemo?"

"Dr. Rowan gave me a list of side effects to expect." She reached for the paper on her night table.
"He was very honest. But then, he told us from the
start that he would be. Let's hear it for honestly," she
mumbled under her breath. "Anyway, he said that the
chemo causes lots of problems. Losing my hair is only
one. But he also said that once I'm in remission and I
go on maintenance therapy, my hair will grow back."

Michael gently stroked her head.

"It's only *hair* Michael," she said through
clenched teeth.

"That's true. And now that I see it short, I like it.
Although the style leaves something to be desired."

His attempt at humor calmed her. "Jory insisted
she wasn't a beautician, but I made her cut it anyway."

"It's not that bad," Jory said, stepping closer to
the side of the bed. "I mean, with a little mousse, a
little curl, it could be really chic."

Michael hugged Melissa and she squeezed her
eyes shut. "I'm scared, Michael."

"Do you want me to stay with you for your treatment?"

She did and she didn't. "No. It's all right."

"I'll stay," Jory offered.

"You're already skipping school."

"So what? It's not like I've never done *that* before, you know."

"The nurses will be with me," Melissa hedged. She began to sense her illness and treatments as a wall rising between herself and the "well" world. She'd been thrown into a different place the others could not fully enter, and she might as well come to terms with that now. She recalled Ric's message from the night before: *You won't have a whole lot in common with your former world.* "You two leave and come back tonight. I'll probably have oodles to tell you by then," she said.

"If you're sure . . ." She saw a guilty look of relief in Michael's eyes. She knew that hospitals and needles scared him.

"Go on." He was almost to the door when she called him back. "I—uh—forgot to ask . . . How's Mom?"

"She's pretty rung out."

Guilt pricked at Melissa's conscience. "I said some things to her last night I didn't mean. I'm so sorry. You'll tell her I'm sorry, won't you?"

"You can tell her. She's planning on coming by during her lunch hour."

"I really am sorry, Michael."

He nodded, his blue eyes holding hers. "We're all sorry, Melissa. Everything about this business stinks. But we're family, and we'll make it through."

Once Michael left, Jory sighed. "Why do I always act like such a fool in front of him?"

Melissa picked up a lock of hair from the bed and it fell through her fingers. *Lucky Jory.* Nothing more heavy to think about than acting silly in front of a guy she wants to impress. She asked, "Could you help me clean this up before you go? I don't want them to bring me back to a hairy bed."

Neither of them spoke as they scooped up the wads of hair and threw them into the wastepaper basket. Together they brushed off the mattress until no wayward strands could be found on the clean white sheets. When they hugged each other goodbye, Melissa sensed a tension between them. Jory could walk out the door. Melissa could not. Jory had school and friends and everyday life to return to. Melissa had chemotherapy to face. She ran her fingers through her cropped hair and settled against her pillows to wait for the technicians.

The chemo room wasn't anything like Melissa expected. It was painted buttercup yellow, with bold graphic prints on the walls and gray carpeting. There were beige contour chairs that looked to be quite expensive. The only thing that belied the serene comfort of the room was the metal IV stand beside each chair.

"Hi, Melissa," a nurse said cheerfully. "I'm DeeDee Thomas, and I'll be administering your medication."

Feeling more terrified than sociable, Melissa forced herself to acknowledge the nurse's chatter while DeeDee inserted a needlelike contraption of plastic tubing and a rubber plug into a vein in her arm. "This is a heparin lock," DeeDee explained. "Not very glamorous-looking, but you'll wear it for the next few days. That way, we have access to your blood supply and can administer your chemo regime without having to jab you so often."

Melissa wondered if she was supposed to feel grateful. She lay back in the chair and DeeDee hung a bag of liquid on the IV stand next to her bed. "Relax," the nurse said. "This will take about an hour."

An hour! Melissa saw her days dripping away through snaking lines of flexible tubing. "I feel sick to my stomach," she said.

DeeDee patted her shoulder and handed her a small bowl. "In case you need to vomit," she told her. Her eyes were kind, but they didn't even attempt to hide the truth from Melissa.

"It's going to be bad, isn't it?"

"What seems bad now is ultimately for your good. I'll be here for you if you need me."

Melissa swallowed against her own bile and swore to hold back as long as she could. She watched the fluid trickle from the inverted bottle and down the tubing into her arm. She watched as it began its long, steady journey into the microscopic battleground in her body.

That evening Melissa was too sick to eat dinner, too sick to receive visitors. Her mother held her through it all, but Michael had to leave because he couldn't stand to see her hurting. After her mother left, Melissa fell into a fitful sleep, awakening when she had to vomit again.

In the stillness of her room she sensed someone next to her bed. A hand smoothed her bangs from her brow. "I'm here, Melissa," Ric said.

"Go away," she murmured through parched lips.

"It's worse to be alone," he whispered, blotting her cheek with a damp cloth.

She didn't want anyone to see her this way—exposed, vulnerable. Yet his hands were gentle and knowing. "You were right," she said when the violent nausea had subsided. "I do feel like I want to die."

"Haven't you heard?" he chided tenderly. "Only the good die young."

"I hate the way they treat me."

"Who?"

"The doctors. The people here."

"How do they treat you?"

"Like I'm not a person. Like I'm just a blob of cells. Like there's something unclean inside me and they've got to drive it out . . . no matter how much it hurts."

"Should I call up a witch doctor? Or a sorcerer?"

She managed to smile, despite her discomfort. "During treatment today, the psychologist came and taught me about 'imaging.'"

"So what will you use to hunt down and destroy your cancer cells? I pretend I'm manning a ship like Luke Skywalker. I close my eyes and zip through my body firing laser shots at any cancer cells trying to hide and multiply." He demonstrated by pointing his forefinger and making zinging sounds.

Melissa envisioned his illustration and smiled. "I imagine my cancer cells as hairy toads, all black and bony, with large suction cups for mouths. And they're sitting inside my bones sucking out my marrow, getting fat and strong while my marrow gets thinner and thinner."

Ric arched his eyebrow. "Grim picture. So what are you using to destroy them?"

"I . . . I haven't thought of something yet."

"That's the most important part, Melissa. That's what imaging is all about. You've got to see yourself hunting down the cells and destroying them. That's how you turn on your inner healing reserves."

Another wave of sickness churned through her and she clutched the sheets until her knuckles went white. "I . . . I can't think of anything stronger than those toads . . ." she said as her nausea turned into pain.

"You have to," Ric said, uncoiling her fingers from the sheet and making her grip his hand. "Don't you understand, Melissa? Your life depends on how hard you fight."

Chapter Ten

The chemical war intensified, and Melissa experienced battle fatigue. There were setbacks. A reaction to one of her medications that caused a horrible rash. A brief secondary infection that took an extra week to clear up. Melissa's stay in the hospital lengthened, and she felt more and more estranged from her former world.

Melissa knew she wasn't the only one having trouble coping. Her mother came daily with tense smiles and false bravado. Michael came, always nervous and fidgeting, revealing to Melissa that he'd rather be anywhere but at the hospital. Jory visited often, but Melissa adamantly refused to let any of her other friends come up to see her.

Late afternoon sun slanted through the blinds as Jory bounced into Melissa's room, talking nonstop. "Sorry I didn't get by last night. Steve and Melanie and Dirk and I went out for pizza, and Dirk was cash poor so I had to fork it over—boy, did that steam me. I mean, why pay for your own date?" Jory paused long enough to take a breath, and Melissa forced a smile.

Jory's visits were the hardest. She always had stories to tell of school and parties and dates. Melissa listened, hating to hear them, yet longing for them.

"I'm sure he'll pay you back, or at least treat you next time."

"He'd better." She tossed her books on the floor along with a sack. "Listen to me, going on and on. How're things going for you today?"

"Except for chemo, my schedule's open."

"This must be such a drag for you."

"The high point of my day is when they come to disinfect the bathroom," Melissa said.

"How is the food? You really should eat more. You look thinner."

"I know. I've lost twelve pounds in eight days."

Jory grimaced. "Can't keep anything down, huh?"

"I didn't think it was possible to throw up so much."

"And me rattling on about pizza. Sorry about that."

"Let me make my pity party complete," Melissa said, tugging gently on her hair. A handful fell weightlessly to the floor. "How can you stand to look at me?" she asked, touching the sores that erupted on her face.

Jory's green eyes grew wide. "You're not that ugly. I . . . I mean . . ."

Melissa released a short, bitter laugh. "Real homecoming queen material, huh? And how about the junior prom? Who'll want to ask the Bride of Frankenstein?"

Jory picked up the paper bag that lay with her books. "Here. This is for you."

"What is it?"

"Scarves. I bought them in that boutique we used to shop at in the mall."

Melissa momentarily forgot her misery as she fingered the selection of colorful, filmy scarves. "Silk, Jory?" she asked, lifting her hairless eyebrow. She knew that each elegant piece of cloth must have cost double digits. The irony was not lost on her. Jory never had to give a second thought to what things cost. Or who would ask her for a date. She didn't have to struggle with anything more incapacitating than a hangnail. "Thank you, Jory. It was nice of you."

"Do you like them? I picked out what I thought you'd like best. They are okay, aren't they?"

Her eagerness to please touched Melissa deeply. "They're great." Melissa tied a paisley scarf around her balding head.

"Good grief, you look like a bag lady. Here . . . let me do it." Melissa reached for a surgical mask and covered her mouth and nose.

"Why'd you do that?" Jory asked.

Melissa felt overwhelmed suddenly. How could she explain to Jory that the disease was *hers* and she had to join the doctors in the fight against it? Melissa knew that being careful and taking precautions from now on meant helping with her cure.

"Dr. Rowan says I have to be careful not to catch anything. Even a cold could set me back weeks."

"What do I look like? A germ bank?"

"It's nothing personal, really. I just want to get out of here so bad . . ."

Jory slouched in a chair on the far side of the room. Melissa hadn't meant to hurt her feelings and didn't know how to make it up to her.

"So tell me more about school," Melissa said brightly. "Does anyone ask about me?"

"Sure. As a matter of fact, Brad asked me about you today."

Melissa's heart leaped in spite of herself. The afternoon she'd spent with Brad at the country club seemed like a million years ago. And although she didn't want anyone but Jory visiting her, she wouldn't mind if he called. But he hadn't. Not once. "How's Brain Bowl coming? Are they still holding my place open on the team?"

"You mean you still want to do Brain Bowl?"

Jory's surprise irked her. "Of course. Once this part of my treatment is over and I start looking human again, I *will* come back to school."

Jory flushed and stared into her lap. "I—uh—well Brad did say that they were talking about replacing you . . ."

"Don't let them do it, Jory." Melissa grew agitated, twisting the bed sheet into a ball.

"But Melissa, you're so sick. Why does it matter to you now?"

"Because it just does." Her voice went thick with emotion. "Because it's mine. That seat on the Brain Bowl team belongs to *me*."

"Do you want me to ask Mr. Marshall or Mrs. Watson about it?"

"Would you?"

"Well, they've certainly talked with me on enough occasions," Jory observed dryly. "In fact, if you remember, Watson threatened to flunk me last year. I guess I could chat with her on your behalf."

Melissa felt relieved, but the intense emotions had drained her energy and she eased down against her pillow. "I'd really appreciate it, Jory. I mean, I could ask my mom, but I don't think she could handle one more thing. My leukemia is wringing her out."

"How's Michael taking it?"

"He avoids it. I don't think he means to. No one really wants to talk about it with me except the medical types."

Jory picked at the blue polish on her fingernails. "So who do you talk with here?"

"Ric. Sometimes."

"That's the guy with—" Jory paused, "—with the bone cancer."

"The guy with one leg, you mean," Melissa said, knowing Jory was embarrassed. "Don't worry, it took me a while to get used to being honest about it, too. At least once I'm in remission, I'll look normal again. That's what they tell me anyhow. Ricter Davis never will."

"When do you think you'll get out of here? Have they said?"

"My blood work's looking better. My platelet count has stabilized and my white blood count has fallen. My doctors say it's a good sign, but they also say that I still have a long way to go. Once I'm discharged, I have to go on outpatient therapy."

"What's outpatient?"

"I can go home, but I have to come here for chemo and bone marrow exams and blood tests until I achieve remission."

"How long will that take?"

Melissa shrugged her thin shoulders. "They don't know. But once I do go into remission, I'll still have to take some of the drugs for a long time. Maybe years. And I'll have to keep coming to the clinic for testing."

"But you'll be all right?" Jory picked the words carefully. "You'll be well again?"

"I don't know what 'all right' means anymore. I'll still have leukemia. But the longer I stay in remission, the better my chances of being cured. Five years without a recurrence and I'm home free." The smile Melissa offered felt stiff and forced.

"And if you don't stay in remission?"

Melissa studied her friend. She'd turned the statistics and facts over and over in her head for days, ever since she'd asked Dr. Rowan the very same thing. Suddenly she wanted to talk about it, get it into the open and out of the dark corners of her mind. "They're going to do a bone marrow aspiration on Michael next week," she confided.

"Is Michael sick, too?" A look of fear crossed Jory's face and she bolted upright in the chair.

"No. It's for me. To see if his bone marrow is compatible with mine in case I ever need a transplant. They harvest a bunch of his marrow and put it into my bones and wait to see if it will grow and take over for my own." *A bunch.* Is that how bone marrow grows? In an unscientific bunch? Like a cluster of flowers? She cleared her throat. "If it does, no more leukemia. But Dr. Rowan says it's risky. And I could reject the transplant."

Jory's round, green eyes widened and Melissa prayed that Jory wouldn't pursue the next most logical question: *What if you reject the transplant?* "I hope they can fix it the other way. With the chemo and all," Jory finally said.

"Me too."

Jory stood, fidgeting with the strap on her purse. "Well I guess I should be going. I've got a geometry test tomorrow."

Melissa felt childish longing. "I wish I did."

"Are you able to do much studying? I've brought all your textbooks. But maybe you need something special from the library. I'll bring anything you want."

"I'm keeping up. Mom got each of my teachers to outline assignments for me. When I go back to school, I can take a few tests to see if I'm up to par with the rest of the class. It's important that I keep up, you know." She focused her attention on a blank spot on the wall behind Jory.

Jory shifted from one foot to the other. "The PSATs are scheduled for the third Saturday in October."

Melissa's vision zeroed in on her friend. *The PSATs!* How could she have forgotten them? Especially when she pinned her hopes on scoring high enough to qualify as a National Merit Scholar. "In the Lincoln auditorium?" she asked.

"Yes, starting at eight-thirty A.M. sharp. Bring two number-two lead pencils. Don't fold, spindle, or mutilate your IBM punch card."

Melissa sighed. "I've got to get out of this place."

"The test's less than two weeks away."

"I don't care. I'm going to take it."

"They'll have a makeup test."

"No. I'm going to take it with my class."

"Oh, Melissa, do you think you should plan on that?" Jory asked.

"Why not? If I'm an outpatient, like they said I'll be, there's no reason why I can't go."

"But you've been so sick . . ."

"So I'll bring a barf bag." Defiance and anger overwhelmed her. "I'm sick and tired of people telling me what I can and can't do. Don't I get to make any choices for my life?" By now her hands were shaking and she tasted tears in the back of her throat.

"I was just worried, that's all," Jory said.

"Well, stop worrying. I'm going to survive this. I'm not going to fade away like a shadow. I'm *alive*, damn it!"

"I know you are." Jory's voice held a note of hysteria. "It's just all so horrible, that's all. I hate it."

"And I don't?" The burst of anger had sapped her. She shut her eyes as the room spun and nausea overcame her. Fine beads of perspiration broke out on her forehead as she fought against the sickness, but she knew she was losing the battle and said, "Jory, the basin . . ."

Jory clamored across the room and got the basin to her just in time. Melissa heaved until there was nothing left. Jory had dampened a washcloth and wiped her face for her. "Should I ring for a nurse?" she asked.

"No. It's over." Melissa lay back on the bed. She heard Jory moving around the room—flushing the toilet, running water, and returning the basin to her bedside table. When she had the strength to open her eyes, she saw Jory standing next to her, staring at her thoughtfully. "Some friend I am. I throw up all over you." She was too weak to even feel embarrassed.

"I'm glad I was here and that you weren't alone." Jory kept studying Melissa's face, as if seeing her for the first time. Melissa wished she didn't look so horrible.

"Hey, your scarf's twisted," Jory said.

"Will you fix it?" The ulcers in her mouth burned and it was difficult to speak.

Jory eased the surgical mask over Melissa's face. "No use taking any chances on your catching anything. Especially now that you're so close to getting out of this dump." She retied the scarf in a jaunty fashion, with the knot to one side.

"You're a good friend," Melissa said.

Jory's voice turned crisp and businesslike. "And don't worry about Brain Bowl. I'll talk to the powers that be. They won't dare drop you from the team."

"How can you guarantee that?" Melissa was struggling to form words and stay awake.

"Blackmail. How could they even consider dropping a poor, sick girl who's just counting the days till she's able to compete with her team?"

Melissa smiled. "You're devious, Jory Delaney."

"Yeah. I know." Jory wiped her friend's forehead one more time. "And we'll go take the PSATs together. I'll even hold your barf bag if you want."

"I might have to bring a bag to wear over my head, too. Don't want to frighten all my classmates, do I?"

"Who cares? All that matters is that you ace the test for that scholarship."

"You could ace it, too . . ." Her voice was barely a whisper.

"College isn't for me, Melissa. Unless you count the frat parties. Now go to sleep, and I'll be back tomorrow after school." Melissa's eyes were already closed and Jory's voice sounded far away.

When she woke up, the twilight had cast long violet shadows across her room. Ric was holding her hand. "Hey, lady," he said, a half-smile lighting his gaunt features.

"Hey."

Without asking, Ric placed a mint on her tongue. "Rough day?"

"Real rough." Melissa noticed that he was dressed in street clothes, jeans and a polo shirt. "Got a date?"

He placed the back of her hand along the length of his cheek. His skin felt cool and slightly rough. "I've been discharged, Melissa. I'm going home."

Chapter Eleven

～

Melissa filled with envy. *Home.* When would she be able to say the same thing? "I'm happy for you, Ric. Where's home?"

"Upstate New York. But I'm really only returning to my dorm room at USF. After two years of living there, I think of it as home."

"So you'll be here at the university?" In a strange way she was relieved. He was the only person she knew close to her own age who understood what it was like to have cancer.

"At least until the end of the spring term. Then I'll probably stay around for the summer and work until the fall semester starts."

"Don't you want to go back to New York for the summer? And see your family?"

His gaze was direct, and she noticed how dark and piercing his eyes were. "My medical support is here in Tampa. I don't want to leave."

The notion stunned her. *Her* medical support was here too. How would that affect her choice of colleges? Melissa kept her concerns to herself, offering Ric a half-smile. "When you're dressed in jeans, you can't even tell about your leg."

His expression was cynical. "Yeah, this prosthesis is terrific. No one could even guess I'm a cripple unless I break into a run."

"Ric, it doesn't make you less of a person."

"Just three-fourths of one."

"But there're no more signs of your cancer."

He flipped the ends of her scarf. "That doesn't mean it won't come back. There are no guarantees."

Her stomach lurched, but not from chemo. His blunt pessimism made her feel as if she were trapped in a labyrinth of blind alleys and stone walls. "Where's that optimistic guy who sat by my bed while I tossed my cookies every night?"

Ric took her hand. "He's still inside me, Melissa." His scrutiny made her feel uneasy because she knew how horrible she looked, broken out in sores and skin lesions from the medications. "I'm going to call you when you're back home. After the worst is over and you're back in classes."

"Why?" Her heart thudded crazily, but not the way it had when Brad had touched her. She wasn't sure how to sort out the differences between Brad's and Ric's touches and the way they made her feel. And she didn't know why; although she was attracted to both of them, it seemed to be in different ways.

"Because I want to," Ric said. "Because, like I told you before, we're alike."

"Just because we both have cancer doesn't mean we're alike." She wasn't sure why his comparison put her off.

He grinned beguilingly. "All right, then, because I think you're one foxy lady and I want to date you."

Surprised by his confession, she said, "I look totally gross, and you know it."

"But you won't always look 'totally gross.' Once they get you into remission, you'll look just like you did before. Very pretty."

Her hand automatically touched her head.

"Except for my hair. I'll never be able to grow it that long again." Secretly she still mourned for it, but she didn't regret having cut it. At least *that* decision had been hers and hers alone.

Ric's eyes grew somber and he stared long and deep into hers. "Take care, Melissa. I'll be calling you. You can count on it."

She watched him leave, feeling a strange mix of emotions. Part of her felt dependent upon him. Part of her felt freed from having him checking on her, identifying with her, as if he knew what was inside her mind and soul when she grappled with having cancer. The truth was, she wasn't dealing with it. "It," the cancer, was an alien creature that had invaded her body and was gorging itself on her good health.

The doctors, the psychiatrists, the lab technicians—they were foreigners, too. She knew they were trying to help her, but they also seemed like invaders. They had assaulted her dignity—uncovering, poking, revealing, peeling layers of shyness away from her body like dead skin, removing it, strip by strip, until she felt naked and personless. She was still thinking and struggling with her problem when the nurse came to take her down for another round of chemo.

The next morning Michael came to see her. Although she hated for him to see her when she wasn't on top of her nausea, his presence always comforted her. "I'm between work and class," he said, his eyes darting uneasily around her room. "I don't have too much time."

"I'm glad you came anyway. This place is the pits and I want out." He placed the surgical mask over her mouth for her and sat next to her bed, leaning on the mattress and resting his chin on his fist. He reminded her of a forlorn puppy. "When was the last time you went ballooning?"

"I don't remember."

"You need to go soon. You look earthbound."

A smile started at the corners of his mouth. "Will you go with me when you get home?"

"Haven't I thrown up enough latcly? You know how I react to heights."

"Then will you drive the chase car like before?"

"Can I bring Jory?"

He made a face. "You still trying to fix me up with her?"

"Who else is there in your life?"

He touched her cheek. "Only you, Sis."

"Are you bothered about them doing the bone marrow test on you, Michael?" She'd wanted to ask him for days, but hadn't found the right moment. "I know how you hate needles."

"It's for *you*. Let them stick me." He sounded braver than he looked about it.

"Maybe we won't be compatible."

"Then they'll find a donor who is."

The idea frightened her. Somehow the transplant seemed less intimidating if it came from her brother. The thought of having some nameless, faceless stranger living inside her bones made her shudder.

"But we will be compatible," Michael said, trying to comfort her. "And besides, this chemo stuff is going to work, so you won't even need a transplant. You shouldn't even be thinking about it."

"I hope it works. I'd hate to think I was this miserable for nothing." He grinned at her sullen humor. "How's Mom doing?" Melissa asked. "She acts cheerful enough when she visits me, but how's she really doing?"

"Better. Once you two made up and she stopped feeling responsible . . ."

"Oh, that was my fault. She shouldn't feel responsible. Cancer isn't genetic. That was just a cheap shot I took because I was so angry about all of this."

"I think she felt that she should have noticed something was going on with you. That you weren't well. I guess I should have been more observant too."

Melissa was surprised. It hadn't occurred to her that her family might feel guilty about her illness. "It wasn't anybody's fault," she said.

Michael shrugged as if he didn't quite believe her. "Mom's raided the library and the medical textbook section at the bookstores for every printed word about leukemia. You should see her tackle your doctor—she bombards him with a million questions. He must hate to see her coming!"

Melissa pictured her mother giving Dr. Rowan the third degree. It dawned on her that her mother knew more about her disease than she did, and she was moved that her mother had gone to such lengths to read and ask questions about her treatments. "Maybe I'll read some of her books," she said. Although she was inspired by her mother, she wasn't sure how much more she wanted to know.

"I brought you a present," Michael said.

"You did? But you've already given me three stuffed animals and a vase of flowers. You should be saving your money for ballooning." The cuddly toys had been relegated to the windowsill so she could see them from her bed. Dr. Rowan didn't want them too near in case they harbored any microscopic germs.

She thought it was ridiculous. The animals looked only soft and friendly and innocent.

Michael reached for a bag he'd slipped beneath her bed and removed a book with a handsome cloth-and-leather cover. It smelled faintly of disinfectant, and as she thumbed through the pages she was moved by his attempt to "de-germ" it for her safety.

"All the pages are blank," she said.

"That's because it's a personal journal. You're supposed to write on the pages."

"Like a diary?"

"Kind of. You just write in it when you feel like it. You don't have to write every day if you don't want to."

She ran her palm over the supple, dark blue cover. "It's beautiful, Michael. Thanks. Dr. Moffat—that's the shrink who helps us deal with our cancer—" she rolled her eyes in exaggerated tolerance, "Dr. Moffat says writing down your feelings in letters or diaries is a good idea. She says it's therapeutic, but, I don't know . . . I think it sounds dumb."

"'Therapeutic'?" Michael grimaced good-naturedly. "If you're going to talk ugly, I'm taking my gift back. I just wanted to give you something to keep you busy." He paused, then said, "But maybe the shrink is right. Maybe you need to write about this whole stinking experience. In this book you can tell it like it is. And who knows—years from now, when you're rich and famous, you could have it published and make another million on your memoirs."

She smoothed her palm over the ivory-colored pages. "I'd rather think of it as portable bathroom walls where I can write all kinds of dirty words about these last few weeks."

Playfully, he grabbed at the book. "I didn't mean to create a monster."

"Don't touch my book." She held it against her breast and gave him a menacing glare. "Or I'll be sure and write unsavory things about you in it."

He laughed and stood. "Well, I've got to go. Mom's coming up during her lunch hour and that's not too long from now."

Melissa pulled the mask away from her mouth, allowing him to watch her lips as she said, "Promise me you'll take up your balloon some morning this week."

"I'll try."

"Did I tell you that I'm using your balloon in my imaging therapy?"

"You know you didn't." He leaned against the near wall, his thumbs hooked through the front belt loops of his jeans. "So tell me."

"Well, supposedly it's important for me to use my alpha brain cells to fight my leukemia. Some sort of holistic approach to cancer treatment." She shrugged her bony shoulders.

"It seems like a lot of mumbo jumbo, but I think I read something about that in Mom's books. So how does my balloon fit it?"

Enthused, she hunched forward. "I close my eyes and imagine that I'm riding in your balloon—without getting sick," she qualified. "I'm riding along through my bones, and whenever I see one of my cancer cells, I toss a firebomb at it. It blows up"—she snapped her fingers—"without ever touching me, because the balloon's basket protects me."

"Does it help?"

She heard the skepticism in his tone and said, "Yes, it does. After a really good session, after totally relaxing, I feel better. It helps me not to be so sick to my stomach after the chemo treatments, too."

"Whatever works."

"It does work, Michael. I know it sounds crazy, but it *does* work." She picked at her bed sheet. "I want to go home. I want everything to be normal again. I'll do whatever they want me to do in order to get out of here."

She watched him work his jaw. "It won't be much longer. You're bound to respond to all these treatments soon."

"That's what they keep telling me," she said. "So . . . how's my room at home? Does it miss me?"

His smile was brief and rather sad. "It misses you like crazy." She felt an overwhelming wave of homesickness wash over her.

"You'd better go before I try to crawl into your pocket and leave with you."

After he'd gone, Melissa tried doing a school assignment, but her attention wandered. She thought about so many things—home, the PSATs, Brain Bowl, her illness. Even if she did go home soon, how would she adjust? How could she ever think of herself as "normal" again?

She picked up the book Michael had given her and considered what to write in it. Should she describe what it felt like to stare mortality in the face? Or should she write about more practical things, like fighting to maintain her place on the Brain Bowl team? Or about trying to obtain a National Merit Scholarship that she might never use?

Or maybe she should explore her feelings about her family and friends. About how much she cared about them, and how precious they'd become during her illness. And what about life once she got out of the hospital? Who would ask her for a date? Who would ever kiss her or want her? Melissa sighed and thumbed through the blank pages. *Sixteen is too young to die*, she thought. She tossed the book aside, knowing that she had a lot to say and no earthly idea of how to say it.

Chapter Twelve

That afternoon, feeling stronger, Melissa asked a nurse to help her to the sun room. Located in the oncology ward, the room was lined with windows so that the sun streamed in and reflected off the antiseptically clean linoleum floors. Settling into a green upholstered chair, Melissa opened her history book and was soon lost in the drama of the Civil War.

"Hi. What'chya doing?"

Melissa jumped in her seat. A small girl was standing in front of her, holding a coloring book and a box of crayons tightly against her chest. "I'm reading," Melissa answered.

"What'chya reading?" The child was dressed in hospital pajamas a size too large for her tiny body. She had a fuzzy scramble of strawberry curls and big, bright blue eyes.

"I'm reading for school. It's homework."

"I'm going to kindergarten soon. Then I can read and do homework. My name's Rachael and I'm this many years old." She held up four fingers. A heparin lock was taped to her arm.

Melissa ignored the paraphernalia and concentrated on the child's upturned face. "I'm Melissa and I'm this many years old." She displayed ten fingers, then five and one.

Rachael studied them carefully. "Wow. You're old."

Melissa laughed. "You're right."

"I have leukemia," Rachael announced, dropping to her knees and opening her coloring book on the table next to Melissa's chair. "What have you got?"

Perhaps it was the child's unabashed honesty, her uncomprehending acknowledgment of their unlikely sisterhood, that brought a lump to Melissa's throat. "I have leukemia, too."

"I was in mission but now I'm not anymore."

A shudder ran up Melissa's spine. "You mean 'remission,' don't you?"

"Yup. I don't like it here, but Mommy says I have to stay for a while." Rachael flipped open the crayon box and dumped a rainbow of colored sticks across the table. The warm sunlight softened them, and the room became scented with the familiar smell of crayon wax.

"I don't like it here either, Rachael." Despite the sun, Melissa felt chilled. *A relapse,* she thought. Rachael had survived chemo, lived outside the hospital, then relapsed. Her leukemia had returned.

"I have a baby sister. Do you?"

"I have an older brother," Melissa said.

"Older?" Rachael glanced up from her coloring, her expression registering disbelief. "Are you friends?"

"Yes. Best friends."

"I don't like my sister very much. She cries a lot and keeps my mommy busy."

"You'll like her someday."

"Maybe." Rachael continued coloring and said, "The medicine they gave me makes me throw up."

Her sudden change of topics momentarily confused Melissa. "The medicine makes me throw up, too," she said.

"They stick needles in my back. Do they do that to you, too?"

"Yes."

"I used to think if they stuck me with needles everything inside would leak out. But that was when I was only three and I was still a baby."

Melissa bit her lower lip hard. She reached out and touched the soft, shining curls on Rachael's head. "Your hair's very pretty."

"It all fell out once. But now it's back." She beamed a broad smile. "Are you a mommy?"

The question struck Melissa like a splash of ice-cold water. Confused by a rush of emotions, she fumbled with her history book. The bright, sun-washed room was suddenly making her dizzy. "I have to go back to my room now, Rachael."

"Are you sick? Are you gonna throw up? I brought my dish just in case. Want to use it?" She held up the receptacle Melissa knew so well.

"No, thanks . . . It's just that I—I'm cold."

The child nodded. "Oh, I get cold at night. Sometimes when my mommy can't stay with me, I make the nurse bring me two blankets. She holds my hand till I go to sleep."

As Melissa slowly moved out the door she heard Rachael say, "Come visit me tomorrow, Melissa. Can we be friends?"

Safely back in her room, Melissa crawled between the sheets, her teeth chattering. She felt an overwhelming urge to cry but couldn't. *What's wrong with me? Why am I feeling this way?* She turned on her side and shivered. She squeezed her eyes shut, but she kept seeing Rachael's face.

When she opened her eyes, the first thing she spied on the bedside table was the journal. She reached for it, opening to the first cream-colored, fresh-smelling blank page. She sat up and rummaged in the metal drawer until she found a black felt-tip pen, and began writing in her most graceful penmanship.

> *I met a little girl today named Rachael. She's four and she has cancer, too. She thought I was very old, being sixteen, and I thought she was very sweet and too young for these things they're putting us through at the hospital. She asked me if I was a mommy. Of course, I'm not. But I can't help wondering if I ever will be. Who will want to make love to me now that I'm sick? What would it be like to have a baby grow inside of me? Will I ever know?*

Melissa reread the entry, underscored the last sentence, then put the journal away.

"Good morning, Melissa." Dr. Rowan breezed into her room the next day, his face lit with a smile, a clipboard and a manila folder in his hand.

Warily she lowered the textbook she was studying. "My lab results?"

"Your lab results." He flipped open the folder. "Your platelet count has stabilized and your white count is acceptable. However, there's a marked decrease of polys, which means you're still quite vulnerable to infection, so you'll have to avoid crowds and keep that surgical mask on when you go outside . . ."

"Outside?"

"I'm discharging you. Although we haven't achieved remission yet, I think we're close."

Her mouth went dry over the news. *I should be happy about this,* she thought. But in reality, she was scared. She hated the hospital, but there she was sheltered, and her doctors and nurses were at hand to help her. At home, she'd be on her own. "Is it really safe for me to leave?"

"It's both safe and necessary," Dr. Rowan said, shaking his head of unruly hair. "You need to start leading a normal life again. Get back into the mainstream."

Wasn't that what she wanted too? "But what if I have a problem?"

"Your family will be instructed how to deal with most things. And if there's something they can't handle, or if there are any questions, I'm a phone call away. You aren't being released from therapy, Melissa. Outpatient care is just one small step on the road to recovery."

"Can I go back to school?"

"Not right away."

"When?"

"I can't say yet. Your chemo program will change, but until you're on maintenance, I'd rather not have you in a classroom environment."

"I want to be back in school in another week."

"That's too soon, Melissa."

"When?"

"If all goes well, maybe after Christmas. It'll be safer then."

"Christmas! The school year will be half over by then."

"But you'll be stronger and more able to fight off infections."

Melissa struggled against panic. Dr. Rowan couldn't make her wait so long to return to school.

She'd already missed most of October and part of November. She couldn't stand the thought of staying out until January. "But the PSATs are being given next Saturday. I have to take them with my class. They're for college."

"You're a stubborn girl, Melissa. Of course, I can't forbid you, but it isn't a good idea."

Her palms were clammy. "It's one test for just a few hours. My friend Jory can take me, stay with me, bring me straight back home." She squared her chin. "I'll wear my mask the whole time." She imagined herself sitting in the vast auditorium with a surgical mask strapped to her face. The image caused her to shudder, but she'd do it if it meant she could take the test.

Dr. Rowan was speaking to her, but she heard only part of his speech. ". . . your mother comes I'll have your discharge papers ready. Someone can bring you to the clinic day after tomorrow for your chemo. DeeDee Thomas will administer it, so you'll still be seeing plenty of familiar faces. Feel free to come up here to the floor whenever you want to visit. It encourages the other patients, you know, seeing someone living on the outside. There's a teen support group that meets once a month which you might like to join."

Melissa nodded, unable to sort through all he was telling her. The only thing she cared about was that she was going home. When Jory called and Melissa told her, her friend squealed so loud Melissa had to hold the phone away from her ear.

"Everyone will be *so* glad!"

Melissa wanted everybody to know, but she didn't want anybody to visit her. She knew how bad she looked. "I can't have visitors," she added hastily.

"Oh sure. I understand that. But still, you'll be

home. It can't be too long before you can come back to school."

"Probably not," she lied. "About Brain Bowl . . ."

"No sweat," Jory assured. "Watson was the picture of sympathy and understanding. She said you made the final ten fair and square, and even though you haven't been drilling with them, she's sure you'll be up to speed in no time once you return."

Melissa sagged with relief, twisted the phone cord around her forefinger, and said, "I'm on for the PSATs, too. Dr. Rowan wasn't thrilled about my taking them, but I'm doing it anyway."

"Can I come to the hospital and help you pack up?"

"You don't have to. Mom will be here. Michael, too."

Melissa sensed the disappointment in a long pause and said, "What the heck. The more the merrier. Come on down."

After lunch Melissa changed into street clothes, the first she'd worn since her admission. Her jeans hung sadly on her thin body and she could almost count her ribs through her T-shirt. She didn't care. She was going home. She packed everything in paper bags and a suitcase except for one cuddly teddy bear. She gave it to a nurse at the central nurse's station. "This is for Rachael—the little four-year-old girl with the curly, reddish hair."

The nurse smiled. "Oh, you mean Rachael Dove. How nice of you, Melissa. She's down in chemo right now and this will be a special treat for her when they bring her back up. She's usually pretty sick after her treatments."

Melissa returned to her room and waited silently with Jory while her mother handled the paperwork

and Michael lugged her things down in the elevator.
The Pink Lady, a hospital volunteer, made her ride
down in a wheelchair, and Melissa felt self-conscious
rolling through the lobby. Once outside, she saw both
her mom's and Jory's cars parked beside the curb.
"Which chariot will it be?" Her mother asked.

"Do you mind if Jory takes me?"

Her mother's expression said that she did mind,
but she said, "Of course not. I'll see you back at the
house."

Hastily, Melissa asked, "You are riding with us,
aren't you Michael?"

His blue eyes flashed her a knowing, tolerant
look. "Sure."

"Would you—uh—like to drive?" Jory asked, offering him the keys.

Michael took them. "Why not."

"I'll sit in the back," Melissa said. "There's more
room." Michael settled her in the backseat. The car
felt familiar and comfortable and smelled faintly of
Jory's jasmine perfume. "Can you put the top down?"
Melissa asked.

Jory and Michael exchanged glances. "Is that a
good idea?" Michael asked.

"I've been cooped up inside for two weeks. I want
to feel the sun . . . smell fresh air. Please?"

When Michael lowered the top Melissa turned
her face up to soak in the warmth of the sun. She
breathed deeply the cool, dry autumn air until her
head grew light and her body finally relaxed. "Home,
James," she directed with a snap of her fingers.

Michael drove slowly, cautiously, stopping at
yellow traffic lights instead of barreling through as he
normally might do. Jory sat sideways in her seat, gazing at Michael contentedly. Melissa watched the sun-

light play off her friend's hair and the breeze ruffle through Michael's. "We can go a little faster, you know," she said.

"No we can't," Jory replied. She reached into her glove compartment and removed a yellow diamond-shaped sign with black lettering. She stuck it to the windshield, beneath the rearview mirror. Melissa smiled when she read it: "Slow. Precious Cargo on Board."

Chapter Thirteen

❦

"Do you like what we've done to your bedroom, honey?" Mrs. Austin's question made Melissa pause as she walked around her room.

"It's nice, Mom. Really. I had no idea . . ."

"Michael and I wanted to surprise you. He painted the walls and the woodwork, and I picked out the comforter and curtains."

Melissa fingered the powder-blue spread decorated with printed apricot-and-white long-stemmed lilies. The faint aroma of fresh paint hung in the air. "I mean it, Mom. It's beautiful. Thank you."

"Michael installed the phone, too." Melissa noticed the pale blue stylized headset on the night stand next to her bed. "It's one of those programmable kinds," Mrs. Austin continued eagerly. "He's already put numbers into the memory for my office, Dr. Rowan, the clinic and Jory. All you have to do is punch the memory key and the single digit of whoever you want, and it dials those numbers automatically. Nice, huh?"

"Very nice." Melissa picked up the receiver and studied it. The truth was that she'd be home alone most of the coming days and she needed the phone in case an emergency arose. Forcing away her fear, she recradled the receiver. "I really appreciate all you and Michael have done, Mom."

Mrs. Austin advanced and hugged her. "I'm so glad you're home, baby."

Her mother's sweet gardenia scent filled Melissa's senses as she cuddled snugly in her arms. "I'm going to be all right, Mom. I know I'm going to get well."

Mrs. Austin smoothed Melissa's patchy head of hair. "I know you are, too. Now, why don't you climb between those nice new sheets and let me bring you some vegetable soup."

"Homemade?"

"Just for you."

"I'd like that." Her mother's special soup had sustained her through everything from flu to chicken pox to bad days of menstrual cramps.

After Melissa had settled into bed, Michael came in. "It's really good to have you home," he said, sitting on the edge of the mattress.

"Thanks for painting my room. I like the color. Ivory makes the room look bigger. How come there's no programmed number for you on the phone?"

He shrugged. "Between school and two jobs, I doubted you could track me down. But I'll be home whenever I can."

"Still baby-sitting your kid sister, huh?"

He touched her chin. "Yep. And I'll even leave the baseball bat by your bed."

"Mom says you put Jory's number into the phone. How did you know it?"

"Stop baiting me. I looked it up in the phone book."

Melissa frowned. "You've got to admit, she's been a terrific friend. Oh, she was put off at first, but once she got used to my being sick, she came to see me a lot. She bought me all those scarves. She kept me entertained with stories of her social life and everything that's been going on at school, and she made sure I wasn't kicked off the Brain Bowl team."

"I like her car," Michael said dryly.

"Why are you so stubborn?"

"I like to see the fire in your eyes and the smoke curling out your ears."

"You're going to appreciate Jory someday, Michael. And I hope she won't give you the time of day when you're just aching to be with her either."

"The time off her Rolex watch?"

His grin was devilish, and Melissa felt her anger rising. "Out of my room!" She pointed toward the door.

He rose, laughing, and warded off the pillow she tossed at him. "It's good to have you home. Even if it does mean more visits from Jory Delaney."

"Out!"

"I love you, too," he called as he shut the door behind him.

In spite of her exasperation, Melissa smiled and slipped downward into the cozy comfort of her bed. Her eyes caressed her room. *Home.* She'd finally come home. Now all she had to do was go into remission and get well. Then maybe she could put this entire nightmare behind her and get on with the rest of her life.

"Don't you think we should go inside now?" Jory nervously tapped on the handle inside her car door.

"Just a few more minutes," Melissa told her, glancing first at her watch, then out the car window to see two more students straggle into the Lincoln High auditorium in the Saturday morning gloom. The day had arrived cool and gray.

"They lock the doors at eighty-thirty sharp," Jory said, chewing on her bottom lip.

"I know, Jory. Calm down. I'm not going inside until the last possible minute. Are you sure Mrs. Watson's saving special seats for us in the back row?"

"It's all arranged. We slip into the seats right before the test starts, and as soon as it's over, we get first dibs on slipping out."

Melissa took a deep breath, adjusted her scarf and wide-brimmed hat, and said, "Okay, let's go."

Jory buttoned her denim jacket against a blast of cool wind and stepped aside for Melissa to climb out of the car. "Do you have your"—she stopped—"you know. Your stuff."

"I have my mask and some airsickness bags, if that's what you mean."

"Certainly not," Jory huffed. "I meant the stupid number-two pencils."

"Don't worry. Actually, I feel pretty decent. I didn't go to chemo yesterday."

Jory stopped in her tracks halfway between the parking lot and the auditorium doors. "You what?"

"I skipped chemo. I told Dr. Rowan I'd be there Monday, but I didn't want to take a chance on lousing up the PSATs."

Incredulous, Jory demanded, "And he agreed to that?"

"He didn't have a choice. What was he going to do? Come to my house and pick me up bodily?"

"What did Michael say?"

"He doesn't know. And no one's going to tell him, is she?" Melissa threatened with a growl.

"I don't know why I'm supposed to cover for

you," Jory grumbled. "I'm always the one who gets caught."

Melissa touched Jory's arm at the door of the cavernous auditorium. "Because you're my friend. And because you know how much it means to me to score high on this test."

Jory didn't answer, but yanked open the door and preceded Melissa inside. Mrs. Watson rushed up to them. "Oh, Melissa, how good to see you."

Melissa couldn't help noticing the shock in her teacher's eyes when she saw her. "Thank you, Mrs. Watson." She slipped on the surgical mask.

"I've saved you special seats in the last row." Melissa followed Mrs. Watson keeping her eyes cast downward. She sat on the aisle and Jory sat next to her. "Every other chair, dear," Mrs. Watson directed, so Jory repositioned herself.

Melissa looked up cautiously, dipping the brim of her hat. The auditorium was almost full since the entire junior class was there to take the test. She was relieved to see that few kids had noticed her entrance. Most were whispering to friends or merely staring into space. Her stomach churned, but she knew it was from nerves. She had to score well on this test if her hopes for a Merit Scholarship were to be realized. The results would be sent to her in December, but it wouldn't be until the following September that principals would be notified as to which of their seniors were semifinalists. She rummaged in her purse for a mint, hoping to chase away the foul taste in her mouth. That was one side effect of her medications she could live without—the altered taste of food. Some days nothing tasted right.

Lincoln's principal sauntered across the stage in the front of the auditorium and made announcements about the exam. Feet shuffled. The materials were passed down each row, reminding Melissa of the day she'd taken the test for Brain Bowl. How long ago had that been? It felt like a hundred years.

On command, all the students opened the exam. She prayed she wouldn't get sick since she knew she'd be fighting the clock. She pulled her mask away from her face, took in a big gulp of air, then resettled the mask and started the test.

"So how'd you do?" Back in the safety of the car, it was the first remark out of Jory's mouth.

"I think I did okay. How about you?"

Jory grimaced and gripped the steering wheel, nosing the car out of the parking lot well in advance of the rest of the kids filing out of the auditorium. "It wasn't so tough."

"Thanks for getting me out in a hurry. I didn't want to have to talk to anybody and answer any dumb questions."

"No problem."

"Did I make you rush any answers?"

Jory blew air through her lips. "Get serious. What I didn't know, I guessed at. Big deal. I'm not the one who's so hot to go to college." She gave Melissa a studied look. "How are you feeling?"

Melissa grinned. "Pretty good. In fact, I feel good enough to stop for a milk shake. A chocolate one. Somehow, I've got this terrible craving for chocolate."

"Works for me. How about the Steak 'n Shake?" Jory named the restaurant that provided fifties-style curb service. "Then you won't have to go inside and try and drink through a hole in your mask."

"Let's go," Melissa told her friend. The grayness of the morning had been replaced by a weak wash of sunshine. Outside the air was still cool, so Jory kept the top up and the windows raised. Melissa fiddled with the radio dial until she found a song she liked.

At the drive-in restaurant, Jory parked to the far end despite a scowl from a waitress on roller skates who whizzed over to the car. "What'll it be, girls?"

"Two large chocolate shakes and one large order of fries."

The waitress eyed the expensive auto and muttered, "Big spenders."

"Tell the chef to go heavy on the grease on those fries," Jory called as the woman skated away. "And don't slip bringing it back."

Melissa giggled. "She's worried about her tip, you know. Two shakes and fries won't pay her rent."

"So let her take up brain surgery with the rest of the centerfolds working here."

When the food came, Melissa tasted it cautiously.

"Is it all right?" Jory wanted to know.

"Don't mind me. My medications sometimes give food a funny taste."

"And so?"

"And so this is delicious. Tastes just like liver."

"You're kidding." Jory's mouth dropped open, causing Melissa to laugh out loud.

"I'm kidding. It's good. Thanks."

They nibbled on the fries and listened to the music. "You know," Jory observed, "this is just like old times."

Melissa tapped the brim of her hat. "In some ways."

"It won't always be like this, Melissa. You're going to lick this thing."

"Thanks for the vote of confidence." Melissa straightened suddenly at the sight of a bronze-colored

car. Brad Kessing parked his Firebird across the concrete median dividing the two parking areas. Brad was
not alone. Melissa slouched low in the bucket seat of
Jory's vehicle. "Let's split."

"But I'm not finished with my . . ." Jory's sentence trailed as she followed Melissa's line of vision.
"Why that creep."

"Stop it, Jory." Melissa's tone sounded wooden.
"He's a free agent. I have no claims on him."

"He's still a creep."

Curiosity gnawed at Melissa, and she peeked out
the window for a better look at the girl with Brad. She
was pretty, with wispy blond curls. "Do you know who
she is?"

A guilty look crossed Jory's face that Melissa
couldn't miss. "Sarah something or other."

"You've known about Brad and her for a long
time, haven't you?"

"Not that long," Jory said with a self-conscious
shrug. "A few weeks."

"It's all right you didn't tell me. I have no hold on
Brad. He made me no promises."

"He really *did* ask me about you a few times. I
mean he was really interested in how you were
doing."

A sad smile turned up Melissa's mouth. "It's all
right. You don't have to make me feel better about it."
She set the milk shake on the car's console. "I think
I'm finished with this thing. It's lost its flavor."

Jory flashed her lights, and when the waitress
came she paid her. As she backed the car out, Melissa
saw Sarah climb from Brad's Firebird, throwing him a
provocative smile and words she couldn't hear. Brad,
handsome and athletic, gave Sarah a thumbs-up signal, and Melissa fought a rising sadness.

The last thing she saw as they drove off was Sarah flipping her beautiful head of hair, laughing. "She's pretty," Melissa told Jory, straightening in her seat and adjusting her seat belt. "Pretty and perky—just Brad's type." To herself she added, *And healthy, too.*

Chapter Fourteen

~~~~~~~

December 10

I don't think I've ever been so bored in my entire life. Funny, when Dr. Rowan told me that my lab results showed I'd gone into remission, I thought they'd break out the brass band. But it was purely routine. Business as usual. Now that I'm officially in remission, it's just a matter of getting my white count up enough to fight off normal germs before I can reenter the "real" world. Since it's almost time for the semester to end I guess it doesn't matter much. I'll just slip back into school in January . . . if such a thing is possible. I look really gross.

Christmas is coming and I haven't bought anything. If it wasn't for Jory, I'd have nothing to put under the tree this year for Mom or Michael. Of course, Jory loved buying Michael's gift. She says she sniffed every men's cologne in the mall before picking one. She said the money I gave her was enough, but I know it wasn't. Anything that smells like that, in a glass bottle as fancy as the one it's in, couldn't have cost what I was able to afford. I made Michael get something really nice for Jory. He was a pain about it,

*but he did find a sweater that's funky enough
for her. I hope she likes it.*

   *Now that I'm on maintenance and don't
have to go to the clinic so often, I'm feeling
better. But I still get sick after every visit.
Will it ever go away? I see that little girl,
Rachael, sometimes. She's so cute and she
talks my ear off. Why do kids have to get
sick, anyway? Maybe it's one of the questions
I'll ask God when I see him . . .*

Melissa stopped writing in her journal. The psy-
chiatrist had been right—there was something
therapeutic about putting down her thoughts and feelings. Although talking to herself on paper about everyday matters was now a habit, it still surprised her
when thoughts about God and faith and the whys of
sick kids slipped out. She sighed and and shut the
book. Time hung heavy for her. The days and nights
were too long, and she knew that so much introspec-
tion was getting her down.

She tucked the journal into her desk drawer and
studied her clock radio with a frown. Her mother
wouldn't be home from work for another hour.

The melodic chime of her phone made Melissa
jump. Annoyed by its ability to startle her, she
snapped "Hello."

"Melissa? Hi. It's Ric Davis."

Her hand squeezed the handset tightly and her
mouth went dry. "Why, Ric . . . How are you?"

"More to the point, how are you?"

"I'm doing all right. I look like a newborn baby,
the way my hair's coming back, though." She touched
the dark silky down on her head as she spoke. "But

I'm taking the oral medications now and only going in for tests and some IV chemo. You know the routine."

"Yes, I know it. What have they got you on?" She told him and he said, "Watch that last one. It makes you eat like a pig and before you know it, you'll weigh a ton."

"I could use some meat on my bones," she confessed, staring into the mirror on her dresser and wishing she hadn't. Her clothes still hung on her, and the baggy sweatshirt she wore did little to hide the hollow gauntness of her frame.

"Some meat, sure," he emphasized. "But that particular drug will make you bloated. That's what it did to me."

Melissa didn't like the course of the conversation. She didn't want to be told about more problems, more distortions to her body. Abruptly, she asked, "So what's new? Going home for Christmas?"

"Yeah, I am. I'm wrapping up exams tomorrow, then catching a plane home. I'll be back after New Year's."

"Sounds like fun."

"If my prosthesis doesn't set off the metal detectors at the airport."

Same old, Ric, she thought. "It's nice of you to call and check on me, Ric."

"I told you when you were still in the hospital that I wanted to go out with you. I still do."

Her dry mouth felt like cotton. "I'm not sure I'm ready to face the world yet."

"You're going back to school aren't you?"

"Yes. But that's almost a month away. I . . . uh . . . I'm hoping I look better by then."

"In other words, there's a guy you like and he's been sort of cool since he found out you have cancer."

She would have dropped the phone if she hadn't been gripping it so tightly, yet the uncanny accuracy of his comment made her defensive. "That's not what it is."

"Come on, Melissa. It happened that way with me. Her name was Megan."

She thought about Brad and tan, healthy Sarah. Her shoulders drooped. "I know that the kids at school will have to adjust to the new me when I go back. After all, I look so different now." She raised her chin and slipped in a note of defiance. "But I'm still *me*."

Ric's low-throated chuckle came through the line. "I know, Melissa. And that's the girl I'm interested in dating."

She felt herself softening toward him. Ric did understand, and he had already traveled the road she was about to take. "So call me when you get back to campus. Okay?"

"You're on," he said. "Now take good care of yourself, and have a Merry Christmas."

"Thanks, Ric. You too." She hung up feeling a wistful nostalgia she couldn't explain.

Later, when Jory stopped by and she'd told her about Ric's call, her friend asked, "Ric's older, isn't he?"

"Nineteen."

"Thought you didn't like 'older men,'" Jory needled.

"Be kind, Jory. I don't feel very witty today."

"Well, do you want to date him?"

"I'm not exactly deluged with offers you know."

"Yeah, but that's going to change once things level

out for you. In a few months, no one will even think of
you as having been sick."

"What do you do? Sit around and compare notes
with Michael? That's exactly what he says." Irritation
had crept into her voice.

"I wish I could sit around and compare notes with
him." Jory rolled her eyes and reached for the bowl of
popcorn resting between them on the floor of
Melissa's living room.

Melissa pursed her lip. Why couldn't Jory and
Michael and her mother understand how she felt
about herself? Her body had turned on her. Without
warning, it had begun making cancerous cells and
changed all the rules of her life. "Forget it. If Ric calls
again, I'll decide then if I want to date."

"You need to get your confidence back."

"You're right," Melissa said, resigned. "I don't
feel like dating because I don't feel like a decent-look-
ing girl any more."

Eagerly, Jory leaned forward, her green eyes
dancing. "What do you say we retire the scarves and
go wig shopping. I know just the place. It's private.
The saleslady is sharp and knows her stuff. You'll love
it. You can try on everything in the store. What do you
think?"

"Mom told me I could get whatever I wanted for
Christmas," Melissa said, trying hard to catch Jory's
enthusiasm. "I guess I might as well start with new
hair."

Two days later, Jory dragged her into a secluded
salon, tucked away in a corner of the mall's most pres-
tigious department store. The lights were bright, mir-
rors and wig stands lined the walls, and Styrofoam
heads and round boxes clustered on shelves and
pieces of furniture. A vanity table with chairs on ei-

ther side and a swivel mirror in its center dominated the floor area. Settling into one of the chairs, a saleswoman with a soft southern accent and long, slim fingers jotted notes on a pad as she questioned Melissa about her tastes. Without her mask, Melissa felt somewhat exposed, but she was glad she didn't have to wear it in public any longer.

The woman eyed her with keen, professional interest and noted, "If you want to go through these swatches, you can show me the color that's closest to your natural hair. And if you tell me a little about the style, I can show you something so similar to your own that you'll be hard-pressed to tell the difference between your real hair and your new wig." The idea that she had an option hadn't occurred to Melissa. "Long or short?" The woman asked.

"Oh, long," Jory interjected. "And dark. Melissa had hair all the way down to her waist. And none of this fake stuff either. Melissa wants real hair."

Nervously, Melissa licked her lips and shot Jory a pleading glance. "Whose hair is this, anyway?" she asked with a tense laugh.

The saleswoman intervened. "Natural human hair that long would be very expensive and we'd have to special-order it from the Orient. They seem to be the only women growing long hair these days. Human hair is also harder to maintain, and it's color can fade. You can buy it," she added hastily, "but believe me, synthetic hair is much less costly and just as attractive."

"No," Melissa said hastily. "I don't want long hair. And I'm not so sure I want something just like I used to have." She ignored Jory's surprised expression.

"Many women want a wig that most resembles

their natural hair, but the choice is yours. And we do have many choices," the clerk said gently.

"I have an opportunity to change my image, don't I? So why not?"

Quickly the woman crossed to the shelves and returned with a variety of wigs in a range of colors. "Would you like to be a blond?"

"They have more fun, right?"

She smiled and placed a saucy, curly wig on Melissa's head. The hairpiece felt warm and clung to her scalp, but the tight curls clustered about her face only emphasized the hollowness of her cheeks. "I don't think so," Melissa told her.

"How about this?" Jory asked from across the room, where she was searching the merchandise at random.

"That's our Dolly Parton look," the clerk said, settling the almost white, bouffant-style wig on Melissa. "We do a big business in theater and stage performers." One look in the mirror and Melissa cracked up.

"All you need is a guitar," Jory said, laughing hysterically.

Melissa glanced down at the front of her bulky knit sweater. "A guitar and two watermelons," she corrected. She turned to the saleswoman. "Maybe something a little less 'show biz.'"

Laughing herself, the clerk removed the wig and selected another, more sedate one. An hour and twenty wigs later, Melissa finally chose a thick chestnut fall with a little curl that hung just below her ears. It was soft to her touch, but felt odd, too. It was strange to run her fingers through the hair and not have it tug at her scalp. The saleswoman taught Melissa how to care for it, to clean and brush it and secure it to its Styrofoam head when not in use. Melissa paid for it, placing the crisp bills in the saleswoman's hand, then carried the box through the store, ignoring the festive twinkle of lights and decorated Christmas trees. Outside in the parking lot, she tugged her trench coat closer against a raw, gusty wind.

Beside her, Jory said, "It looks good on you."

"Sure." Melissa's teeth chattered slightly. "Almost like the real thing." They drove home in silence because Melissa wasn't sure she could talk without bursting into tears.

Michael made her model the hairpiece when they returned. His expression was reserved, studious. "It's . . . uh . . . different."

"Beats bald," she said tersely.

"I like it," Jory babbled. "Don't you think it was smart to go with a shorter look? I mean, we're the only ones who know about her real hair. This way, it just seems like she's cut it short. Even the color's just like her own . . ." Jory's animated voice trailed off and Melissa glanced at her. Her friend was looking straight at Michael and, as usual, was wearing her heart in her eyes.

Michael hooked his thumbs through the belt loops of his jeans. The sleeves of his navy blue sweater were pushed up, and Melissa noticed his forearms corded with muscle from hard physical labor. Melissa felt sorry that he had to work so hard. "Well, it's better than the haircut by Delaney," he finally said with a softness in his tone.

Rising to the gambit, Jory huffed, "I'll have you know that haircut was a work of art, Michael."

"More like graffiti," he fired back, good-naturedly.

Melissa stepped between them and held up her hands in mock surrender. "Please, I don't think I can referee another round. How about a truce?"

Michael slipped his arm around her shoulders and hugged her to him. "You win, Sis. By the way, you got some mail."

"Where?" Michael grabbed an oversize envelope from the kitchen counter and handed it to her. Melissa's heart hammered. Through the glassine window, she read her name, neatly typed by an impersonal computer in Illinois. "It's my PSAT scores."

"Aren't you going to open it?" Jory asked anxiously.

Melissa tore it open and Jory grabbed for the sheet labeled "Interpreting Your Score" while Melissa read the numbers on the printout. "Raw scores: Verbal 55, Math 41. Scaled scores: Verbal 64, Math 67. Selection index: 195. Percentile ranking: 98." She glanced up.

"You're a genius," Jory interpreted quickly. "According to this, ninety-eight percent of all high school juniors in the country scored below you." She paused before adding sheepishly, "Including me."

"You got your scores? You never said a word."

"What's to say? Only seventy-five percent of all juniors scored below me."

"But that's terrific." Melissa concentrated on Jory's scores because she still hadn't absorbed the impact of her own.

Michael had taken the information sheet from Jory and was reading it for himself. "You know what this means, don't you?" He didn't wait for a response. "It means you have a real shot at a Merit Scholarship."

Melissa had always assumed that the news would elate her. Hadn't that been her dream for over a year?

But instead, she felt strangely let down, out of sorts. The thing she'd wanted so badly, worked for for so long, seemed unreal and unrelated to her life right now. "Good for me," was all she could say. "I won't know until after the SATs next fall if I'm smart enough to advance," she told them.

"Yeah, but it says here '. . . about 50,000 high scorers will be given the opportunity to be identified to two colleges of their choice by the Merit Program in the spring.' You *have* picked two colleges worthy of taking you, haven't you?" Michael joked.

"Not yet," she hedged, her look warning Jory to keep quiet about Princeton. "When you have cancer, your options are different." She fled the kitchen, jerking the wig from her head.

In the living room she paused to stare at piles of Christmas decorations Michael had brought in from the garage. The boxes were frayed and tinsel hung sadly from one of them. He'd moved aside the easy chair and cleared a space for the tree. She stroked the synthetic hairpiece gathered in her fist. "Merry Christmas," she whispered to the pile of dark fibers. "Merry Christmas."

Chapter Fifteen

"Welcome back, Melissa. It's good to see you again."

Melissa acknowledged the greeting in the crowded halls as she had all the others her first day back in school. She waved and smiled at people, but she didn't feel it in her heart. She stopped in front of her locker and fumbled with the lock, concentrating so hard on the combination that she ran through it twice before she realized the locker was open.

"How's it going?" Jory's voice in her ear caused her to start.

"Fine," she lied.

"Everybody's asking about you . . ."

"I know," Melissa snapped, more sharply than she'd intended. "Geez, Jory. I feel like a freak. I can't even go to the girls' room without everyone staring, and when I walk into a classroom, there's instant silence. When I went into homeroom today, everything stopped and the entire class watched me walk to my desk. I felt like a murderer on death row walking to the electric chair." Melissa's blood raced with the intensity of her tirade, but having blasted off her pent-up emotions, she felt mollified. "Sorry," she said sheepishly. "I didn't mean to take it out on you."

"No problem," Jory shrugged. "The novelty will wear off as kids get used to having you back. Cancer's a

121

crummy thing to have happen, that's all. People just want to know how you're coping."

Melissa wanted to tell Jory that people's interest in her was ghoulish, similar to the chasing of ambulances, being drawn not out of compassion, but out of the morbid. Instead, she gazed into the hand mirror she'd hung on the inside of her locker door. Her face looked puffy, a side effect of the medicine Ric had warned her about. Her makeup looked unreal, too. *Why not?* she thought. *Fake face, fake smile, fake hair* . . . She touched the ends of the wig softly framing her face, and wished she'd opted for one with curls.

"Have you seen Brad yet?" Jory interrupted her dismal thoughts.

"No, not until sixth-period study hall. He's got soccer practice after school, so he won't be at Brain Bowl drill either." Truthfully, she was dreading seeing him. She looked so awful and she was acutely aware that he'd not contacted her once since that single phone conversation when she'd been in the hospital. And Jory had arranged for that.

"Will you be in the cafeteria for lunch?" Jory asked.

"Could we go out for lunch?"

"Sure. Where?"

"McDonald's . . . the drive-thru. We can eat in the car." Her tone turned pleading. "I can't make it through the rest of the day any other way."

Jory's wide green eyes swept her. "No problem. Meet me at my car."

The warning bell sounded and the halls emptied rapidly. "We're late," Melissa observed. "I'm sorry I made you late."

"Tardiness is my modus operandi," Jory said, with

a wave of dismissal. "I learned that phrase once in civics class. Does it impress you?"

"Deeply." Melissa squeezed her friend's arm gratefully. "Thanks, Jory. Thanks for everything." She hurried off, struggling to keep her throat from closing up with tears. At the door of her classroom, she squared her shoulders and entered, conscious that all eyes had turned in her direction. She passed down the aisle to her desk, hearing only brief snatches of whispered words. "Cancer . . ." the nameless voices said. "What a bummer . . ." and "Remember how pretty she was . . ."

Melissa arrived at study hall before anyone else and sat down quickly. At least this way, she could avoid an entrance. She could also watch for Brad.

When he came into the room, he was talking to another guy and didn't look up before sliding into his desk. She swallowed hard, absorbing him secretly with quick, stealthy glances.

His blond hair had darkened since the summer and it was longer, too, brushing his collar. A vivid turquoise sweater stretched across his broad shoulders. As always, his legs were too long for the cramped area beneath his desk. A flash of gold from his wrist caught her eye—an ID bracelet with solid gold links. She was torn between wanting him to turn around and yet hoping he wouldn't see her. For whatever reason, he never did, keeping his attention riveted on the pile of books in front of him. As a senior, he'd probably already chosen his college and wistfully, she wondered which one. There was so much she didn't know. So much she wanted to know.

At the Brain Bowl drill that afternoon, Melissa

was sharp. Mr. Marshall said, "You did well, Melissa.
I'm very impressed."

"Thank you. I studied a lot over the break." She
carefully avoided references to the hospital.

"It shows."

She was pleased by the teacher's praise, but
didn't delude herself for a minute that she wasn't low
person on the totem pole to make the final team. I'll
just have to work harder, she told herself grimly as she
hurried down the deserted halls to meet Jory, who was
serving detention in the girl's locker room.

Melissa peeked inside and saw her snapping gum
and doodling on her notebook while the gym teacher
concentrated on paperwork. Jory waved her away,
mouthing, "Fifteen minutes." Melissa nodded and
eased out, hoping the teacher didn't catch Jory with
gum in her mouth, or the punishment might stretch
into another fifteen.

Feeling weary, Melissa deposited her load of
books at her feet and lounged against the wall. She
was mentally reviewing her day when the doors of the
boys' locker room burst open, releasing a boisterous
group of guys. Her eyes grew wide as Brad sauntered
out. Seeing her, he stopped short. His blue eyes
swept over her, then down the empty halls. *Trapped.*
That's how he looked to her. Cornered and trapped.

"Uh—hi, Melissa."

She straightened automatically. "Hi." Her heart
seemed wedged in her throat.

He took a few cautious steps in her direction, his
eyes darting away from hers. "How have you been?"

One of the guys called, "You coming, Kessing?"

"In a minute," he said. "Wait for me outside."

Another one scrutinized Melissa. "Don't take all

day, man. I told my old lady I'd be home right after practice."

Once they had gone, Melissa felt the silence of the corridors press around her. Brad heaved his books on his hip and gestured with his free hand. "So, it's good to see you back. I looked for you in study hall, but missed you."

Liar. "I was there."

"How was Brain Bowl? Did the drill go okay? I hate missing it, but Coach is real strict about soccer practice—if you miss one, you don't start in the next game."

"Brain Bowl went fine." She noticed his hair, still damp from the shower, making his shirt collar wet.

He licked his lips. "You . . . uh . . . look real good, Melissa. How're you feeling?"

"All right."

"I guess it's been a while since we've talked."

"Yeah. A while." She hoped the bitterness didn't sound in her tone. She wanted to shout, *You didn't call me, Brad. Not even once. Why?*

"Your hair's different. Too bad you had to cut it short."

Her fingers toyed with the soft ends of the wig, which felt artificial and not like "real" hair as the saleslady had insisted. "I figured it was time for a change."

Brad fidgeted. "Did you have a good Christmas?"

"One of the best."

"That's good."

She let her eyes fall on the ID bracelet. "Christmas gift?"

"From my grandfather."

"The Rhodes Scholar?"

"One and the same." He smiled but shifted nervously to his other foot. "Are you . . . um . . . you know, all right now?"

She pinned him with a look. "If you mean do I still have leukemia, yes, I do. I'm still on medication, but I'm in remission." He knitted his brow and she could read the anxiety on his face. For some perverse reason, she wanted him to squirm. She wanted to punish him for not calling her. For not sending a card. For everything.

Brad took one step closer, reminding her of a childhood game. *Simon Says, take one tiny baby step.* "Melissa . . . I really do want you to be okay. I wish . . . you were . . . well . . ." His voice broke and for the briefest moment she thought he might reach out and stroke her hair.

Panicked, she pressed closer to the wall, feeling its hardness against the small of her back. She remembered summer sunshine and bright green leaves and cool, quiet water laced with goldfish and blossoms. She recalled how Brad had undone her braid and raked his fingers through her tangled hair, gathering it into handfuls and then letting it fall against her skin. She knew she couldn't stand to have him touch her hairpiece. For one desperate second, she held her breath and mutely challenged him with her eyes, saying, "Don't touch." She wasn't sure why, but she wanted him to have this last illusion. She *needed* him to have it.

Brad dropped his hand and backed away. "I gotta go. The guys are waiting."

"Sure." She tossed her head, longing to feel her cascading hair against her shoulders and back.

"See you at Brain Bowl drill."

"See you."

He retreated down the hall and she deliberately

turned away so she didn't have to watch him go. Moments later, Jory burst through the girls' locker room doors. "Geez! What a drag! Sorry you had to wait."

"No problem," Melissa said, scooping up her books. "Ready to head home?"

"You better believe it." Jory cocked her head. "Are you feeling all right? You look a little pale."

"I'm tired, that's all. It's been a long day."

Together, they trudged outside into the pale winter sunshine and biting fresh air. "Free!" Jory exclaimed, lifting her face skyward.

Free. Melissa wondered if she'd ever feel free again. "Want to come over for dinner?" she asked, remembering that Jory's parents had flown to the Bahamas that morning on some real estate deal.

"Am I invited? Will Michael be there?"

"Aren't we choosy?"

"Just wondering how to dress, grungy or designer jeans." Jory's smile was brief. "Not that he notices either way. But it's fun to hope."

Across the parking lot, Melissa saw Brad's Firebird gathering speed, heading for the highway that ran in front of Lincoln High. Her hopes for him had fled. The wind ruffled her hair, blowing it across her mouth. She pushed it back, but the taste lingered, dry and false.

Chapter Sixteen

After supper, Melissa and Jory sat together on Melissa's bed, pouring over homework. Melissa felt distracted and her mind kept wandering. It must have been obvious because Jory finally asked, "What's the matter? You keep staring off into space. Where's the scholar who's going to knock the world on its butt?"

Melissa managed a half smile. "I couldn't knock a fly off a wall."

"Level with me, Melissa. What's wrong?"

"It was harder going back to school than I thought it would be. Everything's different."

"I told you people would stop talking about you in a few days. It's no big deal."

"I saw Brad while I was waiting for you." Her voice sounded small.

Jory closed her book and nodded thoughtfully. "So, that's it."

"Not just Brad," Melissa balled her hands into fists, searching for a way to explain her feelings. "It's what Brad represents."

"Which is?"

"Jory, remember when we didn't have anything more complicated to think about than what color shirt to go with a pair of pants? Or who was taking who to a party?"

Jory frowned. "Is there a party you want to go to with Brad?"

Agitated, Melissa shook her head and began to pace her room. "Fat chance that Brad Kessing will ever ask me anyplace."

"You mean you don't think he'll ask you for a date?" Jory pulled up her legs and rested her chin on her knees. "Is this what's got you in such a tailspin? You've finally decided that something matters besides grades, but now the guy you were 'sort of interested in' might be interested in someone or something else?"

"Hardly." Melissa locked eyes with her friend. "I have cancer, Jory. People treat me like I'm some sort of *untouchable*. What guy is going to date me?"

"Ric?" Jory ventured.

"What *regular* guy?" Annoyance edged Melissa's question.

"So what?" Jory shrugged. "Being asked out is nothing. I go out all the time and mostly it's dullsville."

Of course Jory got asked out, Melissa thought. She was fun and full of energy and always ready for a good time. "But I *want* to be asked. Who wants me? Or my cancer?" Melissa's words hung in the air between them. The silence was so deep that Melissa could hear the faint sounds of the TV coming from the living room, where her mother was watching it.

"I know what you're talking about, Melissa. But why should it matter now? Four months ago all you wanted was a college scholarship and no involvements. I practically dragged you to meet Brad. Now, you're that far away from college." She gestured with her thumb and forefinger. "You're getting better and stronger every day. Why should Brad matter so much to you now?"

"Because four months ago I didn't have leukemia.

And Brad looked at me like I was beautiful. Today he looked at me like . . . like I was a leper. Like if he touched me, he would catch it."

Jory's voice grew very quiet. "That's his problem."

"No. It's my problem, too. Because it's happening to *me*, Jory. Not to some stranger, but to Melissa Austin."

Melissa parked Michael's truck in the hospital lot, entered the outpatient oncology clinic, and weaved through the maze of children and toys scattered on the floor of the waiting room. It always amazed her to see how many children had cancer. Some were bald, others looked perfectly healthy, yet what touched her most was not how they looked, but how much they acted like normal kids. They fought over toys, they pitched tantrums, they shed tears over hurt feelings. Their mothers often sat stony and withdrawn, but the children never forgot to be children.

Since she'd come for only a blood workup, Melissa walked straight into DeeDee Thomas's office. The diminutive, dark-haired nurse offered a beleaguered smile. "Hi, Melissa. It's a madhouse around here today, but I can work you up in a few minutes. Do you mind waiting?"

"Of course I do. But I will. Just for you."

The nurse poked her playfully. "You're too kind. Oh, incidentally, there's someone in the chemo room who's been asking for you, Rachael Dove. I told her you'd be in today and she's been waiting for you ever since."

Melissa felt a softening sensation. "She's such a doll. How's she doing?"

Nurse Thomas's hands kept busy, sorting through piles of paper on her overloaded desk. "Now where's that form? Ah . . . Here it is . . . Second remissions are even tougher to achieve and maintain. It's a battle, but she's holding her own."

The nurse's honesty caused a chill to go through Melissa. She said with brightness, "I'll go visit her now, and you can come get me when you're ready to draw blood." She walked quickly down the hall to the chemo room—the contour chairs and IV stands seemed all too familiar to her.

Rachael lay in one of the chairs, curled on her side and coloring. "Hi, Rachael."

The tiny girl glanced up and gave her a toothy smile. "Hi, Melissa. I'm coloring this just for you." Melissa looked at the scene from *Cinderella*. "This is Cinderella after her fairy godmother dressed her in her ball gown. Do you like it?"

"It's beautiful. I like pink."

"I've still got some more to do." Rachael sounded disappointed.

"Oh, I'll be here a while. You can finish it."

The little girl grinned. Her skin looked paper thin, and she'd lost all her hair. Her blue eyes seemed too large for her tiny face. "I picked this page," the child explained, "because you're all grown up and can go to balls and dances and stuff like that."

"I'd rather read a book."

Rachael giggled. "I'd rather go to a ball and meet a prince."

Deciding to change the subject, Melissa asked, "So how's your baby sister?"

Rachael made a face. "She cries a lot. But sometimes Mommy lets me hold her and give her a bottle. It was fun till she wet on me."

"Isn't that just like a baby? Do you like her any better than you did the last time we talked?"

"I guess so . . ." Rachael admitted with a sheepish shrug. "Sometimes she smiles at me. There!" Rachael announced triumphantly. "All finished."

Melissa reached down, took the book, and carefully tore out the page. "I'm going to hang this in my bedroom, and every time I look at it, I'll think of you."

The child beamed. She reached over to a small metal table and fished a clump of red curls off the top. "See what Mommy bought me? It's my new hair."

"So it is. Why'd you pick red?"

"Because I watch *Annie* on the VCR all the time. It's my favorite movie. Will you help me put it on?"

Melissa nestled the wig on Rachael's head. "You look just like a little movie star."

"I do? Justin Malone in Sunday school says I look like a clown."

"He's just jealous. You look lovely."

"I want to be a movie star when I grow up. What do you want to be?"

Melissa felt herself stiffen. A million thoughts tumbled through her head. High school graduation, college, her name on a brass nameplate. Would she see them all? "I've always wanted to be a lawyer," she said.

"You do? But you're so pretty. You could be a movie star." Touched, Melissa stooped down and hugged the child to her. "Thank you, Rachael. That's the nicest thing anyone's said to me in ages."

DeeDee Thomas leaned into the room. "I'm ready for you, Melissa."

"Coming," she said. "You take care, Rachael, and I'll see you again real soon. Thanks for the picture."

"I wish you were my sister," she said.

"I am, Rachael," Melissa said. "Because of all the

things we share, I *am* your sister. Don't ever forget
that, okay?"

The Brain Bowl session hadn't gone well and
Melissa knew it. She'd been slow on the buzzer and
twice her mind had gone blank. She assumed it was
because Brad was at the drill. The minute Mrs. Watson released the team, Melissa bolted for the door,
eager to get away as quickly as possible.

"Melissa! Wait up!" Mrs. Watson's voice hailed
her as she hurried out into the bright wintry afternoon. She reluctantly stopped and turned to the
teacher. Forcing a smile, she said, "Yes, Mrs. Watson.
What's up?"

"Nothing much. It's just the first opportunity I've
had to talk to you since you've returned to school. I
wanted to discuss Brain Bowl with you. You seemed a
bit off today."

Is that what her teacher wanted? To criticize her
performance? "Sorry. I know I've done better in other
drills."

"Yes, you have. What was wrong?"

"Nothing. I'll do better tomorrow."

"The school board has scheduled the Brain Bowl
round-robin between area high schools for the week
following spring break in April."

"It has?"

"That means we'll be choosing our final panel the
week before the round-robin match."

Melissa added up the remaining time. There
were two and a half months until the panel would be
chosen. "Why tell me this now?"

"I want you on it."

The teacher's forthright honesty caused Melissa to raise her eyebrow. "And I want to be on it."

Mrs. Watson smiled. "I didn't start this project to fail, Melissa. I didn't think you had either."

The insinuation annoyed her. "I didn't. I had a bad day, that's all. Am I the only one who can't have a bad day?"

Mrs. Watson studied Melissa for a long moment. "I want a winning team, and you're one of the best in our group."

Melissa was confused, unable to grasp the purpose of the conversation. "Is this a pep talk? I have every intention of making the team. I've probably worked harder than anybody for a spot. I can pull my own weight if I make the team, so don't feel you have to carry me."

"We *can't* carry you. So please don't stop working this close to the final selection process."

An inkling of Mrs. Watson's objective began to drift through to Melissa. She thought about the four other teachers responsible for choosing the team— Mr. Marshall, of course; Dean Crane; Mr. Wilson, the assistant principal; and Miss Judd, a science teacher. Counting Mrs. Watson, there was a total of five, so there could be no deadlocks on their votes. "Do the other faculty advisors think that my cancer may affect my ability to perform?" When Mrs. Watson said nothing, Melissa added, "It won't, you know. I've missed a lot, but I can do it."

"I know you can," Mrs. Watson said kindly.

"But some don't, is that what you're saying?"

Mrs. Watson touched Melissa's arm. "Prejudice isn't limited to race or religion, Melissa. I won't belabor the point." She waved her hand in dismissal. "But please, keep pouring yourself into this effort.

Now, remember, this conversation was between us girls, and I never would have said anything unless I wasn't pulling for you one hundred percent." She backed toward the faculty parking lot. "Tomorrow, Melissa . . . give it everything you've got."

Melissa watched Mrs. Watson hurry away, not sure whether she felt encouraged or defeated. Her teacher liked her and seemed to be on her side. But who wasn't on her side, and why? With a weary sigh, she crossed the vacant parking lot, unable to deal with it at that moment. Suddenly she heard someone calling her name and saw a guy leaning out of a blue van. She took a deep breath, recognizing Ricter Davis.

Chapter Seventeen

~~~

"Surprised to see me?" Ric asked as Melissa approached the van.

"Very surprised."

His face had filled out and his hair was stylishly cut, but his eyes were as dark and soul-piercing as she remembered. "Hop in," he said.

The van was carpeted in blue and outfitted with a small table and cushioned benches. "Looks like a home on wheels," she told him.

He chuckled. "In case I don't pay my dorm bill, I'll always have a place to stay."

His jeans hid his artificial leg, and she looked away immediately, afraid he'd think she was staring. "How did you find me?"

"I watched the school empty and kept an eye out for the pretty girls. I'd almost given up."

"I had Brain Bowl drill."

He glanced to the side. "Actually, I've waited for you before, but you always seemed to be with that girlfriend of yours."

"Jory." Melissa wasn't sure if she was flattered or not. "You could have called and come by my house."

He ignored her comment. "And then I saw you out front once with some blond-haired guy who looked pretty important to you." Her cheeks flushed, remembering how she and Brad had attempted to sidestep each other but wound up nearly colliding. "So I was right. He *is* important," Ric said when she didn't respond.

His condescending tone was irritating. "Ric, this is really silly. There're a hundred guys at Lincoln High."

"But only one you care about?"

She leaned forward, suddenly angry. "I think I resent this. You have no right skulking around the school, spying on me."

He drove with one hand and reached over and squeezed her shoulder with the other. His tone was apologetic. "I was just checking out my competition, Melissa. A guy has a right to know what he's up against."

"There is no competition," she said icily. "Brad Kessing is nothing to me."

Ric's grin was wide. "Good. Then there won't be any obstacles to our relationship, right?"

"We have no relationship," she told him, wishing he'd never come for her.

"I hope we will, Melissa," he said.

It seemed to Melissa that dating Ric was inevitable. And once she got over her initial animosity toward him, she really did have a good time with him. Her mother was hesitant at first. "He's older than you," she'd said. "I'd rather see you date some boy from your junior class." Melissa didn't have the heart to remind her that most boys from her school avoided girls with cancer.

Michael, however, was more adamant. "Why the hell is he interested in a sixteen-year-old? Can't he get girls his own age?"

"He likes me. Is that a crime?"

"He's almost my age, for God's sake."

"You're not my father, Michael. I'm old enough to choose my own dates."

"If he comes on to you . . ."

"Forget it. He's really just a friend."

Jory, on the other hand, had been philosophical about the matter. "I think you should date him and have a good time. Go enjoy yourself, but don't forget: I want details of every date, every party. Do I make myself clear?"

Melissa did tell Jory everything, but she also wrote in her journal.

February 20

It's been a month since Ric and I first went out—a fast month, too. I like being with him and it makes me even more positive that I want to go away to college. He took me up to his dorm room and I met his roommate, Doug, and Doug's girlfriend, Cheri. Ric used a special knock before we went inside. It's funny, the way everyone's so casual about sex. It still makes me a little uptight. Ric and I aren't doing it, of course, but everyone just assumes we are, and I guess there's nothing I can do about that.

Ric's frat parties get crazy at times. I don't drink because of my medications, and when you're the only sober person in a roomful of bombed people, it's weird. Ric drinks some, but never as much as the other guys, and if things get too wild, we leave. Last Saturday night they had a toga party and some guy stripped naked, so Ric got me out fast. Jory would be having a blast, but I'd hate to see her waste herself that way.

> *Lincoln seems so tame by comparison.*
> *Brain Bowl is still my top priority. It hardly*
> *bothers me anymore to be around Brad.*
> *Maybe because I have someone else to con-*
> *centrate on, or maybe because I know it*
> *can't work out and that Brad still can't ac-*
> *cept me because I'm less than perfect. Ric*
> *accepts me, but sometimes I wonder what it*
> *is I really want. I like Ric, but . . .*

Melissa did not write in her journal about the first time Ric kissed her because it would have seemed too juvenile and because the kiss was hard and deep, serious and a little rough. He tasted faintly of beer, and her heart thudded like a jackhammer. She didn't want him to know how limited her experience was in that area, so she returned his kiss with far more passion than she felt. He pulled away, studied her briefly, then kissed her again, this time more lightly. He said, "You give me hope, Melissa."

"Hope for what?" She was grateful for the surrounding cover of the night so that he couldn't see the faint tremors in her hands.

"For us, of course."

"I thought we were just having fun, Ric." Rock music drifted from the fraternity house as they stood under the sprawling oak tree on the front lawn.

"We are. But there's fun and there's fun."

She brushed aside his innuendo. "And I thought you were attracted to my fine mind."

He chuckled and locked his arms around her waist. "If there's one thing I've learned because of having cancer, it's to go after what you want in life."

"Why?"

"Because life's too short to stand around and wait for things to come your way."

She leaned into his palms, which rested in the small of her back. "Are you ever going to forgive life for dealing you cancer?"

"What's that supposed to mean?" His eyes narrowed in the moonlight.

"Ever since we first met, you've seemed really mad about what's happened to you. Why are you so angry all the time, Ric?"

"Why aren't you angrier?" He fired back.

"I am angry. Every time I go to the clinic and see those little kids and know what we're all going through together, I get very mad. But being mad doesn't change it."

"And being so accepting doesn't make it any easier," he challenged.

"I don't think I'm accepting of it, Ric. I'm not sure what I am about it."

"I know one thing you are," he said, his voice softer, smoothing over the anger that had reared between them.

"What?" She asked suspiciously.

"You're pretty." He brought his mouth to hers.

She caught her breath. "Don't do that."

"Why?" He traced the outline of her lips with his finger. "Sometimes I think this is all there is, Melissa. Feeling, hearing, tasting, seeing . . . What else can there be?"

She slipped from his grasp and waited for her pulse to stop racing, her blood to stop pounding in her ears. "I don't know what else there is, but I just think there's more."

His expression grew cynical. "Well, even if there is 'more,' this is where I want to start—with what I can touch and hold on to." He took her by the waist again and pulled her against him. She felt the hard outline of his body against the length of hers. Where their legs touched, she sensed his prosthesis through her jeans, and Ric relaxed his hold, knowing that she felt it. "Sometimes I forget my leg isn't there," he said. "Even a year after the amputation, I can still feel pains in my leg, still feel my foot. Ghost pains they call it."

Eager to help him forget, she said quickly, "I remember my hair in the same way. I sometimes reach to lift it when I sit down like I used to do so it wouldn't get caught on the back of a chair. And when I brush my wig, I often drop the brush because I expect my hair to be longer. Just for a moment I wonder why it isn't. Then I remember."

Ric fingered the tips of the wig. "This doesn't feel false," he whispered, burying his face in the side of her neck. "And it smells like you. Like fresh flowers."

The tingling sensation started in the pit of her stomach and diffused through her body with the warmth of his breath on her skin. "Thank you."

His mouth found hers again and this time his kiss was long and slow. She slipped her arms around his neck and let him stroke the contours of her body. She felt like satin inside. "We're a lot alike, Melissa."

He'd told her the same thing months before, when they'd been in the hospital. At the time, she'd resented the comparison. Now, she agreed with him. Their illness bound them together with invisible bands and they *were* alike. More alike than she and Brad would ever be. "Let's go inside," she said to him while her mind swirled and spun with the sensations his touch was arousing.

"All right," he said, his voice husky. "But I won't

always let you back off this way, Melissa. I'm not some high school kid, and I know what I want."

Melissa understood, but she didn't know what she wanted. She only knew she *wanted*. Deep inside her heart, she wanted.

"So how's college life?" Jory asked, taking a bite of apple.

"Why do you ask?"

"We never talk about you and Ric, that's all. I'm curious."

Melissa picked at the thick pile carpet in Jory's family room, ignoring the VCR movie that blared in the background. "There's not much to talk about."

"Come on, Melissa. You can talk to me. I'm not your mother. Haven't I spilled my guts about every date I've had this year? I expect the same courtesy from you."

Melissa smiled. "I don't know what you want to hear. I've told you all about the frat parties. I've told you where he takes me, what we do."

"But not how you *feel*," Jory said. "Do you care about him?"

"In a way," Melissa said.

"Ugh! You talk but you say *nothing*!"

"It's a good trait for a lawyer to have," Melissa joked. She knew she was putting Jory off and it bothered Melissa because they'd shared everything over the years. But these were thoughts and feelings she'd never known before, until Ric had brought them out. She couldn't talk it out, she couldn't share it, not even with her best friend. Jokingly, she raised her right hand and said, "I solemnly swear to tell Jory Delaney all my future plans from this day forth, so help me Hannah."

* * *

By the middle of March, the Brain Bowl drills were going like clockwork. Melissa and Brad and a science whiz named Lyle Vargas were the backbone of the team. She hadn't really known Lyle until Brain Bowl started, but she liked him. He was not only sensitive to her, but he seemed to like Jory, and Melissa thought they would make a nice couple if only she would give him the time of day.

Melissa was sure that the Lincoln High Brain Bowl team had a shot at advancing through the round-robin. Following a grueling practice session in late March, Melissa trudged out onto the grassy area in front of the school and looked around for Ric's van. It wasn't parked in its usual place, which meant he was late. She crossed her legs and dropped to the ground, running her palm over the spring growth of fine green grass. The soft blades reminded her of the hair sprouting beneath her wig.

The sun beat warmly on her shoulders, and she could smell the rich, loamy earth she sat on. She saw someone approaching and squinted. The girl stopped a short distance from where Melissa was sitting.

Melissa tried to place the face. *Sarah*. The girl waved, and a bronze Firebird pulled up alongside of her. But it wasn't the car or its driver that caught Melissa's eye. It was the gleaming gold ID bracelet locked on Sarah's wrist. Sarah was Brad's girl.

Chapter Eighteen

～

Brad drove off and a lump wedged in her throat. "This is stupid!" she said out loud, standing and dusting her jeans furiously. Hadn't she known for months about Sarah and Brad? It was silly for her to react to it.

A horn blew and Ric hailed her. She jumped into the van, slamming the door hard. "Who rattled your cage?" Ric asked.

"No one. It was a long day."

"Brain Bowl didn't go well?"

"I said it was a long day. Don't go reading something into nothing."

Ric shrugged and pulled away from the curb so fast that the tires squealed. "How about a hamburger?"

"Mom's expecting me for dinner."

"How about going out later to the library at the university? I've got a research paper to get moving on."

"I need to spend some time at home. Mom's starting to get on my case about going out all the time."

"You're avoiding me."

She gritted her teeth. "I just need some time to myself, Ric. That's all." Without warning, he pulled the van onto a small, dusty road that wound its way into some woods. "Where are you going?" she snapped. "I told you I needed to get home."

144

He ignored her until they reached a clearing and he shut off the engine. Opening her door he hauled her out. "Come on. Let's walk."

"Ric . . . please, I don't want to walk."

Taking her elbow, he led her along, past trees dripping with Spanish moss, toward a river, where he stopped and turned her to face him. "It's nice out here, Melissa. I sometimes come here to study and think."

Still angry, she took a few deep breaths before scanning her surroundings. Wild azalea bushes burst with fuchsia and pink blossoms, and water gurgled over rocks. "You're right. It's very pretty out here."

He lifted her chin and looked hard into her eyes. "I'm sorry you had a bad day."

"I overreacted. Forget it."

"But you still don't want to tell me about it?"

"There's nothing to tell. Honest."

He let it drop and Melissa was grateful. They stood in the clearing, quiet except for the sounds of the woods. Ric finally broke the silence, his voice hesitant and gentle. "Melissa, I want to ask you something. I was going to wait till Saturday, but I'm going to ask you now."

Suddenly she was alert. Her mouth went dry, but she forced some levity. "Ask away."

"Spring break's coming up."

"I know."

"Some of the guys from the house and the dorm floor are planning a trip down to Sarasota to spend a few days on the beach."

"I thought everyone went to Fort Lauderdale."

He grinned. "Highly overrated. Who wants to be stepping over bozos from Michigan and Ohio?" He brushed a wisp of her hair off her cheek and the gesture moved her. Ric never thought twice about her hair being a wig. "Doug's aunt has a place on Sanibel Island and he's taking Cheri there. Doug wants me to come along. And I want you to come with me."

Startled, she stared into his dark, coal-colored eyes. She knew what he was asking. She dropped her gaze and stared at the ground, where she unearthed a rock with the toe of her shoe. "I . . . I don't know . . ."

"I want to make love to you, Melissa. I want to sleep with you and wake up with you." He'd slipped his hands into the back pockets of his jeans but he somehow made her feel as if he were holding her.

"Ric . . . I . . . just can't take off for a weekend. What would I tell my mother? Michael?" She tried to swallow her rising panic.

"If you asked, I know your friend Jory would cover for you."

He'd already thought about the details for her, but she shook her head. "I don't know . . ."

Then Ric touched her, taking her gently by the shoulders. "You don't have to answer now. But will you think about it?"

"Ric . . . I don't—" She stopped, groping for the right words. "I mean . . . I've never . . ."

"I know you haven't, Melissa. But when you do, I want it to be with me."

Her cheeks burned, not from modesty, but from the overwhelming emotions she felt. Hadn't she wondered about what making love would be like? Hadn't she read passages in books that told how it felt? Watched old movies that aroused romantic feelings? "I don't know . . ."

He unbuttoned the top button of her blouse and gently ran his fingertips over her skin. Her knees went weak and she thought her heart might explode. "I've always thought you were pretty . . . from the first time I saw you. You were sitting in that hospital bed and you were combing your hair. That beautiful hair . . ."

She took a step backward, surprised that her legs could support her. Her brain whirled back to some long ago conversation, and she asked, "Who was Megan?"

Ric let his hands drop. "Why do you ask?"

"You mentioned her once. I wondered at the time, but didn't ask."

"She was just a girl I was dating when I was first diagnosed."

"And?"

"And she couldn't handle it." His expression darkened and his mouth pressed into a hard line.

She thought of Brad. Big and blond and so totally attractive to her. "Why can't anyone ever handle it?" she asked, but she didn't expect an answer. She raised her hand and laid her palm on Ric's cheek. "I will think about it, Ric. I'll think about it very hard."

He turned her palm and kissed it. "Two weeks," he told her. "We'll leave the weekend after next."

"You awake, Mom?" Melissa peeked into her mother's bedroom. Mrs. Austin was reading, propped up with pillows, a pile of file folders scattered over the bed.

She smiled and pushed her reading glasses on top of her head. "Come on in, honey." She shoved aside the folders, making a place for Melissa to sit. "This is a nice treat. To what do I owe the honor of such a visit?"

Melissa curled onto the bed and shrugged. "No reason. Do I need one?"

"You never needed one before. Actually, I've missed your visits. Remember how you'd always come in after dates and fill me in? And we'd pig out on cookies and milk?"

Melissa remembered. So much had changed for her over the past six months. "I guess most of it sounded pretty stupid."

"*Au contraire* . . . it kept me young." Melissa allowed a comfortable silence to stretch between them. Finally, her mother asked, "Got a problem?"

"No. Why do you ask?"

"Between school and Ric, you're very busy, honey. Is everything going all right for you?"

Melissa felt her inner defenses go up. She wasn't sure why she'd come into her mother's room. She certainly couldn't bare her soul about Ric's invitation to spend the weekend with him. "Everything's fine, Mom. Don't make a big deal out of a simple little nighttime visit." Melissa felt guilty for sounding short. "I was lonesome, that's all."

"No need to feel lonely. I'm always here."

Melissa nodded. "Yes. You're always here." She longed to tell her mother about Ric. Longed to have her tell her what to do. *She'll say no,* she thought. *It was a mother's place to say no to such things. But I have leukemia,* her reason argued. *I might never face this choice again.*

"Is this a private party or can anyone come?" Michael asked.

"Boy, this is my lucky night," Mrs. Austin said with a warm smile. "Both my kids at once. Come share the bed," she said.

"Can't—I'm too grubby," Michael said, sinking to the floor. "So what's up?"

"Nothing," Melissa said. "Just girl talk." Her heart went out to him. "How's your balloon club?"

"You make it sound like a kiddie club." His grin was impish.

"That's what I get for making polite conversation with a man." She emphasized the last word as if it were a dirty one.

"Watch it, woman, or I may gag and tie you and take you up with me this weekend."

"Thanks for the invitation," she said, "but I hardly ever have a good time when I'm nauseated."

The three of them laughed and Mrs. Austin tossed off the covers. "Cookies," she said. "This occasion calls for cookies and milk. You two wait right here and I'll bring back a tray."

Michael held her robe and Melissa watched them, feeling how much she loved them both. She remembered the early days of her diagnosis and hospitalization. The angry words she'd hurled at her mother and the way Michael had always retreated from any conversation about her illness. None of them had really accepted it yet—especially her brother—but right now, in the comfort of her mother's room, it seemed that nothing could hurt them.

Melissa shook her head to clear it. She would think about Ric and cancer and choices tomorrow. Tonight she would be the little girl who used to sit on her mother's bed and share her heart's secrets.

"Lots of cookies," she called. "Chocolate ones. And make sure the milk is real cold."

Melissa sensed a tension in the clinic. DeeDee Thomas was a jangle of nerves, dropping the tourniquet she was trying to tie around Melissa's arm, contaminating the sterile needle and having to pop open another.

"What's wrong?" Melissa asked, watching DeeDee hunt for a vein along the inside of her arm.

"Just a typical crazy day. Don't mind me."

"It's always crazy around this place. But today seems crazier and you're kind of distracted. Are you sure nothing's wrong?"

DeeDee looked up, half-smiling, and her eyes looked tired. "I was working half the night upstairs in oncology. Then two people called in sick down here and someone had to fill in. I'm wiped out, that's all."

"My blood work's still looking good," Melissa said, trying to make conversation.

"Good. I want you to be well, Melissa. I want all of you to be well," DeeDee said.

"All of us?"

"The kids. All the kids." She gestured vaguely and taped a cotton ball across Melissa's vein.

Usually when her lab work was complete, Melissa tore out of the place, trying to escape the anti-septic smells and reminders of this other world she belonged to. But today she hesitated. "Know what?" she said to DeeDee. "I think I'll go up and visit the floor. Dr. Rowan said that it was a good idea to go up every once in a while so that the really sick kids can see that that part doesn't last forever."

"No, Melissa. Don't go up. Not today."

DeeDee's sharp directive surprised her. "Why not?"

The nurse's eyes were evasive. "It's just a bad day up there."

An icy cold feeling seized Melissa's heart. "What's wrong? What's happened?"

DeeDee straightened and absently tried to tuck

some wayward hair behind her ear. "We had a death," she said. "It was a long fight, but we lost it."

"Who?" Melissa felt her stomach churn.

DeeDee sagged. "The little girl, Rachael Dove. We put her on a respirator yesterday, but today there was no brain activity. We turned off the machine less than an hour ago."

Chapter Nineteen

〜〜〜

The ride in the elevator was smooth and silent. Melissa shivered at the haunting familiarity of the oncology floor. It was as if she'd walked into a time warp. Everything was exactly as she had left it months before. Almost.

The atmosphere was subdued. Nurses moved efficiently, their voices softened, their expressions grim. Melissa hadn't expected the loss to have affected all of them so obviously. She'd figured that they must be used to it, conditioned to it. Yet grief was etched clearly in their faces. She'd never thought of them as anything other than trained professionals, just doing a job, but she saw them now as people, *grieving* people.

She stood near the nurses' station, momentarily confused, unable to decide what to do, where to go. Which room had been Rachael's? She wanted to ask one of the nurses, but couldn't bring herself to approach anybody. They might ask why she wanted to know, and she had no reason. She began to walk slowly down the hall painted with a gay circus theme, glancing into doorways, inexplicably drawn. She didn't want to go. She *had* to go.

She knew she'd found the right room the second she peeked inside. Machines banked one wall, and a hospital bed stood in the center of the floor, empty. Melissa entered, her heart pounding so hard, she felt sick to her stomach.

"Can I help you?" The unexpected voice caused Melissa to jump. "I'm sorry. I didn't mean to scare you."

The girl was about Melissa's age, dressed in a pink striped uniform, preparing to make the bed. "I-It's all right. I didn't think anybody was in the room."

"My name's Laura Lopez. I work here as a volunteer."

Melissa felt disappointed that she wasn't alone. "I'm Melissa Austin."

Laura shook out the sheet and smoothed it across the forlorn-looking bed. "My father's a doctor here at the hospital and my brother's a physical therapist. I guess you might say this place is in my blood." Melissa watched Laura expertly tuck in the corners of the sheet. "Did you know Rachael?" Laura asked.

"Yes. We sometimes had our clinic appointments at the same time."

Laura straightened up from her bed-making. "Oh—you're *Melissa*."

"Yes."

"Rachael talked about you a lot. She called you her 'big friend with the nice eyes.'" Melissa felt a lump in her throat. Laura continued, "I used to read to her at night when her mother couldn't stay. Even when I wasn't on duty, but just studying here in the hospital library, I'd stop by to see her." Laura smiled. "Rachael had a way of growing on you, didn't she?"

"Yes, she did." Melissa cleared her throat. "I didn't even know she was back in the hospital. The last time I saw her she seemed better."

Laura continued fluffing the pillow. "When it happens, it happens quickly."

"'It'?"

"Dying." Laura said the word solemnly.

Melissa dug her fingernails into her palms and turned to gaze at the monitors and machines. They were mute and indifferent. There was no life force for them to measure now. "Did she hurt before she died?"

"No. She was even a little excited. At first, she was afraid of going away. That's what her mother had told her—that she was going to a beautiful place where she could play and never hurt again. She wanted her mother to come with her, or at least one of the nurses."

"But, of course, no one could go with her." Melissa said the words absently. "It's something everyone has to do on her own."

"She slipped into a coma and died."

"Thank you for telling me. I'm sorry I didn't know sooner so I could have visited with her."

"There's a few of her things left in a bag," Laura said kindly. "I gathered them up to send to her family. Would you like to look through them?"

Laura handed her a plastic sack. She saw the teddy bear first, the one she'd given Rachael. It was worn in places, the fur rubbed off, and it was missing an eye. Its red felt tongue was half pulled out. "Looks like she loved it a lot," Laura observed.

Blinking furiously, Melissa sorted through papers with scribbles and pages from coloring books. She saw one of Prince Charming holding the glass slipper for Cinderella and her breath caught. "Do you think it would be all right if I kept this one? You see, I have the one of Cinderella in her ball gown, and . . ." Her voice cracked and Laura touched her shoulder.

"Take it. I'm sure it's fine."

With trembling fingers, Melissa folded the piece of paper and tucked it into her purse. She shivered. Rachael Dove had lived four short years and left behind a wounded teddy bear and a handful of colored papers. "Thank you." Her voice was barely audible. "I . . . I guess I should be going."

"Nice to meet you, Melissa."

When she reached the doorway she looked back at the room. Everything was there except Rachael, life. Yet Melissa knew that the child had left one more thing behind. She'd left an unforgettable memory of herself. Melissa ran down the hall to catch the elevator, tears coming in violent waves.

"Melissa! What are you doing here?" Ric stood so abruptly from the desk in his dorm room that his chair tipped over.

She closed the door behind her. "Are you alone?"

"Yeah, Doug's out with Cheri." He grabbed handfuls of clothes off his bed and shoved books and papers and soda cans out of the way to make a place for her to sit. "I thought you said you were getting together with Jory tonight."

Melissa paced, too restless to sit. "I went by the clinic this afternoon for lab work and then went up to the oncology floor."

"And?"

"And they told me that Rachael Dove had died."

He looked blank for a moment, then nodded. "The little girl you told me about. Gee, Melissa, I'm sorry. I know you liked her."

"I called my mom and told her I was eating out tonight, but really all I've been doing is driving around. And thinking."

Ric walked over to her and pulled her to his chest. "I'm glad you came to me, Melissa."

She leaned against him briefly, allowing one moment of softness and comfort to pass between them, then gently pulled away. "Maybe you won't be."

"Why?"

"I'm not going to Sarasota with you, Ric."

Stunned, he blinked. "Why not?"

She took her time answering, staring thoughtfully into space. "Before I got leukemia, I had so many plans. I wanted to make the Brain Bowl team—no junior has ever made the final panel. I wanted to be a National Merit Scholar. I wanted to go to college and study law. I wanted so many things, Ric."

"You were robbed," he said with a shrug. "We were both robbed. I wanted to run track."

"But I still want all those things, Ric. In spite of everything that's happened."

He reached for her, but she held up her hand to stop him. "What's that got to do with our spending the weekend together?"

Melissa searched for the right words to tell him what she felt. "You aren't my only option in life, Ric. Please don't make me your only one."

She saw anger in his eyes. "That doesn't make any sense. My life doesn't revolve around you."

"What does it revolve around?"

Agitated, he shoved his hands deep into the pockets of his jeans. "School. The fraternity. Things."

"But no track."

He scoffed. "Get real, Melissa. What kind of future does a one-legged runner have?"

"Make one. Be the first."

"You mean, 'If life gives you lemons, make lemonade'?" His tone was sarcastic. "Your romantic outlook is so sweet I could catch diabetes."

She laughed. "My brother calls me a hopeless romantic, too. And speaking of Michael, I thought of something else while I was driving around tonight."

Ric raked a hand through his hair and scowled, but he seemed resigned to listen, so Melissa continued. "When Michael was twelve he had a friend named Corley. I hated Corley's guts." She crossed her arms. "We'd always play board games at his house. Corley had every board game money could buy.

"Anyway, I began to notice that every time Michael or I began to win, Corley would make up a bunch of new rules. One day I got so mad, I wrecked up the board, called him some names, and stormed out of the house. Michael caught up with me and tried to calm me down. When I told Michael I was angry because Corley was cheating, you know what he said? He said, 'I know. But when someone changes the rules of the game, you either play by the new rules, or you don't play.'" She paused to let her statement sink in. "I remembered that tonight even though it happened years and years ago." She reached out and touched Ric's arm. "Ric, I didn't ask for cancer. Or for all the chemo and tests and hospital time. The rules of my life got changed, horribly changed. But I still want to play."

"And going to Sarasota with me, committing to me, isn't part of your game plan?" His question was bitter.

"No." A fine film of tears welled in her eyes. "But being asked was the nicest thing you could have done. You made me feel really good inside," she added shyly.

He stroked her cheek and let his fingers brush her wig. "I didn't do it to be nice."

"And that's what made it even more special. Because you cared. You really cared about me." She squeezed his hand and moved toward the door, until she felt the hard knob touch her spine. "Goodbye, Ric."

He started forward and stopped. "Melissa, if you ever change your mind . . ."

"You'll be the first to know." She closed the door behind her, then leaned against it for support. It was the hardest conversation she'd ever held, and it meant closing a chapter in her life that might never be opened again. She remembered the fire she'd felt when Ric had caressed her body.

"At least leukemia didn't dull your hormones," she told herself wryly under her breath. She left the dorm quickly and headed home, knowing that the next afternoon held one more giant hurdle for her to overcome.

Chapter Twenty

Melissa fidgeted with her belongings until everyone except the faculty advisors had left the Brain Bowl drill session. The names of the final panelists would be posted the next day, and Melissa knew deep down inside that her name wouldn't be on the list.

When the last student had left the room, Melissa took a deep breath and approached the teachers, who sat at a conference table comparing notes—Mrs. Watson, Mr. Marshall, Dean Crane, Mr. Wilson, and Miss Judd. She cleared her throat and they all looked up at her.

Mr. Marshall asked, "Did you want something, Melissa?"

With a calm voice that in no way reflected the panic she felt, she asked, "Would you please tell me now if I'm going to be on the panel or not?"

Mrs. Crane said, "Now, dear, that wouldn't be fair, would it? Everyone wants to know, and besides, that's what our meeting now is for—to decide."

Melissa gritted her teeth and refused to back down. "You aren't going to choose me, are you?"

The teachers exchanged glances. "We've made no decisions, Melissa," Mr. Wilson said, but without meeting her eyes.

Her stomach sank, like a fifty-foot drop on a roller coaster. Her suspicions were confirmed—they had no intentions of selecting her. "Why?" She asked.

"Why what?"

"Why won't you choose me?" Her anger fueled a boldness she didn't know she had. "I'm good at the game and you know it."

"You're the best," Mrs. Watson said, and received a sharp look from Mrs. Crane.

But the words buoyed Melissa. "I've worked harder than anyone. And my specialty is math. No one's quicker at solving problems than me. I'm always first on the buzzer with a math problem."

"Balance, Melissa," Miss Judd said. "We pick the team for balance."

Melissa straightened. "It's because of my cancer, isn't it? You're afraid that I'll get sick or something."

The quick exchange of looks between the advisors told her she'd guessed correctly. *Prejudice.* Isn't that what Mrs. Watson had tried to warn her about weeks before?

Mrs. Crane tapped her pencil on the table. "Melissa, your illness is a factor. You were out for such a long time . . ."

"But I've not missed one session since January. Not one!" She felt small tremors course through her body. "You have no right to hold that against me."

"If our team advances," Mr. Wilson said, "the pressure will be very intense. We can't afford to have a panelist drop off."

Mrs. Crane added quickly, "And you're just a junior, Melissa. You do have next year, you know."

Melissa crossed her arms and attacked their logic. "So in other words, I may be too sick to be on the panel this year, but not so sick that I won't be around to try again next year." From the corner of her eye, she saw Mrs. Watson slip her a thumbs-up signal. Encouraged, Melissa let the words tumble out. "Who of you can say, 'I'll be here next year'? Or next week? Nobody's tomorrows are a sure thing. If I make no plans for a future, then I'll never have a future. Don't you see? Don't you understand?"

The room had gone quiet, so quiet that Melissa could hear the clock on the wall when its hand jumped to pass another minute. Sweat trickled down between her shoulder blades. How had she ever found the guts to say those things to teachers?

Mr. Marshall cleared his throat, and his appraisal of her was both direct and pensive. "You're right, Melissa. You need to know right now if you'll be selected for the panel or not." He glanced down the row of startled faces. "I personally recruited Melissa last September because I thought she had what it took to participate in Brain Bowl. Nothing has happened over the past few months to change my opinion. I want her on the final panel."

"Me too," Mrs. Watson added emphatically.

Miss Judd nodded, then Mr. Wilson. Melissa's heart pounded. Mrs. Crane pressed her lips together, but finally offered a brief, terse nod. Melissa felt her legs trembling as Mr. Marshall stood and shook her hand. "Congratulations, Miss Austin. But please hold off telling anyone until all the names are posted tomorrow. All right?"

"It's a deal," she whispered, not trusting her voice to hold.

Mrs. Watson leaned forward. "By this time next year, you'll be a veteran. Imagine how strong we'll be when we have someone on the team two years in a row."

Two years in a row. Tomorrow. The future. Melissa flashed her a winning smile. "Yes, next year. When I'm a senior."

Chapter Twenty-one

∼‿∾

Melissa slipped on the bright green jacket, smoothed her palms over the fine linen fabric, and examined the intricate green-and-gold Lincoln High School crest sewn on the breast pocket. Her bedroom mirror told her she looked every inch the exclusive representative of the Brain Bowl team that she felt she was.

With satisfaction she inspected her makeup, then her hair and figure. Gingerly, she touched the ends of her wig, smoothing them under, close to her ears. Few traces of her ordeal with leukemia remained, and unless someone had known her before, no one could tell she'd ever been sick. Yet, she cautioned her reflection, remission didn't mean the disease was over, but simply that it was held in check.

She thought about the night ahead of her. In two hours, she'd be sitting on the stage of the Tampa Civic Center Auditorium facing every other high school panel in the Bay area for round one of Brain Bowl. Butterflies fluttered in her stomach, but they were welcomed. Her nerves tingled, but they also felt sharp and alert. Melissa knew that she was ready for the competition.

She thought back to the week before, when the names had first been posted and read over the school PA system. All day long, kids had stopped her in the halls and congratulated her. And late in the afternoon, when she'd been waiting for Jory by her car, Brad had hailed her.

"Wait up, Melissa," he'd said, jogging toward her. He still had the power to make her heartbeat quicken, and she guessed some things would never change. "I'm really glad you made the team and I just wanted to say, congratulations and I told you so."

"Congratulations to you too, Brad. I'm glad they picked you to be captain. We're gonna win it, you know."

"Of course we're going to win it."

An April breeze ruffled her hair, blowing it across her cheek, and he reached out to smooth it. This time, Melissa did not withdraw from his touch. "The wind can't do much damage," she said, holding his gaze. "It's only a wig."

"I figured. I had an aunt who went through chemo, and she lost her hair and had to wear a wig, too."

Suddenly, she felt a jumble of hopes and illusions and wishes. She glanced at his wrist and noticed that the ID bracelet still belonged to Sarah. Then, setting her mind at ease, she let go of her longings for Brad. She slugged him playfully on the arm. "My real hair's growing out well, and by the end of the summer, I'll bet it's past my jawline."

"I'll check you out before I go away to college," he told her. They talked for a few minutes and she watched him head toward his car. Now, days later, Melissa could really shrug off the last vestiges of yearning, and refocus her energy on the evening ahead.

There was a knock at her door and Jory breezed in, her green eyes dancing. "All set?"

"What do you think?" Melissa twirled, showing off the jacket, white pleated skirt, and white pumps.

"Preppy," Jory said, then added with an impish smile, "but on you, it's sensational."

"You look different," Melissa observed, scrutinizing her friend from head to toe. Jory's standard funky look had been replaced by polished sophistication. Her dress was simple, but elegant, the green perfect for her auburn hair. Her usual wild shade of nail polish had been exchanged for a soft shade of apricot.

Self-consciously, Jory dropped her gaze. "I decided it was time for a new image. Even Peter Pan had to grow up."

"I'll bet Michael will approve."

"Do you think so?"

Jory asked the question so quickly and with such eagerness that Melissa intuitively reached out and squeezed her friend's hands. "Let's go dazzle him with our combined beauty. I'll bet he and Mom are waiting for our grand entrance right now."

Jory hung back slightly. "In a minute. First, I want to give you a present."

Melissa noticed the small bag Jory was holding. Surprised, she asked, "For me? What is it?"

"Close your eyes." Melissa obeyed, more excited than curious. "Okay, open them."

Jory held a wig, a fall of hair that was rich and black and incredibly long. Melissa stared, open-mouthed. "Oh, Jory . . ."

"It's *real* hair, Melissa," Jory began to babble. "I sent for it ages ago, through a salon in New York that specializes in only the finest. I sent them pictures of you and had them make up the hairpiece just for you. It's just like your real hair, don't you think, Melissa? I

insisted that it had to be perfect. Tell me you like it.
Tell me you'll wear it."

Mesmerized, Melissa reached out and touched
the hair, sifting it through her fingers. Tears gathered
on her lashes. "I-It must have cost a fortune . . ."

Jory dismissed her remark with an impatient
wave. "It's my money and I can spend it however I
like."

Unable to take her eyes off the hair, Melissa whispered. "Help me put it on."

In moments the switch was accomplished and
Melissa could only stare in the mirror at the reborn
image of herself. "I-I'd almost forgotten . . ." She
gathered a fistful of the hair and rolled it through her
fingers, feeling the luxurious weight of it, the silkiness
of it on her skin. It hung to her waist and she tossed
her head to feel the way it brushed her shoulders and
flowed down her back. She caught Jory's eyes in the
mirror and turned toward her. "Thank you."

Jory blinked, haphazardly running her forefinger
beneath an eye. "Don't want to smear my mascara,"
she mumbled, shifting nervously from foot to foot.

Without a word, Melissa slipped her arms around
Jory and hugged her tightly, not caring that she herself
was crying and probably ruining her own carefully applied makeup. "It's the most beautiful gift I've ever
been given. I love you, Jory Delaney."

"Oh, Melissa, I love you, too. You're my best
friend. My *best*."

Melissa might never have let Jory go, except for a
rap on her door and Michael's muffled, impatient
voice. "Aren't you two ready yet? We're going to be
late if you don't light a fire under yourselves."

"Cool out. We're coming," Melissa said. Both

girls quickly touched up their makeup, then Melissa opened the door with an exaggerated flair. "Good grief, Michael, I can tell time and we're not late."

When he saw her he stared, shocked. "It's a gift from Jory," she told him.

He looked at Jory, standing timidly behind Melissa, who stepped aside. "You did this for Melissa?" he asked.

Jory tilted her head, her expression caught between defiance and desperation. "Why not? What are friends for?"

Michael's hand drifted up to touch Jory's cheek. "Thank you," he said. He tipped her chin upward and with incredible tenderness said again, "Thank you, Jory." She blushed, staring into Michael's eyes, unable to speak.

Reluctantly Melissa broke the spell. "Are we ready?"

Michael stepped away from Jory and took Melissa's hand. "Mom's waiting in the car."

Melissa's heart swelled, and she was filled with joy. "Last one out buys milk shakes for everyone after the match," she called. "Chocolate!"

She bounded out of the room and down the stairs, her hair chasing behind her. It caught the lamp glow and sparkled like starlight in the night.

Goodbye
Doesn't Mean Forever

For Rochelle

———

"Now faith is the substance of things hoped for, the evidence of things not seen."

HEBREWS 11:1 (KJV)

Chapter One

~⁘~

"Jory Delaney, you can't be serious! What do you mean you don't want to go to Europe with your father and me next month?"

"Mother, please, give me a break. School starts at the end of August. You won't be back by then and I can't miss the start of my senior year. Besides, I don't feel like exploring ruins and visiting a bunch of moldy castles." Jory faced her mother across the glass-topped table on their patio next to the pool. Her breakfast lay cold and untouched, and butter melted in a crystal dish in the rapidly warming Florida morning.

"Well, that's the silliest thing I've ever heard." Mrs. Delaney tossed her pink linen napkin onto the colored flagstones and pushed her chair backward, making it screech. "You have the opportunity of a lifetime here, and you're throwing it away. Missing your first week of school can't be that big a deal."

"Well, it is to me."

Mrs. Delaney dismissed Jory's words with a flip of her hand. "Your father and I work very hard. This is the first non-working vacation we've planned in years and you don't want to go. That is such an insult."

1

Jory gritted her teeth, biting back the hot words she longed to throw at her elegant blond mother. *Sure, mother,* she thought sarcastically. *Just a cozy little family threesome.* After all the years they'd shuttled off on their real estate deals, leaving Jory under the care of some anonymous housekeeper, now they wanted her to drop everything and take off with them.

"You and Daddy go to Europe, Mother. I'll be perfectly happy to stay here and start school on time. And I'm sure Mrs. Garcia will see to it that I don't starve to death." She emphasized her retort with a toss of auburn curls.

"Well, don't worry. We will." Mrs. Delaney said coolly.

"Fine. Then it's settled."

Silence hung between mother and daughter. The bright blue water of the pool sparkled with the sun. On the far side of the patio a sprinkler spun, tossing water over boxwood and summer flowers. "Jory, your refusal really burns me up. You won't be but a week late in starting school if you come with us. What's a week compared to a monthlong tour of Europe?"

It wasn't over. "I told you," Jory said with an exasperated sigh. "Europe and old castles and quaint cottages aren't my idea of a good time."

"And just what is? Going to public high school with a bunch of riffraff? Honestly, Jory, we'd send you to Tampa's best private school if you'd say the word. And Briarwood School for Young Women doesn't start classes until after Labor Day, so that

would you give you plenty of time to get home before school begins if that's what's stopping you from
coming."

"The word is no, Mother. I *like* Lincoln High."
She stabbed a strawberry from a selection of fresh
fruit arranged on a crystal platter. She didn't want
her mother to dredge up that old argument about
Jory's choice of public over private school.

"Your father and I have worked very hard for all
this." Mrs. Delaney gestured around the patio and
yard, which were carefully secluded behind an
eight-foot security fence. "Money is security,
Jory—not a curse. You certainly have enjoyed its
benefits so far. A new convertible, the latest fash-
ions, a home in the most exclusive area of
Tampa . . ."

Unable to stand her mother's count-your-bless-
ings-speech one more time, Jory jumped up. "I'm
going for a swim." She tugged at the French-cut leg
of the green suit that hugged her body like a latex
glove.

"It's that Austin girl, isn't it?" Her mother's ac-
cusatory tone caused Jory to stop short. "Ever since
she came down with cancer last year, that's all
you've been concerned about."

Jory suddenly became calm and said, "Melissa
Austin is my best friend and has been since the fifth
grade. And yes, I'm concerned about her. Even
though her leukemia is in remission, she isn't
cured. She's the bravest person I've ever known."
Jory wanted to say more. She wanted to remind her
mother that it was Melissa who opened her home to

Jory over the years when her own parents had been
too busy earning money to be available. In some
ways, Jory even thought of Mrs. Austin as her second mother.

Mrs. Delaney arched one perfectly shaped
eyebrow and tapped long manicured red fingernails
against the glass tabletop. "Loyalty is an admirable
quality," she said, "but there's more at stake here
than old friends and returning to high school on
time, isn't there? Face it, Jory, you aren't exactly
headed toward scholastic immortality in your
schoolwork. Have you followed up on any of those
college applications your father wanted you to?"

"No."

"And why not? Most of your friends have already finished their applications and you haven't
even started. Once you graduate next June, just
what do you plan to do with yourself?"

Jory tipped her chin, her green eyes as cool
and hard as her mother's diamond rings. "Maybe I'll
run off with the gardener and get married."

"That's not funny, Jory. You have money—lots
of it in a trust fund. You're seventeen and without
purpose or direction. If you won't choose a college
and you refuse to go to Europe this summer, what
are you going to do? We won't have you sitting
around when there's so much at stake in your future."

Jory was so angry she was shaking, but she
knew that she couldn't speak rationally. Her mother
rose in one fluid motion, her floor-length silk loung-
ing robe billowing around her. "That was an unnec-

essary and tacky comment about marrying the gardener. Use some discretion. Don't make people gossip. We have an image to maintain in Tampa, you know."

"I'll keep your request in mind," Jory said through pressed, white lips. "We don't want people to talk about your shiftless daughter, do we?"

"Don't be so melodramatic. Reputations are important, and what you do now can follow you the rest of your life." Mrs. Delaney glanced at her gold watch. "I have to dress and meet your father at the club. We're entertaining some Arab businessman who's interested in one of the old estates on Bayshore Drive. It'll mean a tidy commission if we close the deal. But don't think this conversation is ended, Jory. I'll let you stay home from Europe this trip, but I expect you to do something about your future. And you'd better get started. Time's running out for you to get into a good college."

Jory swore she saw dollar signs flash in her mother's eyes before she swept through the patio's French doors, leading into the house. Still trembling, Jory plunged into the cool blue water of the pool, balling her body to stay weighted on the concrete bottom.

Beneath the surface, it was quiet, serene. She opened her eyes, allowing the chlorine to sting and take the place of angry tears. Jory wasn't stupid. She knew that her wealth gave her a cushion. She thought again of Melissa, of the horrible cancer that lurked within her body. She thought of the chemo that had stripped her of her hair and her beauty.

Jory also knew her mother was right. Life had
smiled on Jory Delaney. For years, she'd dated and
partied and lived exactly as she pleased. But there
was a void inside her too. In some ways, Melissa
had so much more than she did, in spite of her cancer.

Lungs bursting, Jory struggled to the surface,
gasping for air. She swam to the side and heaved
herself onto the glazed tile border. "Well, Mother,
thanks to me at least she's pretty again," she muttered, remembering with satisfaction the waist-
length wig she'd given Melissa as a gift. She
stretched backward onto the tile, allowing the sun
to warm her golden skin. And as for her mother's
warning about who to date . . .

For Jory, there was only Michael Austin,
Melissa's dark-haired, blue-eyed, brother. He was
twenty-two but seemed older. For as long as Jory
had known the Austins, Michael had been son and
brother and father. When Mr. Austin walked out on
his family, Michael stepped into his role while their
mother worked. Now, between his jobs and classes
at the university and an occasional ride in his hot-
air balloon, Michael seemed to have no other life.
Jory longed to change that. She could be so much to
him if only he'd let her.

"Michael . . ." She whispered his name. He'd
always thought of her as Melissa's spoiled rich
friend, a kid, but she'd prove him wrong. She recalled the one time when he hadn't looked at her
like she was a child, the night last spring when
she'd given Melissa the wig.

"You did this for Melissa?"

"Why not? What are friends for?"

His hand drifted up to stroke her cheek. She gazed at him through thick lashes, her heartbeat fluttering and erratic. "Thank you." He tipped her chin upward and lightly brushed her bangs off her forehead before trailing his fingers over the arch of her cheekbone.

She could have drowned in his eyes. She almost lost emotional control and whispered, "I love you, Michael . . ."

Restless, tingling with the memory, Jory sat up. She would dress and drive over to Melissa's. With school starting in five weeks, they could talk about new wardrobes and what it would be like to be seniors and speculate whether Melissa would be named a National Merit semifinalist. And maybe, if she was very lucky, she'd catch a glimpse of Michael.

"Hey, Jory. How goes it?" Melissa asked as Jory coasted into her friend's driveway.

"Okay. How goes it with you?" Jory climbed over the side of her convertible and walked to the kitchen door, where Melissa waited behind the screen. Melissa was wearing not her waist-length hairpiece but, instead, her own hair, regrown into a sleek black cap.

"They make doors for cars, you know."

"A nuisance." She followed Melissa to the kitchen counter, strewn with the makings for soup and pasta salad. "What are you doing?"

"I thought I'd get a head start on dinner for Mom. She's training a new group of operators at the phone company today and that sort of thing always wears her out."

Jory felt totally comfortable in the familiar Austin house. Her eyes darted from the worn wallpaper to the refrigerator, cluttered with notes and magnets, to the old pine table where she'd shared so many meals with Melissa, Mrs. Austin, and Michael. "Smells yummy," she said, popping a chunk of chicken into her mouth.

"Didn't you have breakfast?"

"Lost my appetite," Jory said, unable to keep the sarcasm out of her voice.

"What happened?"

Jory shrugged, deciding not to mention Europe. "I had a tiny run-in with Mother. She and Dad keep fussing about my going to a private school." Jory silently wished that her mother were more like Melissa's. Mrs. Austin always seemed to have time for her family, in spite of how long and hard she worked. Jory never heard her griping at Melissa about how to live *her* life.

"A private school's name on your diploma would make any college look harder at you," Melissa said, chopping celery.

Jory knew she could never make Melissa understand that an exclusive college campus wouldn't make the idea of four more years of school any more attractive to her. The fact was that while she was innately smart, she loathed disciplined study habits. "I know I've got to decide something soon about my future. But right now, life's too short and the summer's almost gone."

Life's too short. Jory could have bitten her tongue for using that particular phrase. But if her friend noticed, she didn't let on. "You sound like Scarlett O'Hara—'I'll think about it tomorrow.'"

"Oh fiddley-dee," Jory said with a flap of her lashes.

"I saw Brad last week," Melissa said casually.

"Oh, yeah? How's the former captain of our victorious Brain Bowl team doing?"

"Getting ready to head for Yale. And it was an *almost* victorious Brain Bowl team," Melissa corrected, punctuating the air with the tip of her paring knife. "We lost in the state finals, and you know it."

"Wasn't your fault," Jory griped. "The judges were prejudiced toward the Miami team."

"We'll get them next time. Don't forget, I'm going to be captain when Lincoln selects its new team next spring."

Jory grinned. "I thought you had to try out for the panel. Or does rank have privilege because you're one of the few returning players from last year?"

"Lyle Vargas will be back. You remember him?"

Jory puckered her brow. "A science whiz, right? He makes me yawn."

"Really? He speaks highly of you, you know."

"Definitely not my type. Give me dark, handsome, and older anytime."

"What's all the noise out here?" Jory felt her heart pound at the sound of the voice. She turned from the counter to see Michael, rumpled and disheveled and unbearably sexy, standing in the doorway. She smiled at him, but his blue eyes swept past her as if she weren't there.

Chapter Two

"Well, good morning," Melissa said. "What woke you from your long summer's nap?"

"The smell of food and female chatter," Michael rumbled, sticking his head into the open refrigerator.

When he reemerged Jory shifted, trying not to feel hurt. She eyed him covetously. His upper body was bare, tight with tanned muscles from working in the sun. Well-worn jeans hugged his lean hips.

Michael clutched a carton of milk and a small bag of powdered-sugar donuts and wandered to the table. "I worked construction until three yesterday, then took the late shift at the grocery warehouse. I've had four hours of sleep and I chew up little girls who stand around in the kitchen giggling." He opened the carton of milk and downed a swig.

Melissa brandished her paring knife. "Careful, or I'll cut off your ears."

"Watch it, Melissa, he really does look mean," Jory interjected, propping her elbows on the counter. She decided to act flip, desperate to be more to him than a "little girl."

"Can't you two go wander around the mall or something? I need my sleep."

"We'll be out of here as soon as I finish making dinner."

"Do you want to hit the mall?" Jory asked, in no hurry to be away from Michael.

Melissa dropped her gaze. "I can't. I've got a clinic appointment at noon."

Jory saw the muscles work in Michael's jaw while she felt a sinking sensation in the pit of her stomach. Wouldn't her best friend's life ever be normal again? Michael asked, "How are you getting there? Why didn't you work out something with Mom? I can hitch a ride to work if you want to borrow my pickup."

"Mom had a hard day ahead of her and I didn't want to complicate it. It's no big deal, Michael. I go to the clinic twice a month, you know. I'll just take the bus," Melissa said brightly.

"Like hell," Michael snapped. "You got sick last time and almost didn't make it back."

Melissa blushed, obviously embarrassed. "Don't be silly," Jory interrupted hastily. "I've got nothing to do today. I'll take you."

"Oh, Jory, it's a long visit today. They're doing a lumbar puncture, and if I don't lie perfectly still for at least half an hour afterward, I get the world's worst headache. There's nothing for you to do but sit and wait."

"I don't care. I'll read."

"You hate to sit and read."

"Let Jory take you." Michael's command settled the matter instantly. He stretched out in his chair, his long legs crossed at the ankles, and ate donuts. Jory made a stab at starting a conversation, but the good humor of the day had evaporated. Melissa finished quickly in the kitchen, and after she changed Jory drove her to the clinic.

"Keep the top down," Melissa said when Jory started to raise the soft cloth roof of her car.

"But I thought the sun was bad for you."

"Some of my medications react to too much sun, but I doubt I'll turn splotchy in a twenty-minute ride." Melissa's tone was cynical. Jory watched her friend from the corner of her eye as Melissa rested her head on the bright red upholstery and turned her face toward the sunlight. "I'll bet I'm the only girl at Lincoln who returns this year without a tan," she grumbled. "God, I miss going to the beach."

Jory missed going with her. They hadn't been once all summer. "The beach is hot and sticky anyway," Jory said. "Who needs it?"

"*I* need it." Melissa sighed. "It's the ocean I really miss. And the waves."

"And the good-looking guys," Jory joked, in an effort to chase away Melissa's doldrums.

"Aren't I allowed even a small pity party?"

"Absolutely not. You don't see me feeling sorry for myself because your brother acts like I'm part of your household fixtures, do you?" She shook her head as she parked in the clinic lot. "No-o-o. Not Jory Delaney. She just picks her tongue up off the floor every time she's around Michael and keeps on smiling." Jory's speaking about herself in the third person made Melissa chuckle. She couldn't stand seeing Melissa down-and-out. "And incidentally, I'm going to have to get tough with Michael if he's not careful."

"Tough?"

"I'm just going to have to grab him, throw him to the floor, and ravish him. Not that I'm a pushy broad, but I'm tired of waiting for him to ravish me. Lord knows I've been waiting since the sixth grade!"

They entered the clinic, laughing. Melissa signed in and Jory found a seat, moving some toys left by the younger kids. She glanced around the building and shuddered. The place gave her the willies. The smells, the sounds, the sight of so many kids with cancer caused her nerves endings to itch. How did Melissa stand it?

As soon as Melissa was called into the lab area, Jory went outside for fresh air. The July heat was oppressive. In another month school would start. *My senior year,* she thought. She'd be a graduate by the following June. Jory wished she cared.

She would, however, have to think of something to get her mother off her back so that she could enjoy her final year of high school. She glanced toward the beige brick of the hospital and thought about Melissa getting needles poked into her veins and her spine. Jory wished there were something she could do for her friend. *Something* that would make the pain go away and make their senior year memorable.

* * *

"Are you going to be all right?" Jory couldn't conceal her terror. They sat in the blazing sun on the shoulder of the road while Melissa leaned out the open door and vomited. Jory felt helpless, panicked, as she patted Melissa's sweat-drenched back and tried to comfort her friend.

"I'll . . . be . . . fine." Melissa managed between gags.

"This is the pits!" Jory said, raising the convertible's roof. She turned on the air-conditioning full blast to ward off the unbearable heat. Her blouse stuck to her skin. She'd helped Melissa before, but she'd been in the hospital then and there had been nurses close by. Now, Jory knew, there was no one but herself. "I think the cooler air will help," she told Melissa above the roar of the air conditioner fan. *Be all right, Melissa. Please, be all right*, she prayed silently.

Slowly, the heaving subsided and Melissa sagged against the car seat, her face pinched and white. Gently, Jory reached across, closed the car door, and stroked Melissa's clammy forehead. Melissa's eyelids fluttered open. "Sorry about that." Her voice sounded raw and small.

"What's the big deal? You think I've never puked before? Remember that time I had the flu? You were there for me."

"True . . . we've certainly made some lasting memories." Melissa made a stab at humor.

Jory threw the car into drive, checked for oncoming traffic, and lurched the car off the shoulder and onto the road. Gravel spat from under the tires. "Do you feel better?"

Melissa eased upright and nodded. "Yes. Can we stop for a cold drink?"

"There's a mini-mart up ahead. I'll get us a couple of sodas."

After they were back on the road Melissa asked, "Where are we?"

"Just driving around. There's not much traffic out this way, and I thought you might not want to go home right now."

"You're right." Melissa gazed out at her surroundings. "Wait a minute."

"What is it?" Jory grew anxious, afraid that Melissa would be sick again.

"I've been on this road before. There's a place off a dirt road . . . Ric brought me. There!" She pointed. "Turn here."

Jory followed Melissa's directions and maneuvered her car down a twisting dirt lane, draped with drooping tree branches. When she reached a small clearing, she turned off the engine and they sat in the summer quiet. A stream gurgled over rocks nearby. "Not bad," she said.

"Put the top down. I need some fresh air."

Overhead, Spanish moss hung from trees, and they could hear insects chirping. "Ric brought you here?"

"Yes, last spring. It's sort of peaceful, don't you think?"

"Sure do." Jory sipped her soda. "What happened when he brought you?"

Mischief sparkled in Melissa's blue eyes, letting Jory know that she was feeling better. "He asked to make love to me."

Jory's jaw dropped. "Really? What did you say?"

"I told him I'd think about it."

"And?"

"And I thought about it."

Exasperated, Jory squealed, "Don't do this to me, Melissa Austin! What did you *do?*"

"I told him no. It wasn't right for me."

"I don't know what I'd say if someone I really cared about asked me," Jory confessed, thinking of Michael. But then, he'd never ask her.

Melissa swirled the cola can, and Jory listened to the liquid slosh. "So who's asked you who you *didn't* really care about?"

"Are you kidding? I've been slapping guys' hands away since eighth grade. Honestly, a girl gets a reputation for parties and good times, and guys think they can get away with anything."

"Don't tell me you're giving up the party life this school year?"

"Maybe. My mother wants me to 'get serious' about my future."

"What's that mean?"

"To my mother, it's being seen in the right places with the right people."

"A party's a party," Melissa observed. It bothered Jory that everyone, even Melissa, had this image of her as frivolous and shallow. No wonder Michael thought of her as a silly kid.

"Don't bet on it. I like to pick my parties and my friends. Mother thinks that the masses at Lincoln aren't good enough for me. Or rather for our family's position in Tampa."

"Sorry. I didn't mean it like it sounded. You know I think you're terrific." Melissa plucked at lint on the upholstery. "I can't wait for school to start because it puts me that much closer to college. That much closer to law school and a career."

Jory felt pangs of envy. Melissa knew exactly what she wanted—if she could live long enough to achieve it. Jory didn't know anything she wanted— and she'd probably live forever. She sighed, starting the car.

"Michael's taking his balloon up this Saturday at dawn," Melissa said. "Why don't you come with me and help him launch it like we did last summer?" Jory's pulse automatically accelerated and Melissa continued, tenderly, "Who knows? Maybe this time he'll take you up with him."

"Who knows?" Jory echoed, feeling her spirits soar. *To touch the sky with Michael* . . . Well, perhaps she could think of *one* thing she wanted.

Chapter Three

❧

Jory shivered in the damp fog. Members of Michael's hot-air balloon club scrambled to unfurl their nylon ships and launch them before the sun could rise. She nudged Melissa, asking, "Why's Michael late? Will the fog keep him from going up?" Melissa had spent the night at Jory's house, and the two of them had arrived at the field first.

"He said he'd meet us here," Melissa said. "And this fog's nothing. The sun will burn it right off. Besides, it's a low fog and the balloons will be above it in minutes."

Jory listened to the hiss of the propane tanks. She watched a balloon fill and rise like a colorful soap bubble. Once filled with heated air, the balloon strained against ropes as a ground crew held it to the earth and two people climbed into a gondola-shaped basket. Light from the headlamps of parked vans and trucks tunneled through the fog, making the seven-story-tall balloon seem like a ghostly galleon for aliens. "My hands are sweating," she confessed to Melissa in a whisper.

"Why?"

"Because I might get to go up in Michael's balloon with him."

"Now that wasn't a firm promise," Melissa warned. "I said *maybe*."

"'Maybe' was all it took for me to crawl out of bed at four A.M. and drive out here with you, wasn't it?"

"If you do go up, don't get sick like I always do. My stomach is definitely a landlubber."

"That's sailor talk—not ballooning," Jory said with a grin.

"Nausea knows no distinction," Melissa said, holding her palm against her abdomen.

Jory watched as another balloon rose, its pilot adjusting the smaller propane burner aboard his craft. The bright flame shot upward into the neck of the balloon. "You're sure the fabric won't catch on fire?" she asked, feeling apprehensive for the first time.

"Michael says that's what keeps them up in the sky. When a pilot wants his balloon to go higher, he turns up the burner. If he wants to go lower, he lets the air inside the balloon cool naturally, or he releases it through a special valve." Melissa punctuated her explanation with her hands as she talked. "It's tricky though, because it takes time for the balloon to respond. That's why these people have a pilot's license."

Surprised, Jory interrupted. "I didn't know Michael had a license to fly."

"It's the law. And there has to be a chase crew—like us—on the ground," Melissa continued. "In case a pilot gets into trouble with power lines or something."

"The things I do for love . . ." Jory mumbled.

"Here he comes."Melissa pointed to a pickup approaching over the bumpy terrain. The truck skidded to a halt and Michael jumped out and hurried to lower the tailgate.

"Oversleep, Big Brother?" Melissa needled.

"Beth overslept," he corrected, his hands busy hauling out the massive nylon balloon from his truck bed.

"Beth?" Jory asked blankly in unison with Melissa. Then for the first time, she noticed the passenger inside the truck. A girl, blond and still sleepy-eyed, pushed the creaky door open and stepped to the ground. She smiled sheepishly. "Beth Collins. Are you Melissa?"

"Beth's in my macroeconomics class at USF," Michael explained as he worked to lay the balloon out on the ground. "I promised to take her up this morning."

Jory felt twinges of hurt and jealousy. She exchanged glances with Melissa, who stepped toward Michael. "I thought Jory might go up with you."

"Sorry, my basket can only hold two. Here, hold this rope while I drag the propane tank over."

Jory shuffled out of the way, numb and embarrassed. *Stupid*, she told herself. How stupid of her to ever think she had a chance with Michael.

"Can I help?" Beth asked.

"Hold the other rope," Michael directed, aiming the nozzle of the tank at the mouth of the balloon. He turned the valve, the tank hissed, and the yellow-and-red material fluttered and began to fill.

"How'd you get into hot-air ballooning?" Beth asked, her face pretty and attentive in the growing morning light. "I heard balloons like this are expensive."

"I accepted it as a payoff on a bad debt that some guy owed me. I worked a whole summer and the guy's construction company went bankrupt. He gave me the balloon to keep me from blowing his head off." Michael grinned. Jory tried to ignore the way his nearness made her insides turn to jelly. He talked as he worked. "And yes, it is expensive. But it's my only vice."

By now, the balloon had filled, and its bright panels of fabric stretched and reached toward the sky. "It's beautiful," Beth shouted, holding fast to the rope.

"Come on. Get in the basket before we miss what's left of the sunrise."

With envy, Jory watched Beth scramble into the wicker gondola, followed by Michael. "Toss off the ropes," he commanded Melissa and others who'd gathered to help with the launch. Michael released a blast of propane from the tank on board the balloon, and the great airship rose. "Hey," he called down to Melissa. "You two will be my spotters won't you? You and Jory follow in my pickup, and after we land I'll treat everybody to breakfast."

"Jory and I'll follow," Melissa shouted.

The balloon floated up, and as it climbed Jory felt her fantasies floating away with it.

"I'm sorry." Melissa's voice interrupted her thoughts.

Jory turned and forced a smile. "What's the big deal? You told me all along that it was chancy that he'd take me with him."

"I didn't know a thing about this Beth."

"Well, aren't you always saying he needs more of a social life and I need to concentrate on guys my own age?"

"Yes, but . . ."

"Then that's just what I'm going to do." Jory got inside the truck and slammed the door a little too hard. "After all, school starts in a few weeks and there's a whole army of senior guys waiting to be conquered." Suddenly, she half wished she'd gone to Europe with her parents.

"That's the spirit," Melissa said, sliding behind the wheel and starting the engine. "We'll come back for your car later," she added, putting the truck into gear and heading across the field.

Jory gritted her teeth as the vehicle bumped along, forced down a lump of bitter disappointment, and scanned the sky. The fog had evaporated and dawn had broken out in shades of pink and violet. The balloon floated on a hazy draft of warm summer air. She watched it recede, carrying her hopeless love for Michael along with it.

"You're awfully quiet, Jory. And you didn't eat much at breakfast. Was it because of Beth?"

Melissa's question stirred Jory long enough for her to adjust her rearview mirror and realize that she'd passed her exit on the expressway. "It was gruesome," she confessed. "I didn't like sitting there watching Beth make nice-nice with him. But it's more than that."

"Like what?"

Jory shrugged, not sure she was able to verbalize her churning thoughts. "I feel like Rip van Winkle. I woke up one day and discovered that life had passed me by and all I was was older."

"I don't get it."

"You have all these dreams and plans, Melissa. I don't have anything. No goals. No stars to shoot for." She released a short, derisive laugh. "Do you know how awful it makes me feel to admit my mother's right?"

"Geez, Jory, you're seventeen. You've got a million years to make plans."

Jory glanced toward her friend. "That's what *I've* been telling *you* for years. But you kept telling me that life was more than one long party. That I needed to think about my future and college."

Melissa flushed. "I'm not contradicting myself. You do need to think about those things. I guess I hate to see you down, that's all. And all because Michael showed up this morning with a girl."

"It just made me realize how I get focused on one thing and forget about everything else."

"That's not true. You're just loyal."

"I'm a dope," Jory corrected.

"Well when school starts, something or someone will come along and make you happy again."

Jory saw Melissa's hand resting against the seat. It was thin and pale, and it reminded Jory of her best friend's battle against cancer. Again, the unfairness of life smacked her conscience. "So help me dedicate this year to 'finding myself.' Okay?"

Melissa poked Jory's shoulder. "Only if you smile and tell me you haven't given up on Michael."

"But you're *always* after me to give up on Michael."

"I've changed my mind. Beth doesn't deserve him."

Jory slowed the car, taking an exit back toward north Tampa. "And you say I'm fickle," she said. "Now that Brad's graduated and Ric's out of the picture, what's Melissa going to do with her libido?"

"Absolutely nothing," Melissa said. "I told you, it's books and studying for me. College scholarships are my only true loves."

Jory shook her head. "Which brings us full circle. Melissa chasing substance . . . Jory chasing rainbows."

Melissa squeezed Jory's arm. "Chase the rainbows for both of us."

The tone of urgency in her voice gripped Jory's heart. She eyed her friend and bit her lower lip as she noted the look of sadness on Melissa's face. "I will, Melissa," she said, swallowing her fear. "I promise, this will be the very best year any two seniors at Lincoln High ever had. We'll leave 'em laughing. Is it a deal?"

Melissa's eyes softened. "It's a deal."

Jory lowered the car window to allow the humid summer heat inside and combat the sudden chill that had swept through her. "Then how about some lunch?"

"It's ten o'clock. We just had breakfast."

"Correction. You and Michael and Beth just had breakfast. I didn't eat a thing."

Melissa laughed, and Jory drove into a fast-food drive-thru lane laughing too. *The best senior year ever.* She'd made Melissa a promise she would keep. No matter what.

Chapter Four

The start of school wasn't nearly as exciting as Jory had hoped. The halls looked the same, the classes were just as boring, the faces of new freshmen just as bewildered and lost-looking. There were no seniors to look up to, either. "We're it," she'd told Melissa after the first day of classes. "So why don't I feel important?"

It was lonely coming home to an empty house, too. Except for Mrs. Garcia, who cooked and dusted and kept the place immaculate, the house seemed lifeless and hollow. Jory almost began to miss her mother's constant nagging. A few postcards describing the "beauty of the Thames" and the "rugged Irish Moors" were all she had to remind her that she did have parents.

Jory went to Melissa's often. First out of loneliness, then, once her parents returned, out of a need to escape, and by mid-September her days had settled into a monotonous routine. She was at Melissa's the afternoon her friend received a letter notifying her that she'd been named a National Merit semifinalist. "Didn't I say you would be one?" Jory asked with an indulgent expression.

Melissa was stunned and continued to look

dazed, even after Jory had poured her a cola and ushered her to the pine table in the Austin's kitchen. "I . . . I should call Mom at work . . ."

"Catch your breath first." Jory took the letter, read it aloud, and hugged Melissa. "How does it feel to have a dream come true?"

"Anticlimactic. What do I do for an encore?"

"Get one of the scholarships. According to the letter, they notify school principals in February who the finalists are and then award the scholarships in March and April." She glanced up from the letter, her green eyes wide with respect. "It says here that only fifteen thousand high school juniors in the *entire* country get to be semifinalists. I'm impressed, Melissa."

Melissa's face broke into an ear-to-ear grin. "So all I have to do now is score incredibly high on the SATs, get a teacher to write a glowing recommendation on my finalist application, and not let any of my grades fall this school year." She snapped her fingers. "A cinch."

And keep going for chemotherapy and hope that your cancer doesn't go out of remission. Jory heard the unwelcome thought inside her head as loudly as if it had been spoken. "When they go public with the names of the kids who made semifinalists and print your name in the *Tampa Tribune*, you'll become a celebrity," she said.

"Fame, but no fortune," Melissa mused. "Four years of college is expensive." She waved the letter under Jory's nose. "This is my only hope."

Jory felt guilty because she knew she could afford to attend any university or college she wanted, grades permitting. "So where will you apply? Yale?"

Melissa arched her eyebrow. "You mean because Brad's there? If you recall, dear-but-meddling-Jory, Brad Kessing had a girlfriend when he left for college. You *do* remember Sarah of the golden hair and innocent blue eyes, don't you?"

Jory wrinkled her nose. "She was so All-American clean, she squeaked."

Melissa laughed. "And even if Brad and Sarah are no longer an item, I'm certain he's discovered some gorgeous Vassar girl by now."

"Then why don't you apply to Vassar?" Jory asked brightly.

"I'm over Brad. And before you go spending all my scholarship money, how about if I first win the scholarship?"

"You will. But you're right—first things first." Jory scrunched her brow. "To celebrate this first coup—becoming a semifinalist—we need to have a party."

"Jory . . ."

"I'll throw the party. It'll be a bash—a blow-out!" Jory rubbed her hands together, warming to her plan. "A beach party," she said, slapping her hand against the table with a smack.

"Now, you know I can't be out in the sun."

"There's no sun at night," Jory countered. "Water's still there. Sand is still warm. We can build a bonfire, roast hot dogs, marshmallows, maybe a few senior boys . . ."

"The beach at night? Bonfires? It's illegal."

"Don't be a party pooper. My parents own a strip of beach real estate south of Clearwater that they're selling for condos, so it's private property and we can do whatever we like."

"But it's almost October . . ."

"So what?" Jory interrupted. "This is the *perfect* time of year for a beach party. Not too muggy. Not too cold. I'm telling you, it's perfect." She took a long sip of cola, her brain tumbling with ideas. "And besides, it's my party. And I want to give it in your honor."

Melissa squirmed. "It's too much fuss . . ."

"I don't think so. Anyway, how will I maintain my party girl image this year at school if I don't whoop it up once in a while?"

"But I thought you were going to get serious about your life."

"I've got forever to get serious about the rest of my life. I only have one senior year."

Melissa smiled tentatively. "I guess one party can't hurt . . ."

"Good. Then I'll start making the plans. First, I need to pick a date." Jory stood, crossed to the bulletin board on the kitchen wall, and studied the calendar. "When's your next clinic visit?"

"Two weeks."

Jory wanted plenty of time between the visit and the party. She wanted Melissa feeling her best. She poked the calendar, a Saturday in early November. "This looks like a good date to me. Let's designate it 'P-day.' I'll get the word out."

"Do you suppose anyone will come?"

"Get real, Melissa. Who would refuse an invitation to a party thrown by Jory Delaney?"

"Sorry. It was a momentary lapse into insanity," Melissa giggled.

"Then it's settled. I'll throw a party. And believe me, it will be a party to remember. Lincoln will be talking about this party long after we're dead and gone . . ." The innocent words were out of her mouth before she could stop them. *Dead and gone*. What a stupid thing to say.

Melissa offered a wistful smile. "We all die, Jory. You don't have to feel bad about reminding me. Forget it."

Jory nodded, still fighting the prickly sensations that were turning her face red and making her squirm. "Anyway, it'll be a great party. Trust me."

"Of course it will. What else would I expect from my best friend?"

Jory's mother was less enthusiastic about Jory's party. "The beach at night? On our property? Really, Jory, can't you come up with a better idea? Why not the country club?"

Jory wrinkled her nose in disdain. "These are the 'common folks,' Mom. We want to have fun, not be hemmed in at some snobby club."

"But on our property? It's so isolated. There's nothing out there for miles. What about legal liabilities? And what about chaperons?"

Jory clenched her teeth but forced a sweet

smile. "I'll get everyone to sign waivers for your insurance company."

"Don't be a smart-mouth. You know what I
mean."

Mrs. Delaney tapped her heel on the thick
pile carpet of Jory's bedroom. She crossed her arms
over the front of her vivid pink silk shirtwaist dress.
"Perhaps we could make a deal."

Jory sensed disaster but asked, "What sort of
deal?"

"Gasparilla's coming up in February."

Jory grew wary. Gasparilla was a holiday
unique to the Tampa Bay area. In the 1600s, the
pirate José Gaspar sailed into the bay and captured
the city. For some reason, in later years, the socially
prominent of the city had turned the anniversary of
the event into a festival that centered on balls, parties, parades, and even a nationally recognized mar-
athon that garnered some of the world's top
runners. The highlight of the day was when a socially elite crew consisting largely of men with Old
Tampa money and influence sailed into the bay
aboard an authentic pirate ship and "captured the
city."

"So what about it?"

"Your father has been invited to be part of the
crew this year, and there're umpteen parties and
galas for us to attend."

"No reason why you two shouldn't."

"*You're* a part of this family, Jory, and you will
be expected to be a part of the festivities."

Every fiber of Jory's being rebelled. "I can't think of anything I'd rather *not* do."

Her mother's face darkened. "This is quite an honor for our family, Jory, and I won't have you spoiling it by your flip attitude toward polite society."

Jory rolled her eyes in indignation. "Well, excuse me."

"Your attitude doesn't make sense, anyway," Mrs. Delaney continued. "You want to give a party, yet you don't want to attend parties for your father's and my sake. Parties where you'll meet the right people, dress in beautiful clothes, and have a wonderful time. Honestly, I just don't understand you."

I know you don't, Mother, Jory thought. "So our taste in parties is different."

"Don't be cute," Mrs. Delaney said shortly. She studied Jory, who lifted her chin defiantly. "Why don't we compromise?" she asked.

"Meaning?"

"I'll let you throw your party on our beach property if you'll cooperate with me over the next few months about the functions I want you to attend."

A warning bell clanged in Jory's head. "I have to keep my grades up," she hedged.

Her mother chuckled derisively. "I'll be certain not to cut into your study time. And the Gasparilla party circuit won't really begin to heat up until after Christmas."

"How many functions?"

"As many as I think appropriate for you."

Jory's temper flared. "That's not fair! I want to give one party and you're locking me into as many as you want."

"Don't act childish, Jory. I'll only accept the invitations I feel will be useful to us and our position in the community."

Her mother's perspective sounded cold and callous and made Jory cringe inwardly. She wondered whom her mother deemed the "right" people for her to mingle with. She knew it wouldn't be the Austins. The thought of her plans to help make this the best year of Melissa's life cooled Jory's anger. "Do you have escorts to these events picked out for me?"

"Of course not. Not until I know which specific events you'll be attending. Then we'll decide. But I won't stick you with losers, Jory. It'll be only the nicest of young men." .

I'll bet, Jory thought bitterly. An image of Michael floated into her mind. *Definitely not the right type*. But what did it matter? Michael was the impossible dream and always had been. But the hopes and plans Jory had for Melissa were not impossible. Her mother was right—all it took was a little compromise. "And once Gasparilla's over, the deal's off?" she asked.

"Please don't make it sound so cut-and-dried. This is for your own good, even if you can't see it now."

My own good . . . Jory was glad that the custom of arranged marriages was no longer in vogue. "All right, Mother. I'll make the trade, but don't bug me about how much time I spend with my other friends." Mrs. Delaney nodded her agreement. "And notify me in plenty of time when one of these little events is coming up. And if I need a special dress for one, you pick it out." Jory knew she was safe in that area. Her mother did have good taste and an infallible sense of style. "And now, please let me have the rest of my senior year to myself."

Mrs. Delaney smoothed the front of her silk dress, and her wrist full of gold bracelets caught the light. Mollified by Jory's compliance, she asked, "How is Melissa, anyway?"

"She's still got cancer." Jory had to clip the words in order not to spit them out. "She gets chemo every six weeks. She gets stuck with needles and has her bone marrow sucked out, and sometimes she gets so sick, she throws up for hours."

A momentary frown knitted Mrs. Delaney's brow. "I am sorry, Jory, that she's having it so rough. I truly am."

"But she does have a shot at a National Merit Scholarship and she's at the top of our class."

"That's nice." Her mother toyed with her jewelry. "I want you to have a good time during your senior year, Jory. I want you to continue your friendship with Melissa. But I also want you to realize how much you have and how much more you can have if you'll only take it."

Her mother had shrugged off Melissa's Merit semifinalist status as if it were nothing. To Jory, the gulf between herself and her mother had never seemed wider. "I'm going to start planning my beach party right away. It'll cost money."

"Money is no problem."

"Right." Jory turned and crossed to her bedroom window, where she lowered the miniblinds against the glare of the sun. To the Delaneys, money never was.

Chapter Five

⌒

"Hey, Delaney! Great party."

Jory flashed a smile at the anonymous shout coming from a group of classmates, and shielded her eyes from the glare of sunlight off the bright green water of the gulf. The sun hadn't even set and already the party was in full tilt. She hadn't expected such a huge turnout, but news of the party had spread like wildfire and half the senior class had shown up. The weather had cooperated, still balmy with a dry tropical breeze and only a hint of autumn in the November air.

Jory was making her way through the warm sand toward the food tables when Lyle Vargas fell into step beside her. "How you doing, Jory?"

She glanced up at the thick brown hair that always seemed to be hanging over Lyle's forehead. His eyes were almost amber in the waning light. "Fine."

"Haven't seen much of you since school started."

"Been busy." She recalled telling Melissa that she thought he was boring. Actually, she didn't know him at all, except that he had a reputation for being smart and friendly. He played on the varsity basketball team, although he was never a starter, and he'd been on the Brain Bowl team with Melissa the year before. Jory had actually caught him staring at her a few times in the halls at school or at parties.

"It was good news about Melissa's making the National Merit semis, huh?"

Lyle's comment both surprised and touched her. Jory doubted that anyone there even cared that the party was for Melissa's achievements. "I thought so." They passed through a pickup volleyball game and dodged the ball as it smacked the sand in front of them. She stopped at the food tables long enough to grab a cola out of a washtub of ice. "Have you seen Melissa?" She asked a group of girls.

"I saw her heading down the beach with Tony Perez," someone answered.

Jory strained to see down the shoreline in the fading light. She searched vainly for the familiar sight of her friend, but saw only gentle waves lapping the hard white sand.

"Looking for Melissa?"

With a start, Jory realized that Lyle had spoken. She'd almost forgotten that he'd walked with her. Slightly embarrassed, Jory said, "Melissa's seemed out of it ever since I picked her up this afternoon and brought her to the party."

"Yeah. I noticed that too."

"I can't figure out what's got her down."

"She'll probably be back in a few minutes," Lyle offered in a way that made Jory suspect that he understood Jory's concern about her friend's absence better than the average person.

Before she could comment, Pam Hughes interrupted. "Jory, some of the guys are building the bonfire. Where're the hot dogs?"

"I'll get them." Jory turned to Lyle. "Catch you later. Okay?"

His expression fell, but he agreed and wandered off toward the volleyball match. She rummaged through the ice chests shoved beneath the tables. By the time she'd dragged the Styrofoam box to the hollowed-out pit in the sand, the heaped-up firewood was glowing brightly. Several guys were toasting their accomplishment with beer.

Jory frowned, wishing they'd left the beer behind, but knowing it appeared at every party even though no one was of legal age. *Except Michael.* Where had that thought come from? Michael Austin was miles away, and she'd done everything she could to keep from thinking about him for months. Jory sighed and wondered again where Melissa had disappeared to. When she saw Tony Perez dancing with Felicia Garton, she grew concerned. "Tony, have you seen Melissa?"

"Not since we got here."

"I thought you two went for a walk."

"We did, but she told me to go on back, that she'd rather be by herself for a while."

This doesn't sound right, Jory thought. Melissa had been looking forward to the party and had even helped shop for the food. "Which way did she head?"

The dark-haired boy offered an annoyed shrug. "Lighten up, Jory. She'll be back."

"Which way?"

He pointed southward and Jory headed down the beach in an easy jog. Her bare feet slapped the sand, the gentle wash of salt water occasionally brushing over her toes. The sounds of the party receded in the night, and soon all she saw when she looked behind her was the glow of the bonfire. Jory tugged her windbreaker to her, grateful that she'd taken the time to put it on.

The moon came out, only half full, but bright enough to cast an eerie light on the sand. Scattered seashells caught the moonlight and glittered, moist and cool. Jory felt her pulse quicken and her tension evaporate when she saw Melissa sitting alone in the sand, her knees pulled up to her chest, her chin resting on them. Her waist-length hair fluttered in the breeze.

Slowing, pausing for breath, Jory approached her friend. "Is this seat taken?"

Melissa turned slowly and gazed upward. If she was surprised to see Jory, she didn't show it. "No. Sit next to me."

Jory obliged, plopping down with a long exhalation and crossing her legs. Questions crowded her mind. She resisted the urge to be irritated with Melissa for going off without a word. Instead she stared out at the swells and whitecaps, and the lull of the surf calmed her.

Melissa asked, "Why does the ocean always make you feel small and insignificant?"

"Maybe because we are," Jory answered with a shrug. She wasn't in the mood to delve into the mysteries of the universe. "You're missing a good party," she ventured cautiously.

"I'll head back in a few minutes."

They fell silent. Jory sensed that something was wrong, but couldn't bring herself to ask what just yet. "Tony Perez is cute. You took a walk with him?"

"A short walk." There was silence. "Do you ever wonder where God is, Jory?"

"He's in heaven," Jory said matter-of-factly. "What does it matter?"

"I've been thinking about Him lately. I wonder what part He plays in our lives. Do you think He knows us by name? And if He does know each of our names—does that give Him the right to pull us around like we're puppets on strings?"

"I hadn't ever thought about it. It seems to me that He'd be too busy with things like world hunger and world peace and stuff like that to have time for plain old me." Jory picked up a shell and scooped out a hollow in the sand. Loose grains immediately filled the hole and she abandoned the project as hopeless. "Let's see. . . . Does God have a long list with everybody's name on it and check us off one by one?" Jory attempted to lighten Melissa's mood.

"You've got God mixed up with Santa Claus, Jory. No, I think God plans what's going to happen to us even before we're born."

Jory wrinkled her nose in dissatisfaction. "Doesn't sound like we get much of a chance to make decisions about our lives, huh?"

"No. Therefore, I guess it doesn't really matter if we're good or bad, does it? God's already decided what's going to happen to us."

"Now *you're* making Him sound like Santa Claus." Jory poked Melissa's arm playfully. "I don't know why you're thinking such heavy thoughts, but personally, I think everybody gets a choice about how he wants to manage his own life. You either do what's right or you do what's wrong. But I'll bet God knows what choice you're gonna make before you do. That makes sense to me. How about you?"

"But what about the things that just happen to people. Things you don't get a choice about? Does God decide those things for you in advance?"

Like getting cancer, Jory thought, the conversation weighing her down. A fiddler crab ventured out of his burrow and scampered to the waterline. A wave broke offshore, sending a rush of water toward him. He attempted a retreat, but the water caught him, tumbled him wildly, and pulled him out to the sea. "So what did God decide about us?" Jory asked lightly, wanting to chase away the unanswerable and the unfathomable. "You're the National Merit scholar."

Melissa turned her face toward Jory. Her eyes were dark hollows and her skin looked pale, ethereal. "God decided that you're going to be rich and famous."

"No kidding? And I just thought I had to figure

out what to do over the rest of the school year." She smiled nervously and pushed her hair behind her ear. "What did He decide for you?"

A wry smile hovered on Melissa's lips. She leaned sideways and whispered from the corner of her mouth, "That I'll go to my grave a virgin."

Jory laughed at Melissa's sudden turn to humor. "Not if Tony Perez has anything to say about it, you won't."

Melissa sobered and pulled the luxurious length of hair over her shoulder and stroked it. "Last spring, when Ric asked me to go to bed with him, it was the funniest feeling. I mean, I wanted to. I really did. I wanted to know what it felt like. To be with a guy that way." Jory squirmed in the sand. She'd seen enough movies and read enough books to have wondered the same thing. "But in the end, I decided I wanted more than to just satisfy my curiosity. I wanted to be in love."

Bewildered, Jory still couldn't figure out where the conversation was leading. "I guess we all want to be in love before we try making love. I know I do." Sometimes she thought she was in love with Michael, but he'd never even so much as held her. "So maybe when you get to college, you'll fall in love. I have to agree that it's slim pickings in our senior class."

Melissa leaned back on her palms and let her head drop back. In the moonlight Jory could see she looked troubled, and she realized that Melissa still hadn't touched on what was really bothering her. "So we've talked about God and love. What else? We need to get back to the party before they send out a search party."

"Do you think they've even missed us? Do you think anyone even cares?"

"Of course," Jory volunteered. "In fact, Lyle Vargas was asking about you. He seems more sensitive than most of the clods in our crowd."

Melissa smiled. "If he asked about me, it was just an excuse to have a conversation with you."

Jory waved her hand. "Sure. All the guys like Jory but the right one."

"You're a good friend, Jory, and the party's super."

"How would you know? You've missed practically the whole thing."

"I got a call from the clinic today."

Jory started. Her breath caught in her throat, and her heart began to hammer. *A call from the clinic.* "And?"

"And they said that my blood work showed signs of an elevated white count again."

Jory licked her lips nervously but her mouth was dry. "An infection?"

Melissa faced her, and immediately she was hidden in shadows. "It means I'm out of remission. It means my leukemia has come back."

Chapter Six

"There must be some mistake," Jory said. "They must have gotten your lab work mixed up with someone else's. Why, I saw a story on TV just the other day about a woman whose baby got mixed up with another woman's in a hospital nursery. I mean, if they can get a real live baby mixed up, what chance do they have with a blood sample?" Jory knew she was babbling, but she couldn't stop.

"There's no mistake, Jory."

"Well then, they've just misinterpreted the results. Maybe you really do have an infection. Infections can cause white blood counts to go up. I know for a fact . . ."

Melissa laid her hand on Jory's arm. "It's not an infection. It's a relapse."

Jory struggled to her feet, agitated, restless. Her legs had cramped from sitting so long and she stumbled when she tried to pace. "Well, I don't believe it. You've been feeling great for ages. You look terrific too. They've made a mistake." She was angry at the nameless, faceless doctors who were ruining Melissa's life.

Melissa stood and dusted off the seat of her

jeans. "It's all right, Jory. You don't have to be so upset about it."

Jory whirled. "No it isn't all right. Now you've got to start that stinking chemo stuff again. You'll lose your hair. You'll be sick all the time."

"No chemo this time, Jory."

Jory halted her tirade and stared at Melissa's face. She realized that she was seeing Melissa through a mist of tears. "The chemo worked the first time. Why won't they do it again?"

"Because achieving second remissions with chemo is difficult."

"Then what will they do?"

"Dr. Rowan says they want to try a bone marrow transplant."

Jory had heard the term when Melissa had first been diagnosed a year before, but she couldn't remember what the treatment involved. "Tell me about it."

"It's when they take healthy bone marrow from a donor and put it into my cancerous bone marrow. The theory is that the new marrow will begin to grow and take over from the bad marrow, and I'll be cured."

"Why didn't they do that to begin with?"

Jory watched Melissa shove a seashell around with her big toe. "It's risky."

"How risky?"

"Fifty-fifty chance of its working."

The implications of Melissa's words momentarily tied Jory's tongue. Finally she said, "Sounds like they're calling a coin toss. Heads, they win. Tails, you lose."

"That's about the size of it."

"And if they don't do the transplant at all? What are the odds then of your being cured?"

"Twenty percent."

"Stinking odds." She took a long, shuddering breath and faced Melissa fully, crossing her arms as if to ward off the impracticality of the math equation. "So where do you get this marrow?"

"Dr. Rowan says that anyone's best chance comes when the marrow is received from a biologically compatible donor."

"Meaning?"

"Michael."

Jory's heart lurched. *Double jeopardy.* What if they both lost? "Is it dangerous?"

"More for Michael than for me. For him, it means an operation to remove the marrow and a recovery period. There's a risk whenever anyone goes under general anesthesia. It's uncomfortable for the donor because they put a needle into his hipbone to extract the marrow."

Jory trembled and for a second felt queasy. "Then what happens?"

"Once they remove it, they bring the marrow to me in IV bags and let it drip into me, just like the chemo. I'm awake the whole time and won't feel anything. Mom can even sit with me. We can read

or play Monopoly. 'Do not pass Go. Do not collect
$200' . . ." Her attempt at humor didn't help Jory.

"How does Michael feel about donating his
marrow?"

"You know Michael. . . . Bring on the lions."

Jory smiled wistfully, thinking of Michael. "You
said there were risks," she said.

"Well, it's more complicated than just dumping
Michael's marrow into my body. It has to do with
genetic compatibility."

"I thought you said you and Michael were compatible."

"We are. Mostly. But there's always the threat
of rejection. And complications."

"You could reject his marrow?"

"Our cells' genetic codes are different. My
body will attack his marrow the minute it gets inside."

"But I'll bet the doctors have a solution for that
problem too." Jory knew she sounded sarcastic, but
she didn't care.

"How'd you guess?" Melissa stooped and
picked up the shell and ran her fingers over the
smooth, sea-worn surface. "They put me in the hospital and do testing to see if I'm a candidate for the
operation in the first place. If so, they put me into
isolation, in a germ-free room, and start me on massive doses of autoimmune suppressant drugs. They
destroy my body's ability to fight germs, *and* it's
ability to fight off Michael's bone marrow. Then
they do the transplant. Then we have to wait to see
if it takes, and hope there aren't any complications,

like a secondary infection. As I understand it, even a common cold could kill me because I'll have no resistance to fight it."

"And if it does take?"

"I get to go home and go on a different kind of maintenance program. Ultimately, I can be cured."

She cleared her throat. "So how long will all this testing and suppressing and operating take?"

"Six to eight weeks."

"So if you go in now, you could be out by January."

"I haven't said I'd do it."

"What?" Jory leaned forward, as if she hadn't heard correctly. "I don't understand."

Melissa flung the shell far into the sea. It shattered the path the moonlight made on the water. "It's my body and my treatment, and I haven't decided to go ahead with it."

"But . . . you have to!" Jory's eyes grew wide, her palms clammy. "The odds . . ."

"Screw the odds." Melissa's voice had gone calm and steely. "I'm not sure I want to be part of some grand experiment."

"But they must do this operation all the time. I read where they transplant whole hearts and livers. Surely a little bone marrow—"

Melissa interrupted, "But this time it's *me*, Jory. It's not some stranger in the newspaper."

"What are you gonna do?" Jory couldn't keep her voice from wavering as she asked the question.

"I don't know . . . Which brings us back to our original discussion, doesn't it? Maybe God's already decided what I'm going to do. Just like He decided that I was going to have leukemia."

Jory felt the darkness of the night closing in on her. She was afraid. Afraid because she could do no more to change the course of Melissa's life than she could to change the course of the tide. "You will tell me when you decide, won't you? No matter what you decide?"

Melissa hooked her arm through Jory's. "You know I will. You're my best friend."

Jory felt a lump wedged in her throat. "Come back to the party with me and I'll roast you a marshmallow."

"You're on."

They walked together slowly toward the party and the bonfire's flaming fingers. As they walked the water washed their footprints away leaving no trace of their existence on the shell-strewn beach.

"Your father's furious, Jory. How do you think we felt when the police showed up at two A.M. to tell us that they'd busted a bunch of minors for drinking on our beach property?"

Jory faced her mother in the luxurious living room of their house, too weary to do much more than shift from foot to foot. "For the tenth time, Mother, I left at midnight to take Melissa home and I didn't go back to the party. I just came on home."

"But it was *your* responsibility and *your* friends."

"I said I was sorry."

"Sorry doesn't cut it. We allowed you to throw that party, but we'd never condone drinking by minors."

Jory knew she should have hung around and supervised the party, but after hearing Melissa's latest news, neither of them had been in the mood for it. "Look, I'll go back today and make sure the property is cleaned up. I never meant for things to get out of hand."

"It's going to be a long time before we allow you to have another party, Jory, so don't ask." Mrs. Delaney glared and tapped her nails on the marble mantle of the fireplace.

Jory sighed, impatient to escape her mother's foul temper. She didn't know what else to say. She couldn't tell her about Melissa's problems because her friend had asked Jory to keep it secret until she decided what she wanted to do about the transplant. "Don't worry. It'll be a long time before I want to throw another party. Can I go now?"

"Not yet. I want to discuss your schedule for the upcoming holiday season."

"What schedule?"

"The party agenda and where we'll be expected to attend."

Jory groaned. "Do I have to?"

"Yes, you do. There's a dinner dance at the University Club that highly placed educators from all over the state will be attending. I told Beverly Hotchkiss that her son Steve could escort you."

Jory rolled her eyes, remembering Steve as

conceited and mouthy with roaming hands. "Not him," she groaned.

"Beverly's husband chairs the state committee on education and is very influential. For a girl who may need all the influence she can gather simply to get into college, this particular party is a must."

"Kids get into college on their grades and test scores, Mother, not on who they know."

"Don't you bet on it," Mrs. Delaney said. "Besides I think your father has his sights set on your attending the University of Miami, his alma mater."

Jory's mouth dropped open. Her parents had already decided her future! "Since when? Cripes, I haven't even made up my mind about *going* to college yet. That's not fair!"

"We're only trying to do what's best for you, Jory. If you do decide to go to college, at least this way you'll have your foot in the door. Your father's already begun your paperwork."

"How dare you and Daddy do this without my permission!"

"Why can't you see that we are not your enemies, Jory? We only want what's best for you."

Jory felt that the world was crumbling. Melissa was facing a risky cure, Jory was expected to date boys she disliked and go to parties she didn't want to attend, and her parents were negotiating her life like a real estate deal. "You can't *make* me do something I don't want to do," she said stubbornly. "And I still haven't made up my mind about college, much less where I want to go. So stop it!"

"Well make it up," Mrs. Delaney said, her tone angry. "Decide something by January, because that's all the time I'm going to give you to start being sensible about the rest of your life."

Chapter Seven

On Monday, the school was buzzing about Jory's party and the raid by the police. Without meaning to, she'd achieved minor celebrity status at Lincoln. "What did they do to you?" she asked a group of guys at lunch.

Billy Warren lowered his dark glasses and grinned. "Not half of what my dad did to me. I'm on probation until 1999."

"Glad you can make light of it, Warren," another boy said. "I got my car taken away and I'm walking to school for the rest of the semester."

Jory propped her elbows on the table and rested her chin on her palms. "Sorry it got out of hand."

Billy shrugged. "It was still a cool party, Jory, so don't sweat it. The cops have us going before a judge next month and we'll probably all be assigned some sort of community service."

"I guess it could be worse," she told him. "Maybe it won't go on your record." After the guys left, she found herself sitting alone with Lyle Vargas. "You get busted too?"

"No. I left before the action started."

"Smart move."

"Why'd you and Melissa leave so early?"

She was surprised that he'd noticed when she'd taken off. "Melissa was tired and she wanted to leave." It was a half-truth, but the whole truth wasn't any of his business.

"Are you her keeper?"

Jory sat up and stared him straight in the eyes. "What's that crack supposed to mean? No, I'm not her keeper, but she's my friend and she's sick and I brought her to the party. When she wanted to go, I took her home. That's all."

Lyle's expression was serious. "When we were on the Brain Bowl team together, I saw how much determination she had and I admired it. I feel sorry for her too."

"I don't feel sorry for her." Jory bristled. "I respect her. She knows what she wants and she goes after it. *She's* a National Merit semifinalist," she added pointedly.

Lyle grinned sheepishly. "So am I."

He caught Jory completely off guard and she felt herself blush. "Congratulations," she said. Then a thought occurred to her. Lyle was brilliant. Would he be capable of taking away a scholarship from Melissa? "Are you applying for a scholarship?" she asked.

"Yeah. I'd like to go to medical school. How about you?"

Jory suddenly felt nervous. She'd never considered that someone else from Lincoln might get the award. She decided not to say anything to Melissa, since her friend had so much else on her mind, but she *would* keep tabs on Lyle. He wasn't bad-looking, Jory thought. A bit serious, but tall and lean with an angular face and intense amber eyes. He was no Michael, but he was handsome in his own way. "I haven't decided where I'll go," she said. "Maybe the University of Miami."

"It's a good school."

"It's close to the beach."

"I haven't decided where I'll go either. A lot depends on getting a scholarship. Even if I don't get the National Merit, I need to get some sort of scholarship, and since I want to be a doctor, I need to do pretty well wherever I end up going."

She shrugged, feeling irritated. Did everybody in the world know what he wanted from life except her? "It takes years and years to become a doctor," she said. "I couldn't stand all that studying. That's the problem with college—you have to study. Maybe I'll just go for the frat parties."

"You can have anything you go after," Lyle said, his eyes holding hers.

"Thanks for the vote of confidence. I'll keep it in mind." She shifted, feeling self-conscious. "I've got to scoot. If I cut one more English class, I'll flunk this six-week grading period."

Lyle scrambled up when she stood. "Maybe we can talk again, Jory."

"Sure, Lyle. Sometime." Jory hurried off to class without a backward glance.

Jory had a fling with Doug Swanson during football playoffs, which kept the next few weekends tied up, but by Thanksgiving, the infatuation had run its course. On Thanksgiving Day, she ate a quick and boring meal with her parents at a restaurant, then went to Melissa's to watch the college games.

Sunk in a comfy beanbag chair, Jory was profoundly aware of Michael stretched out on the sofa near her. He seemed to have returned to his solitary ways and Jory was secretly glad that his relationship with Beth had broken off.

"Popcorn?" Melissa asked, passing Jory an oversized bowl of buttered white kernels.

"I can't eat one more thing."

"Not even chocolate chip cookies? Mom's got a batch in the oven."

"On Thanksgiving Day?"

"She bakes when she's agitated," Melissa said, but offered no other explanation.

"Chocolate chip cookies? Well . . . maybe I could force one down."

Melissa rose from a matching beanbag. "I thought so. I'll be back in a flash."

Alone in the room with Michael, Jory attempted to concentrate on the game, but it was a losing battle.

"What do you think she'll do?" Michael's abrupt question startled her.

"Do about what?" Jory sat up and faced him.

"About the bone marrow transplant. I know she's told you about it."

Jory nodded. "But she hasn't made up her mind yet."

"You'd tell me if she had, wouldn't you? I know she tells you everything."

"Yes, I would," Jory said.

"I mean, it involves me too. It's my bone marrow."

"I think it's a great thing you'd be doing."

"I'd give her my right arm if I thought it would make her well."

Jory heard his anguish and longed to comfort him. If only she had the nerve to put her arms around him. "I know what you mean," she said.

Michael snapped, "How could you? She's just your friend. She's *my* sister. Why are you so helpful to Melissa, anyway? What's in it for Jory?"

His sudden animosity surprised and stung her. "Nothing's in it for me, Michael. I . . . I just care. That's all."

Michael stood abruptly and paced. "Some people get positive strokes from helping life's underdogs," he said accusingly.

Jory's temper flared. "Is that what you think? That I get some sort of kick out of hanging around Melissa?"

"Look at yourself, Jory. You've got money and a rich family and you can have most anything you want. Why Melissa?"

She wanted to shout, "Because she's like a sister to me. Because your family has been more of a family to me than my own. Because I love you, Michael!" Instead, she said, "Sometimes there's no explaining why you like some people more than others. It's just the way things are."

Michael raked his fingers through his black, disheveled hair and rocked back on his heels. "Forget it, Jory. I didn't mean to take it out on you. It's just that I can't stand this waiting around."

"Melissa needs time to decide, Michael. It's not something she can change her mind about halfway through."

"I know, dammit. It's all or nothing." He rotated his shoulders and pressed his eyes closed. "If she tells you first," he asked hesitantly, "if she says anything to you, let me know. Please."

Jory almost reached out and touched him, but instead tucked her hand into the pocket of her jeans. "Okay. But I don't think she will. I think she'll tell you first. You're her brother."

"I'm going for a drive," Michael said. "Tell Melissa to let Mom know. Tell them not to wait up. I'll be gone for a long time."

Jory watched him leave and felt like crying.

Jory and Melissa went Christmas shopping the next day. "Biggest sale day of the year," Jory said as they plowed through the crowded department store in the mall. "Did you bring your list?"

"Yes, but I can't stop long enough to fish it out or I'll get trampled."

"Where's your sense of adventure? Come on. There's a sale rack of sweaters and jeans."

An hour later, Jory led Melissa to the food area in the center of the mall for a soda. She heaped their packages on a chair and sat next to Melissa.

"What a ratrace. Have we gotten through your list yet?"

"I've got a blouse for Mom and two tapes for Michael." Melissa paused. "Remember last year? I was in the hospital and you had to do my shopping for me."

Jory remembered. Melissa had been receiving chemo and she'd lost her hair and was sick as a dog. Jory had brought everything back to the hospital for Melissa's approval. "I did a good job, didn't I?" Jory asked, above the babble of voices around them.

"Michael still wears that cologne you picked out."

The mention of Michael made Jory recall his hostility toward her and she gave an offhanded shrug. "I had fun choosing it."

"Wonder what we'll be doing this time next year."

"Shopping, of course."

"Will we?" Melissa withdrew her straw from the cola and let a few drops puddle on the table.

A shiver went up Jory's spine. Melissa's mood swings were frustrating. One minute she was involved and happy, the next minute she was distracted and pensive. "We've done this post-Thanksgiving ritual for four years," Jory reminded her.

"Except last year."

"Ah, come on, Scrooge, where's your Christmas spirit? We'll be here shopping again next year. We were born to shop!"

"I might not get home for Thanksgiving, depending on where I go to school."

"That's a possibility," Jory said.

"Then again, if I don't get a scholarship . . ."

They stopped talking because Jory wasn't convinced they were really discussing Christmas shopping. From speakers, Christmas music played. A small ficus tree stood decorated with white lights and the stores were decorated with bright green plastic wreaths with red bows. Suddenly the mall looked too bright. There were too many people and too much noise. "You want to get out of here?" Jory asked.

Melissa plucked at her straw with her thumbnail. "Would you take me someplace special if I asked you?"

"You know I will. Name it."

"Don't freak out on me, all right?"

Puzzled, Jory began to gather up her packages. "Would you like to drive over to the beach? It's chilly, but at least the sun's shining."

"Not the beach." Melissa caught Jory's eyes and held them. "I want you to take me to Memorial Gardens. I want to visit Rachael Dove's grave."

Chapter Eight

The grounds of the cemetery were beautifully kept, and a gravel road wound through sections of headstones and monuments. A cloudless blue sky stretched overhead and the afternoon sun warded off a chill in the air. "Are you sure you want to do this?" Jory asked, driving slowly in the direction of Rachael's gravesite.

Melissa glanced up from the map she'd been given at the entrance. "I'm sure. Take a left."

Jory obeyed, but didn't like the idea one bit. She'd never met the four-year-old Rachael and knew of her only through Melissa. Yet she did remember how devastated Melissa had been when the child had died the previous spring. Rachael had given Melissa a page from her Cinderella coloring book and it was still pinned to her bedroom bulletin board. "This place is creepy, Melissa."

"I don't think so. I think it's sort of restful."

"*Too* restful for me."

"Stop, Jory," Melissa directed. "I think it's over there, by that tree."

Melissa was out of the car before Jory could turn off the engine. By the time she caught up, her friend had found the bronze marker with Rachael's name on it. Jory eyed the embossed rose at the bottom. It seemed indecent to see the dates of Rachael's birth and death—too short a time span lay between the two numbers. Other markers stretched row upon row, in both directions. The plots seemed small and crowded together. "You ready to go yet?" Jory licked her lips nervously.

"Not yet." Melissa stared down for several minutes before she spoke. "I read a poem in English Lit. last month by Gerard Manley Hopkins called 'Spring and Fall.'"

"Could we discuss this someplace else?"

Melissa continued as if she hadn't heard Jory speak. "It was about a little girl named Margaret who's crying becuase the leaves die in autumn. I don't remember it word for word. But the last part goes, 'Now no matter, child, the name: Sorrow's springs are the same. . . . It is the blight man was born for, It is Margaret you mourn for.'"

Jory felt goose bumps on her arms. "We're all born to die. Is that it?"

"So it seems," Melissa said.

"Are you going to have the transplant?" Jory asked quietly.

Melissa's eyes were wide and troubled. "I don't know. I'm scared, Jory. Real scared."

"I'm scared too."

"My doctor said he found lymphoblasts in my blood work last time. The chemo isn't doing the trick for me anymore."

"The transplant *is* a chance," Jory observed.

"They shut me in a sterile room, Jory, with machines and monitors."

"Can you have visitors?"

"Yes, but everyone who comes in has to dress in those sterile green hospital gowns and wear a mask."

"I look good in green," Jory ventured, hoping to break the tension.

Melissa looked around the cemetery. "This might be the only way out of that room for me, Jory."

Jory swallowed hard. "Maybe not. Maybe you'll beat the odds."

"Rachael didn't."

"But you're not Rachael. And she didn't have a bone marrow transplant."

Melissa nodded slowly. "That's true."

"You can lick this thing, Melissa," Jory said. "I know you can. Didn't I predict you'd be a National Merit semifinalist? Didn't you beat the odds on that?"

"Yes."

"Then you can do it again."

Melissa sighed and gazed up at the bright blue sky. "We can go now," she said.

When Jory got home she called Doug, even though they weren't dating anymore. "There's a party over on Davis Island," she told him, forcing a happy voice. "Want to go?" They ended up at a mansion with white pillars and a circular, shrub-lined driveway.

"Who owns this place?" Doug asked in genuine awe.

"Friend of a friend." Jory led him inside, where music screamed and kids danced in tight bunches, shouting above the noise. She wanted to laugh and dance and have a ball. She wanted to forget about the cemetery and Rachael and Margaret, the girl in the poem. Doug nuzzled her neck, but she shied away. "Cool it, Doug."

"Well, excuse me. I thought we were here to have a good time." He tried again to pull her close.

"I plan to have a good time, but hands off. Okay?"

"What's with you, Jory? First you're hot, then you're cold. I don't like being jerked around."

Jory stepped out of Doug's grasp. "Look, this was a bad idea. I don't really feel like partying after all, but there's no reason you shouldn't stay." Before he could do anything, Jory escaped into the crowd and headed for the door.

Once outside she took in big gulps of air and squeezed her eyes shut, because she suddenly felt like crying. "You're being stupid," she told herself aloud. "You like parties. Parties like you." But no matter what she said, she felt only like going home and being by herself.

The atmosphere at the Austin's dinner table was tense. For Jory, it didn't seem much like Christmas Eve. Melissa was withdrawn, Michael was sullen and brooding, and Mrs. Austin was overly chatty, insisting everyone have seconds, when they hadn't even finished their firsts.

"Tell me, Jory, what's your family planning for Christmas Day?"

"My mother's got a party lined up in the late afternoon. I'm not sure where." She did, but hated thinking about spending a tedious afternoon with her parents' friends. Naturally, Mrs. Delaney had seen to it that a "charming young man" would be there for Jory. Their fight over it still rang in her ears, but she was going.

"I was thinking that we might go to a movie," Mrs. Austin said. "You know how long Christmas Day can be. After the gifts are unwrapped and the dinner's eaten, what's left to do?"

Jory envied Mrs. Austin's plans. There were no parties to attend, just family togetherness. She'd have given a million dollars to go to that movie with them.

"Would you like more lasagna, Michael?"

"No, thanks. I'm full."

"But you hardly ate anything and it's your favorite—"

"No, Mom." His abruptness caused a strained silence to fall.

"This isn't fair." Melissa spoke. "Everybody's on edge and it's all my fault."

"That's not so . . ." Mrs. Austin began.

Melissa slammed her fork against her plate. "Yes it is. This is Christmas Eve and it's worse than a funeral around here." She backed away from the table and left the kitchen. Michael exchanged glances with his mother and the two of them hurried after her. Jory had no choice but to follow.

In the living room, Melissa stood fingering the needles on the decorated Christmas tree. Jory hung back, fidgeting, while Mrs. Austin went to her daughter. "What can I do to help, Melissa? Tell me, please."

"Nothing. There's nothing anybody can do." Melissa's voice was soft and Jory had to inch closer in order to hear.

Michael came up on the other side of his sister. "Remember the Christmas we went to Disney World?"

Melissa nodded. "I was ten and you rode Space Mountain with me and didn't even hassle me afterward when I threw up."

"You never did have a strong stomach."

Melissa turned her head and smiled wistfully at him. "You told me that I should go ride it with you one more time. That it was like falling off a horse. You had to get right back on and ride again." With sudden swiftness, Melissa spun and said to her mother, "What should I do, Mom? Please tell me what to do."

Mrs. Austin held her daughter and stroked her hair, which by now was almost past her jawline. "You're my baby, Melissa. It's killing me watching you have to make this decision. But I believe it's your decision to make. I want you to grow old, Melissa. I can't stand the thought of your not living a full life."

Melissa buried her face in her mother's shoulder. "Old and wrinkled sounds wonderful to me." She pulled away. "But we all know there are no guarantees if I have the transplant."

Michael cleared his throat and shoved his hands in his pockets. "Are you saying my bone marrow might not come through? I only manufacture primo stuff, you know."

"Does it come with a money-back warranty?" Melissa asked.

"A 'life-back' warranty," he said, his voice barely above a whisper.

Jory inched toward the door. She felt intrusive, like an eavesdropper. How differently Mrs. Austin treated Melissa from the way her mother treated her. Jory wasn't even allowed to make a simple decision about college, and Melissa was being entrusted to make one about her very life.

"What do you think, Jory?"

Melissa's question so surprised her, that Jory felt her cheeks flush, and her feet seemed rooted to the carpet. Her gaze flitted from face to face. "I . . . I . . . don't know . . ."

"You once told me that we all get choices about how we want to manage our lives," Melissa said.

Jory recalled their conversation on the beach. "I still think that's true." She chose her words carefully because Michael and Mrs. Austin were watching, and her heart was pounding and her palms were sweating. "It's sort of like if we don't choose whenever we get the chance, then we have nothing to complain about if things don't work out the way we want them to in our hearts."

Melissa shrugged and dropped her eyes, miserably. "I don't feel like I have much of a choice."

Mrs. Austin put her arm around Melissa's shoulders. "I'll support any choice you make."

Jory studied the faces of the three Austins. Same dark hair, blue eyes, and pointed chin. The Christmas tree lights twinkled behind them, making patterns on their skin. She ached inside, longing to be a part of them.

"I'll do it," Melissa said softly. "I'll call Dr. Rowan right after New Year's and tell him I'll do the transplant."

Mrs. Austin sagged with relief and Michael broke out in a grin. "That's a girl," he said. "We'll beat this thing, Melissa. With my marrow and your guts, we're going to win."

Jory walked toward the door, pausing long enough to take one last look at the three of them. Though her heart begged to stay with Melissa and Michael and their mother, her common sense told her she was intruding.

Outside stars burned in the sky, and Christmas lights shone from neighborhood houses. She shivered. In one week her best friend would begin a journey into the unknown. Jory swore to God that, one way or another, she would not go alone.

Chapter Nine

❧

"Jory, wait up. I want to talk to you."

Jory turned in the school's crowded hallway and spotted Lyle. "What do you want?" She wasn't in a good mood and knew it.

"I heard Melissa is back in the hospital. Is that true?"

"Doesn't anyone have anything else to gossip about around this place?"

"It's not gossip, Jory. I'm interested."

The sincere expression on his face made her regret her sharp remark. "Everybody's asking, Lyle. I'll bet I've been asked about Melissa a million times today." Jory stopped beside a bank of lockers. "She went back right after New Year's. They've been putting her through a bunch of tests and plan to do a bone marrow transplant real soon."

"Are they using her brother's marrow?"

"Yes. But first she has to undergo autoimmune suppression. It'll take a couple of weeks before her body's ready for the marrow. Rejection," Jory said. "That's the problem."

"I'm sorry, Jory. I know she's your friend."

Jory felt tears well in her eyes and she shifted uneasily. "I've got to go."

Lyle's hand shot out and touched her shoulder. "Would you like to go someplace after school and talk about it?"

She shrugged nonchalantly. "What's to talk about? There's nothing to do but wait and hope that the transplant takes."

"You act like it doesn't bother you."

"It bothers me plenty, but I don't go around discussing it with every Tom, Dick, and Harry."

"Or Lyle," he said with a quick smile.

For some reason, his concern made her want to bolt. "The bell's about to ring. Can't be late," she said with forced enthusiasm.

"I wouldn't want to make you late," Lyle said, shifting forward.

She stepped back, feeling a tightness in her chest, and all she wanted to do was get away.

"If you change your mind . . ." Lyle said.

"I won't, but thanks for the offer. I'll be just fine." She forced a carefree smile. "There's plenty to do without sitting around and speculating about Melissa. I'll tell her that you were asking about her, though." Jory stepped into the flow of students, scurrying to class before the morning bell sounded. She smiled and waved to everybody all the way to her classroom.

"Welcome to my clean, germ-free universe. They scrubbed it down with disinfectants and sprayed it with ultraviolet light. What do you think?"

Jory entered Melissa's room through a cubicle,

pushing up the sleeves of an oversized sterile gown. She felt freakish in mask and bonnet. "To quote Kermit the Frog, 'It isn't easy being green,'" she said.

Melissa giggled. "You can always make me laugh, Jory." She was sitting up in bed, but at least she looked normal, not bloated and splotchy as she had the first time she'd been in the hospital undergoing chemo.

Machines and apparatus lined the walls. "Have they started the drugs?" Jory asked, adjusting her mask, thinking her voice sounded muffled.

"Tomorrow." Wires attached to Melissa's chest led to a monitor that registered a regular green blip on a small screen.

"What's that?"

"My heart monitor. There's been some damage to my heart from the chemo. They have to keep close tabs on it."

"And that?" She pointed to a small cart with paddles.

"A crash cart. In case my heart goes haywire." Jory grimaced. Melissa seemed resigned now and, in some ways, eager to get on with the program. She added, "You just missed Michael."

Jory wasn't too sorry she'd missed him. Ever since the day he'd questioned her motives for being involved with his sister, she'd felt awkward around him. Still, it hadn't lessened how deeply she cared for him. "Is he nervous about going under the knife?"

"Worse than a two-year-old. Why are men such babies about needles and hospitals?"

"I wouldn't like it much myself," Jory confessed. "When does he check in?"

"Day before surgery. They prep him early the next morning, extract the marrow, and rush it over here to me. He'll go into the recovery room and then back to his hospital room. They say he'll be up and around in no time. Two or three days, max."

"They probably need the bed for sick people," Jory said with a nervous laugh, because her stomach felt funny whenever she thought about them sticking syringes into Michael's bones.

"I got my SAT scores," Melissa said, changing the subject. "And Mrs. Watson is writing my recommendation for the Merit Scholarship."

The information brought a sense of normalcy into Jory's thoughts. "Mother's making me apply to the University of Miami," she told Melissa.

"Is that what you want?"

"No, but I don't know what I want, so I'm just biding my time and trying to go along with her. Mother can be very determined." She didn't want to burden Melissa with how much the two of them yelled at one another. Jory went on quickly. "A lot of the kids at school are asking about you. Lyle too."

"He likes you, Jory."

Jory looked skeptical. "I don't like him. I mean, not in that way."

"Is it still my brother?"

Jory dropped her gaze and picked at the front of her gown with gloved fingers. "He's angry with me, Melissa. I don't know why either."

"He's angry at everybody. He's been going to a gym and taking it out on a punching bag."

"Doesn't he ever go up in his balloon anymore?"

Melissa shook her head. "No. I wish he would, but it's like he's doing penance. He won't let himself have a good time while I'm sick."

Jory wrinkled her nose. "That's weird. How's that going to help you?"

"Go figure." They fell silent and Jory heard the hiss of some machine and the steady electronic beep of Melissa's heart monitor. Melissa reached into the drawer of her bedside table and withdrew a small book. "Will you do me a favor, Jory?"

"Anything."

"This is my journal." She handed over a blue leather-bound volume. "I've been writing in it ever since last year. I want to keep writing in it. You know, keep a record of these days."

Jory nodded. "Sounds like a good idea. What can I do?"

"If things don't go well . . . if I get real sick or something, keep it up for me."

The request seemed overwhelming and Jory handed the book back to Melissa. "Cripes, I'm no good at that sort of thing. I can't even keep my class notes in order. Maybe your mother could do it for you."

"No. I want you to do it."

"But what would I write?"

"The facts. Your feelings. Whatever you think of."

"Melissa, I can't."

Melissa jutted her lower jaw. "It's important to me, Jory."

"But why?"

Melissa hugged the book to her. "Maybe because it's the only thing I have to leave behind. Rachael Dove left a whole pile of coloring book pages and I know they must mean everything to her family."

"You sound like you don't think this transplant is going to work." The notion irritated Jory. "You've got to think positive, Melissa."

"I believe in the transplant. But I still want you to do this for me."

"But *you'll* do it for now?" Jory licked her lips and felt sweat trickle down between her shoulder blades. The mask was making it difficult to breathe.

"As long as I can."

"And after you're home, you'll keep writing in it?"

Melissa stared at Jory for a long moment. "Sure. Once I'm home."

Jory felt relieved. Once Melissa went home, everything would return to normal. "It's a deal," she said. Melissa slid the book back inside the drawer and Jory added, "I'd better be going." She didn't have anyplace to go, but the walls were closing in on her.

"See you tomorrow?" Melissa sounded hopeful. "Lying around with nothing to do but read and watch TV gets boring."

"Sure." Jory didn't meet her eyes. She left the

hospital, shaking off the scent of medicine and disinfectants. She decided not to go home. Instead she headed for isolated back roads north of the university. She floored the accelerator, and the engine responded. She blasted down the highway, honking her horn, passing startled motorists she thought were going too slowly.

The radio blared, and the noise and the speed soothed her and made her feel in control. Somewhere north of Tarpon Springs a cop caught up with her. He gave her a lecture and a speeding ticket. She shoved it into her glove compartment, knowing that when her mother found out, she'd be in big trouble. "So what?" she said to her reflection in the rearview mirror. "Who cares?" Life was too short to waste. Let her mother say whatever she wanted. Jory really didn't care.

Lyle called her that night and asked her to a movie. She wasn't really interested in going, but her parents were out of town on business and she was lonely. He picked her up and took her to a film she forgot once the credits rolled. "Ice cream?" Lyle asked afterward.

"It's winter."

"Hot fudge takes care of cold nights."

The ice cream parlor was filled with kids from school, and Jory flitted from table to table, laughing and making small talk while Lyle bought hot fudge sundaes.

They sat across from each other in a booth. Jory felt herself relaxing, buoyed by the animated conversation with friends. She swirled her spoon through a blob of warm chocolate. "Tastes good."

"Did you go by the hospital today?"

She felt herself tensing up again. She didn't want to talk about Melissa. "Why are you always asking me about Melissa? Do you like her or something?"

"I know what her family's going through, that's all." His words reminded her that she wasn't a member of the Austin family. "My mother had cancer, Jory. She went through chemo and radiation three years ago. She's been in remission ever since."

His admission startled her and she grew self-conscious, as if Lyle could read her heart and see the hurt. She didn't want anybody to know how much it hurt.

"Cancer's rough on the whole family. It's expensive too," he said.

She wanted to say it was rough on best friends also. "I-I'm glad your mother's all right now, but I don't know what you want me to say about Melissa." She forced a smile and felt foolish.

His amber eyes seemed to be looking inside her. "When my Mom was diagnosed, our whole family went through a special therapy program to help us deal with our feelings about it."

"Sounds good."

"It *was* good, Jory. I learned a lot about myself and how to accept reality. You need to deal with it too."

She shifted her eyes away. "I've dealt with it. I

want Melissa to go on with her life, and I'll help however I can because she's my friend. There's nothing more to say."

"You can talk about how mad you are about it. And how unfair it all is."

* He was trying to peel off her shield and she resisted. "Nobody knows how I feel. And I don't want to talk about it with anybody."

"Why? I've been there. I almost lost my mother, Jory."

She shoved the half-eaten sundae aside and stopped smiling. "When you called and invited me to the movie, I said I'd go because I wanted to forget about Melissa and all that's going on. I'm sorry I came."

Lyle stretched out in the booth, jammed his hands into the pockets of his jacket, and studied her. "All right, we won't talk about it. So what did you think of the movie?"

Her mind drew a blank about the plot. "It was all right."

"Okay," Lyle said, "let's try another topic. Any word about your getting into the U of M?"

When had she told him about *that*? "No word yet."

"How about nuclear disarmament, Jory? Want to try that one?"

Anger welled inside her so hot, she felt like throwing something at him. "What's with you? Get off my case!"

Lyle stood abruptly. "Come on, I'll take you home. You're right, this date was a bad idea because you really didn't want to be with me, you just wanted something to keep you busy."

The accusation made her squirm because he was right. "Sorry I'm such a boring date," she flung at him and stalked out to the car.

In the car, Lyle said, "I'm sorry, Jory. I really did want to be with you tonight. I'd like to see you again."

She shook her head, feeling a wave of depression swooping down on her. "It's no good, Lyle. I don't know what I want right now. My head's all mixed up about everything."

In her driveway, he reached out and placed his hand on her shoulder. "If you change your mind, if you need anything . . ."

"I won't," she said, sliding out of the car. She scurried up the walk, not wanting him to follow. She didn't look back, but the warmth where Lyle's hand had rested lingered.

Chapter Ten

On the day of Michael's surgery and Melissa's transplant, Jory skipped school. She sat in the surgical waiting room with Mrs. Austin, who kept an anxious eye on the clock. A woman from her office and a minister had come to wait with her, but it was Jory Melissa's mother talked to most often.

"Why do you suppose it's taking so long?" Jory asked, when they'd been there an hour.

"It could take up to six hours," Mrs. Austin said. "They remove the marrow a pint at a time and spin out the platelets because that's what Melissa needs."

Jory's jaw dropped. "Then it'll be after lunch before we hear anything?"

"I'm afraid so. You don't have to wait the whole time, Jory. You can leave and come back," Mrs. Austin said kindly.

"Oh no. I don't mind. Really. I'd go crazy sitting around at school. Besides, everybody at Lincoln is looking to me for a firsthand report." Jory smiled brightly, knowing that she was as nervous as Mrs. Austin, but able to hide it better. The thought of Michael in an operating room and of some doctor sucking out his bone marrow made her knees go weak. "How's Melissa this morning?"

"She's ready for the transplant. I saw her at six and she was awake and waiting. I'll be checking on her off and on."

"Is she all suppressed?" The question sounded stupid, but Jory didn't know how else to phrase it.

"They've virtually wiped out her immune system. I'm so edgy around her, I don't know what to do. What if some germ slips in despite all the precautions? What if she gets a cold? Or pneumonia? It can happen."

"By then, Michael's bone marrow will be working hard and fighting off the germs," Jory said cheerfully.

Mrs. Austin left to check on Melissa and another hour passed. She returned, saying Melissa was fine but bored. "Did I ever say thank you for all the nice things you've done for Melissa?" She asked.

"I've wanted to do things for her. She's my best friend." Mrs. Austin's gratitude made Jory squirm. "I've wanted to do it for you too, Mrs. Austin. It's meant a lot to me the way you've looked out for me over the years."

"Oh, Jory, I've never minded. I knew right from the start that you and Melissa had a special kind of friendship. Besides, I've always considered you one of my own."

"A-And I've felt like yours too," Jory said, honestly, because she'd never felt closer to Melissa's mother. "You've always made me feel special."

Mrs. Austin smiled. Jory saw deep, tired lines around her eyes and mouth and realized that the pressure must be incredible for her. Both her kids were in the hands of doctors at the same time. "Would you like some coffee? I'll run to the coffee shop for you."

"No. I don't think I could keep it down."

"I know what you mean."

As the noon hour approached, Jory began to think the day would drag on forever. She groped for a topic of conversation to keep her mind busy. "I think you've been so strong through all this, Mrs. Austin."

"Strong? Hardly. I've lost it so many times, I can't count them."

Jory was surprised. "I would have never guessed."

"What choice did I have? I couldn't let Melissa see me scared. And Michael's so angry about the whole thing that I was afraid he'd snap if I didn't keep it together."

"Melissa says that too."

"Why not? He's been a father and brother to her all these years. Now, all this is doubly hard for him."

"Sometimes I get so angry, I want to punch someone out," Jory confessed. "But who? Who's responsible for this?" She eyed the minister and lowered her voice. "I always thought God loved us and wouldn't let anything bad happen to us. Why did He let this happen to Melissa?"

Mrs. Austin studied Jory. "Don't think I haven't asked the same thing. Why *my* daughter?"

"Did you get an answer?" Jory asked, hopefully,

Mrs. Austin stared off into the air. "I've looked for answers everywhere, Jory, and the search isn't over. Rain falls on the just and the unjust, Jory. God is God, we are His creation, and we have no right to question His authority."

Jory bristled because she hated arbitrary authority, hated being pushed around by someone bigger and more powerful than she. Like her own mother. "That's not fair," she muttered.

"God isn't fair. And I don't mean that in a bad way. Fairness implies that we have rights. Do we have the right to tell Him how to run the universe?"

Jory furrowed her brow. "Maybe not."

"Then why should we have the right to tell Him how to order our lives?"

"But what did Melissa ever do to deserve cancer?"

"Nothing. I suppose that's where the great mystery lies. People don't get what they deserve—good or bad. Life isn't always so logical."

"The rain falling on the just and unjust?" Jory asked.

"Yes, but regardless, we still have one very real thing going for us. We have hope, and I think that's what separates us from the rest of creation. We get to hold on to hope . . . hope for things not seen."

Jory was moved by Mrs. Austin's faith and she wondered if she'd ever feel that way herself. Would she ever come to accept gracefully what she couldn't understand or change? "All I want is for Melissa to get well and everything to be normal again. When I think of all the plans she's made—of her dream to be a lawyer and all . . ."

"Melissa is single-minded. And she's like a bulldog. Once she latches onto something, she doesn't let go."

"That's good, don't you think? I mean, if she's a fighter, it's got to count in her favor."

"That's what her doctors tell me." Mrs. Austin patted Jory's hand absently. "I'm glad you stopped wearing that blue fingernail polish. You have pretty hands."

Jory glanced at her unpolished nails, unable to remember the last time she had done them. "Just one of my phases." How silly that period of Jory's life seemed to her now—the strange hairdos and outlandish clothes. She'd done it merely to get a rise out of her mother. It had worked, yet nothing was different between them. They were still butting heads and arguing over everything. Jory sighed, shaking off the direction of her thoughts. There were too many other, more important things to think about now. Like Melissa, and Michael, in surgery.

The door swung open and Michael's surgeon

entered. Jory crowded near Mrs. Austin, determined to hear his report.

"Michael did fine. He's young and strong and came through like a champ. He's in recovery now, but we'll send him to his room once his vital signs stabilize." The physician took Mrs. Austin's hand "We removed six pints of marrow through two holes in his backside. He'll be sore for a few days, but that's the worst of it for your son."

"And Melissa?"

"We've sent the bags to isolation."

Jory noticed that Mrs. Austin's hands were shaking. "I'd better go on up . . ."

The doctor started to leave, then turned. "It's a precious gift your son has given his sister."

"I know," Mrs. Austin said. "He's given her a second chance at life." The doctor left, and the minister and Mrs. Austin's friend gathered closer. Mrs. Austin told them, "Thank you for coming. Both of you." Then confusion clouded her face.

Jory asked, "What's wrong?"

"Suddenly, I don't know what to do. . . . I mean, Michael's in recovery and Melissa's waiting for me. I want to be with both of them. But there's only one of me."

Jory said, "Michael would want you to go to Melissa."

"Yes. Of course, you're right." Mrs. Austin headed for the elevators for the ride up to the isolation ward.

"Tell her I'll buy her a five-pound box of chocolates," Jory called as the elevator doors closed behind Mrs. Austin. Alone in the roomful of strangers, Jory picked up her purse and started for the elevators too. She punched the button for the ground floor when an idea struck. She could wait in Michael's room until he came down from recovery. Then she could see with her own eyes that he was fine.

Jory held her breath as she slipped inside the private room where Michael was already asleep. Jory stepped close to the bed. The hollows below his eyes appeared darkened and bruised, showing how stressful the surgery had been on his body. She listened to the soft sounds of his breathing. She fussed over the sheet, pulling it closer to his neck, and let her hand linger on his shoulder, tentatively, careful not to wake him.

His black hair fell over his forehead and she gently brushed it aside, allowing herself the luxury of touching him. He didn't stir and Jory grew bolder. She stroked his cheek and felt the rough stubble of his beard. She placed her palm along the length of his face and her heart pounded. How long had she dreamed of touching him like this? "Michael . . ." she whispered.

She remembered all the times he'd teased her and ignored her. She was a kid—Melissa's "little rich friend." It didn't matter. Nothing mattered but the love she felt that made her pulse throb and her heart ache.

"Prince Charming's asleep," she murmured, amused by this ironic turn of events. Jory glanced around the room. They were alone. Closed blinds held off twilight, and in the soft arms of shadow Jory leaned forward. With measured purpose, she traced the outline of his lips with her fingertips, then bent and kissed him longingly on the mouth.

Only immediate family members were allowed to see Melissa for the first week. It infuriated Jory to have to get information from the nurses' station or from Mrs. Austin. "Nothing yet," Melissa's mother told her over the phone when Jory called. "So far nothing's happening with the transplant."

Jory worked up her courage to visit Michael, who was recovering but still in a lot of discomfort. "I feel sixty years old," he grumbled. "I can't even stand up straight."

A nurse clucked over him and assured him the pain would pass. "Here. I brought you a present," Jory said, placing a book about ballooning on his bed after the nurse had left.

He picked it up and flipped through beautiful color photographs of earth taken from hot-air balloons. "Geez, Jory, this book must have cost fifty bucks."

His comment stung, but she ignored it. "It was on the discount table and I thought it would get you close to the sky until you felt like doing the real thing again."

He closed the book. "Thanks, but I don't know if I'll ever go back up. It all seems so pointless now."

She wanted to protest, but what right did she

have to encourage him? "Will you be out soon?" She asked.

"Not soon enough. Maybe tomorrow. I went up to see Melissa, though."

"How's she doing?"

"Not much change. It makes me mad. I thought for sure they'd be able to tell something by now."

"It's not been that long . . ." Jory said, letting the sentence trail when Michael glared at her. She hated it whenever she said silly, innocuous things. And she hated it when Michael looked at her like she was a child. She remembered kissing him and her cheeks flushed.

"I hate this place," Michael said through clenched teeth. "I feel like I'm in a cage."

Jory shifted from foot to foot, understanding exactly what he meant. She opened her mouth to speak, but Mrs. Austin came through the door. She looked pale, like she hadn't slept in a week.

Michael sat straight up in his bed and blanched. "Man, that hurt," he mumbled. He reached out to his mother. "What's wrong, Mom?"

Jory stepped aside, trying to make herself unobtrusive. Cold fear knotted her stomach, because she could tell something was wrong. Very wrong. "Melissa has a fever," Mrs. Austin said, taking Michael's hand. "She's sick, Michael. And it's either an infection or the first signs of rejection."

Chapter Eleven

"Melissa needs blood. Will you help me?" Jory spoke to Lyle, who was sitting at a table in the school library with books and papers spread out in front of him.

"I'll give blood," he said.

Jory fidgeted. "She needs lots of blood. I've asked permission from the principal to organize a blood drive for her. But I need help." Lyle was watching her so intently that she almost turned and ran off. "You said to come to you if I ever needed anything," she said, almost accusingly. "Will you help, or not?"

Under the table he shoved back the chair across from him with his foot. "Sit down." Jory sat on the edge, tapping her foot impatiently. "What's happened?" Lyle asked.

"I'm not sure. Mrs. Austin just said that she needs blood. She's getting it through the blood bank, but they need to replenish what Melissa uses. I figured it was something I could help with. There're plenty of kids at school who would like to do something. Everyone asks about Melissa. I know people care."

Lyle hunched forward, wrinkling his brow and

nodding thoughtfully. "We could do more than organize a blood drive."

"What do you mean?"

"I told you that my mom had cancer. It almost wiped us out financially. I'll bet the Austins are hurting for money by now too. Can you guess how much all this must be costing them?"

Jory shook her head, but recalled that Melissa often worried about money and what would happen when her mom's insurance ran out. What Lyle was saying made sense. She wished she'd thought of it. "What have you got in mind?"

"A carnival here at the school. Something that the whole community can come to. We'll call it Melissa Austin Day—"

"—and we'll charge a donation of blood for admission!" Jory cried, catching on to his idea.

Lyle grinned. "Two bucks if you're squeamish."

"We can have the newspaper write it up. Maybe some radio stations will give us some time on the air to talk about it. There are lots of stores in this area. We could ask them for merchandise and raffle it off," Jory rambled on, her mind racing with ideas. "We can charge for games of chance. Different clubs here at school can man booths, and all of the proceeds will go toward Melissa's hospital bills. Of course, we'll take straight donations too. We'll have to set up a special account at a bank. . . ."

By now, Jory was bursting. "It's a great idea, Lyle. You and I will be the main committee. Let me get some of the faculty to help too. I know Mrs. Watson will. Melissa's always been her favorite."

Jory scrambled for her notebook and began jotting notes furiously. "If we get right on it, I'll bet we could get it together in two weeks. That's right before Gasparilla. Maybe we could even have a float in the parade . . ."

"Whoa," Lyle cautioned with a laugh. "Boy when you catch on to something, you go all out."

Jory shrugged sheepishly. "Okay. I got carried away. No float. But the carnival is perfect and we can use a pirate theme." She tapped her lips with the end of her pencil. "My parents are wired to everybody in this city. They could help get some nice donations."

"Would they?"

Jory thought back to her party and wondered the same thing. "Sure," she said, with a confidence she didn't feel. "A few things anyway."

Lyle crossed his arms and studied her. "You're really into this idea, aren't you?"

Jory looked straight at him. "Last summer, I promised Melissa that we'd have the best senior year ever. But she got sick again and I feel like I haven't followed through on my promise. This will make up for it."

"You're a great friend, Jory."

She blushed and stood up quickly. "Geez, I've got a million things to do. Let me get started and I'll call you tonight. And thanks, Lyle. I mean it. It's a great plan, and Melissa's family needs it."

Lyle caught her hand and squeezed it. "It's not just for Melissa, Jory. It's for you too."

She felt her breath catch in her throat as she stared into his amber eyes. "Then thanks from both of us," she said and skittered away.

"That'll be one pint of blood. Step into the bloodmobile behind me." Jory flashed a flirtatious smile at the two senior boys waiting to donate blood and get into the carnival.

"I wouldn't do this for just anyone, Delaney," one of them said.

"Don't give me some line about helping Melissa," Jory teased. "You just want the chance to dunk the principal in the water tank at the baseball toss."

The boy grinned. "Hey, now that sounds like fun!"

The boys entered an enormous blue-and-white vehicle, and Jory stacked a pile of dollar bills from the many who'd paid cash to get into the carnival.

"How's it going?" Lyle asked as he came up to her.

"Business couldn't be better. How's it going on your end?"

"The water balloon throw was wet." He shook drops of water from his hair. "And two freshmen won the egg toss."

"When do we raffle off the weekend for two at the beach?"

"After lunch. It was great of your parents to

persuade that resort to make the offer. Are they here?"

Jory dropped her eyes and her smile faded a bit. She thought back to her mother's reluctance to help. "It's not that we don't approve of what you're doing, Jory," Mrs. Delaney had said. "We'd like to help, but . . ."

Jory had gotten angry. "All you have to do is *ask*, Mother."

Jory told Lyle, "They have other plans and won't get by. But who cares? We're doing a booming business."

Lyle closed the cash box and said, "Why don't you take a break and walk around and see the sights with me?"

"But we need someone to man the entrance."

Lyle whistled shrilly and three players Jory recognized from the basketball team jogged over. "Let Larry, Curly, and Moe fill in for a while," he joked. "Can you dudes handle it?"

The guys razzed one another, but sat dutifully at the table. Jory explained the procedure to them and then she and Lyle made their way through the crowds. He took her hand. "Wouldn't want you to get lost."

"I'm a big girl," she said, but she didn't pull away.

Blue sky blended with warm sunshine. The smell of hot buttered popcorn and candied apples hung in the air. Jory inhaled. "We got lucky. February can turn mean, but today's gorgeous."

"I special-ordered it," Lyle said. He stopped in front of a booth. "Want to try your luck knocking down the bottles?"

"You don't think I can do it, do you?"

He shook his head. "It's a game of skill. Girls aren't any good at games of skill."

"Watch this, buster." Jory plopped down a dollar, and the attendant, whom she recognized from her Spanish class, handed her four baseballs. Two minutes later, every stack of bottles lay in a heap.

Lyle raised his hands in surrender. "I take it back. You're terrific."

"And don't you forget it."

He reached out and touched her cheek. "How can I?"

Jory felt flustered, suddenly ill at ease. She glanced away. "What's that long line for over there?"

Lyle followed her pointing finger. "That's the cheerleaders' booth. They're selling kisses for a buck, and making a fortune too."

"Humph," Jory said and flounced over to the booth. She watched a line of guys putting up their money and being kissed. Lyle eased behind her. "They certainly get into their work," Jory said, arching her eyebrow. "Especially Shirley Vaughan. Look at her. If she gets any closer we may have to hire a surgical team to extract her."

Lyle placed his hands on her shoulders and she felt the length of him against her back. It was comforting and she didn't want to move. She leaned into him ever so slightly. His fingers tightened gently.

"Hey, Delaney!" A guy from the line yelled. "I'll give you *two* bucks if you'll kiss me."

She started to refuse, but then an impish grin lit her face. "Make it three."

The kid moaned. "Geez, the things I do for love."

He shouldered his way through the line. As Jory took her place in the booth, she flashed Shirley a smile. The cheerleader tossed her head and stepped aside. Jory kissed the boy and attempted to leave, despite a chorus of cheers for her to stay. "Drop it, fellas," she called. "This was a one time only." Suddenly, Lyle stepped forward and slapped down five dollars.

Startled, she stared and whispered, "Lyle, don't be silly, we're on the committee together."

"Every penny counts." he told her, leaning forward. "Besides, it's not for me. It's for Melissa."

Someone overheard him and began to chant, "Go for it, Lyle!"

Jory's pulse fluttered as Lyle's hands came up and cupped her chin. She caught her breath as his lips came down on hers, very soft and very sweet.

"Are you mad at me?"

Lyle's question and boyish grin almost caused Jory to forget that she was annoyed with him. "That was a dirty trick you played on me this afternoon."

"What trick? I paid five bucks for a kiss." She turned her head, determined to stay miffed, but he dipped into her line of vision. "It's my money and it was worth it."

She warmed her hands on a mug of hot chocolate and watched as several faculty members counted the receipts for the day on the far side of the gym. "Fifty people were watching and it was embarrassing."

"I could arrange a private performance."

Jory fumbled with her cup, confused. Lyle was getting too personal and she didn't want that. This day was for Melissa. The thought of Melissa made her sober. "I called the hospital," she told him, ignoring his offer. "Mrs. Austin says that Melissa's got a rash now and they're working on the assumption that she's rejecting Michael's bone marrow."

Lyle eased beside her in the bleachers. "I'm sorry. But maybe the tide will turn. I've done some reading. Rejection can reverse itself."

Jory shrugged. "Sometimes I feel that we're all on a big merry-go-round and we can't get off."

"Where's Little Miss Optimism?"

"Going down for the count," Jory confessed with a tired sigh.

"We did great today," Lyle said, enthusiastically. "We got gallons of blood and raised a ton of money."

"It *was* a good day, huh?" Jory felt lifted by his good humor and offered a tired smile. "Mrs. Austin was really touched. When I told her what we were planning on doing, I thought she'd break down and cry."

"You'll have to give her a final tally tomorrow. Maybe things will be looking better all the way around by then."

"Maybe so." Jory leaned on the bleacher. "I'm wiped out," she confessed.

"Look, I'll go over and get a ballpark figure from the principal and then take you home. You can call her first thing tomorrow."

Jory watched him cross the gym floor and wondered where he'd gotten his energy. Her thoughts returned to Melissa lying in her hospital room, fighting for her life. She thought of Michael too. Michael, whose bone marrow was to have given his sister a second chance at life. Jory wanted to be with them both.

Lyle returned, his brow knitted thoughtfully. "What's up? Do they need a Brinks truck to haul it away?"

"We got some checks in donations," Lyle said. "From people who didn't come."

"That's good, although this afternoon it seemed like half of Tampa showed up."

Lyle handed her a check. She saw the amount—five thousand dollars—and whistled. Then she saw the signature and gasped. The check was signed by her mother.

Chapter Twelve

"Why did you do it, Mother?" Jory impatiently shifted from foot to foot in her parent's study, a room painted forest green and accented with brass and ferns.

The desk lamp cast shadows on the wall as her mother worked on real estate contracts at her antique desk. "Do what, Jory?"

"I saw the check for Melissa. It shocked me that you would donate so much money to her family. Why didn't you tell me you were going to do that?"

Mrs. Delaney put down her pen and removed her glasses. "I'm not insensitive, Jory. I know how much Melissa means to you and I feel very sorry for her family and what they must be going through."

"It's been going on for a long time. Why are you suddenly so concerned?" Jory knew she was being rude, but she didn't care.

"I've never seen you so involved in anything before," her mother countered. "I was impressed."

"So you were rewarding *me*? A whole bunch of people worked to make this thing happen, you know." Jory wanted to tell her about Lyle, because without him, she would have never pulled it off.

"That's not it. Stop being so defensive. But Jory, you must admit that you put very little effort into things that you do. I simply think you did an excellent job on this carnival for your friend. I heard it talked about on the radio, and the article in the newspaper was good too."

"If you were so impressed, then why didn't you and Daddy stop by?"

"Your father's flown down to the islands on business and I was swamped with desk work and couldn't get away." Mrs. Delaney paused. "How did it go? Did you raise lots of money?"

"Yes. But Melissa's not doing so well. They think she might be rejecting the transplant."

"That's too bad. Really, I'm sorry."

"She knew that was a possibility when she checked in to the hospital. But she had the procedure done anyway. Her mother thought she was mature enough to make the decision herself."

"That is a big decision for such a young girl. . . ." Mrs. Delaney shifted and glanced at her watch. "You should go to bed and get some rest."

Jory felt like screaming. How could her mother bounce so easily between caring and indifference? "I'm tired, but I'm not sleepy," she said, plopping onto a sofa.

"That happens to me sometimes," Mrs. Delaney swiveled in her chair to face Jory. "Maybe you'd like some hot tea?"

"I had hot chocolate already." Jory plucked at a decorator pillow.

"What is it, Jory? What do you want?" Her tone was kind, a bit imploring.

Jory didn't know exactly. Her antagonism waned and she felt restless and unsettled. "I-I want to thank you for the money," she said. "It was a big donation and I know it will help the Austins."

Mrs. Delaney heaved a sigh and pressed her eyelids with her fingers. "I honestly feel sorry for that family. I can't imagine how I'd handle it if it were you."

The remark caught Jory off guard. It had never occurred to her that her mother ever thought about her in any way except as someone to order around. "I don't know how I'd handle it if it were me either."

"I'm glad it isn't you." Her mother's face was bathed in lamplight, and for a moment, Jory thought she saw her eyes glistening.

She recalled all the arguments they'd had over the past months and realized that these were the first gentle words they'd shared in ages. She remembered another scene. One of Mrs. Austin cradling Melissa beside their Christmas tree. She couldn't remember the last time her mother had held her like that. "Well, I guess I'll go to my room." She struggled to her feet, suddenly exhausted.

She got as far as the door before her mother said, "Uh, Jory. There is one thing." Jory tensed. She should have known their moment of peaceful coexistence wouldn't last. "I appreciate the way you've stuck to your bargain about going to all the engagements I've arranged over these past months."

"A deal's a deal."

"I know it hasn't been exactly fun to go out on arranged dates."

"I knew it was important to you and Dad."

"Well, I'm releasing you from that commitment. There's one I set up months ago for the first of March that I'd really appreciate if you'd keep, but after that, you don't ever have to go to something I've arranged if you don't want to."

Jory turned, open-mouthed. "I don't?"

"You don't."

"Gee, Mom—thanks. Really, I mean, thanks a *lot*."

Mrs. Delaney shrugged. "Don't act like you've just been released from prison. I know sometimes it seems that all we ever do is fight. That we always seem to be working at cross purposes. But, Jory, all I've ever wanted for you was the best from life."

Jory's eyes flew up to her mother's. "We've just never been able to agree on what was 'the best.'"

"No, I guess not."

The tick of the antique wall clock was the only sound to break the silence between them. Jory had an overwhelming urge to slip into her mother's arms and rest her head against her. She didn't move. "Well, good night," she finally said, clearing her throat.

"Good night, Jory," Mrs. Delaney said. "Please keep me posted on Melissa's progress."

"I will." Jory slipped into the hall and up the stairs feeling quite alone.

For reasons she didn't understand, Jory spent every night of the next week studying. She was almost finished with an English term paper on Saturday night, when Lyle called. "Want to hit a party with me?" he asked.

She stretched and eyed the paper. "Tell me more."

"Some of the guys are checking out a big bash in the woods north of the university. A couple of them are planning on going to USF next fall, and a few of the fraternities are having a free-for-all out there tonight. I'd like you to come with me."

Jory was tempted. "Gee, Lyle, I don't know . . . I've got this paper due Monday." She toyed with her pen, and inspiration struck. "Tell you what. Give me directions, and I'll meet you out there when I'm finished."

"You're on." She heard the smile in his voice over the phone. She hung up and wondered why she'd agreed. She loved parties, but it was more than that. She'd wanted to be with Lyle. "That's stupid!" she said aloud, flipping through the book to find her place and get back to work. Lyle Vargas was just a nice guy who was sensitive and understanding about her friendship with Melissa. That was all. For Jory there was only Michael. Always and forever. Only Michael.

A few hours later, Jory parked her car and followed the sounds of music to a clearing in the pine trees. The moon was full, its light filtering through the trees, and the night air was cool and crisp. Auxiliary floodlights, fed by a portable generator, had been set up in a haphazard circle. Vehicles were scattered everywhere, and people danced, some on the hoods of the cars.

Her eyes darted about nervously. She didn't recognize a soul of the college crowd, most of whom were drinking. She had almost talked herself into leaving when Lyle called to her. "It's a little crazy around here, but I'm glad you came," he said.

She flashed him a perky smile. "You know me, just a party girl at heart."

Lyle eyed her, shaking his head. "Why do you keep pushing that image of yourself? You're far more than that, Jory."

"Never!"

"Yeah you are. I know you want everybody to think you're only running around looking for a good time, but you're not that way at all. Look at how much you do for Melissa."

"Cripes, Lyle, you make me sound like Mother Teresa." Jory felt silly listening to him sing her praises. Although she'd once wanted to change her image from a good-time girl, she didn't want anything to interfere with her promises to Melissa right now. She slid out of his grasp. "So where's the gang?"

"Skip and Tommy are putting the moves on some girls. I've just been hanging back waiting for you."

"So here I am," she said brightly. "Why don't we dance?"

"Can we wait for something slow?"

She watched several couples whirl in frenzied motion. "Doesn't look like there will be anything slow coming on the pipes for a long time. Come on, don't be a party pooper. I want to have *fun!*"

Lyle danced with her, and in minutes Jory was caught up in music and motion. She welcomed the opportunity to clear her mind, to relax and let loose. When something slow did blare over the speakers, she sighed. Slow meant thinking and talking, and right now Jory didn't want to do either. Lyle pulled her to him, locking his hands behind the small of her back. "This is much better," he said, catching his breath and resting his chin on top of her head.

The air was cool on her warm skin and Lyle was near and his arms were holding her and he smelled of warmth and woodsy cologne. It would be so easy to nestle against him, to bury her face in his chest and float in his arms. "I'm thirsty," she said, holding herself away from him. "Do they have sodas, or is beer the only thing to drink?"

Lyle stopped dancing but didn't release her. "Look at me." She tipped her head upward. "What's wrong, Jory?"

"Nothing's wrong." She offered a brilliant smile. "Can't I be thirsty?"

"Whenever you smile like that it means, 'Don't get too close.' Why can't you talk to me, Jory? I've been there."

"Been where? And I'm so sorry my smile bothers you." Why did he always have to dig inside her? Why couldn't he just leave her alone and have a good time?

She squirmed out of his arms and walked to the edge of the circle of light. He followed. "Look, Lyle, maybe I shouldn't have come. You want to be serious and I want to party. Everybody accepts me just the way I am, Lyle, except you." *And my mother and Melissa*, she thought. "Why can't everybody just leave me alone and let me live my own life?"

"Your best friend is *dying*, Jory. You can't stand by and watch it happen and not have it tear your guts out. *Talk* to me. I can help."

"She's not dying!" Jory yelled. "She's sick and she's having problems with her cure, but she's not going to die." Pressure began to build in her chest as she spoke.

"It isn't your fault that Melissa got sick and you didn't," Lyle said.

"That's stupid," she hissed. "That's never crossed my mind." The tightness in her chest increased and she wanted to bolt. Lyle reached for her, but she shoved him away. "Leave me alone. I mean it. Melissa's going to make it."

"But what if she doesn't? What will you do?"

"I'll be just fine with all my *real* friends around me. Up 'til now, you've been a good friend, but . . ."

He lifted his hands to her face and ran his thumbs along the sides of her cheeks, making her shiver. "I don't want to be your buddy, Jory. I don't want to be just another one of the guys you run around partying with."

Lyle's words had hurt and she wanted to hurt him back. "Let me be real honest with you, Lyle, all right? The only guy I've ever been crazy about is Michael Austin. I've felt that way for years, and even though I date other guys, no one's ever been able to change my mind about him."

Lyle said nothing, but his eyes looked dark and hurt. Jory wished she could take it all back. Lyle had been good to her and kind to Melissa. He said, "In other words, 'Buzz off, Lyle.' Is that the bottom line?"

She raised her chin. "You got it."

"Thanks for being honest, Jory. You get your wish. I won't bother you anymore. You drove yourself here, I guess you can drive yourself home." He walked away and quickly disappeared into the clusters of people.

Alone in the moonlight, Jory swallowed a lump of hot tears. She didn't care. Let him go! She sniffed and ran her fingers through her hair, damp at the temples from anxiety. She glanced about, not sure what to do or where to go.

She heard a familiar voice call her name from across the clearing and her stomach did a somersault. She turned to see Michael Austin coming toward her.

Chapter Thirteen

Michael wore a cockeyed grin as he approached her, weaving slightly as he walked. Jory knew instantly that he'd been drinking. "Hey, Jory. What're you doin' here?"

He'd greeted her like a long-lost friend and she realized exactly how drunk he had to be. Michael had rarely been very friendly to her, especially over the past few months. "Looking for a good time," she told him gaily.

"Then you've come to the right place," Michael said, looping his arm over her shoulders. "We're all having a real good time."

All thoughts of Lyle and their argument fled. "It looks like you've gotten a head start, Michael. How long have you been here?"

He attempted to read his watch. "Hands look fuzzy," he said, tapping the face. "Gotta get the thing fixed."

"Are you . . . uh . . . with somebody, Michael?" Jory asked.

He leaned into her and scratched his head, as if trying to remember. "Just some guys."

Jory was relieved. She felt euphoric over his being nice to her and she didn't want to share him, even if he was smashed and wouldn't remember a thing in the morning. "Why don't we sit down?" she asked.

"In a minute. First, I need to get a beer."

"Don't you think you've had enough beers?"

It was the wrong thing to say. "I know when I've had enough," he said abruptly.

Anxious not to lose him, Jory flashed him one of her most fabulous smiles. "Of course. So why don't I sit here on the car and wait for you?"

"Works for me," he said with a wave of his hand.

She watched him thread through the crowd toward an area with two stainless steel beer kegs and a washtub of other drinks. She knew that it wasn't smart for him to be drinking so much, but she also knew what he'd been through since Melissa's illness began. He deserved to blow off some steam.

A guy came toward her and Jory stiffened, willing Michael to return. "You a friend of Austin's?" He asked.

Jory hesitated. "Yes."

"Me too. I've been trying to get him out of here for an hour. But he won't go."

"He doesn't do this sort of thing often," she said, feeling a need to defend Michael.

"I know. You think you can get his car keys from him and get him home? He's too far gone to drive, and I'm not much better off myself."

Slightly ashamed that she hadn't thought of it herself, Jory asked, "Where are they?"

"In the pocket of the windbreaker he's wearing."

"What about you? How will you get home?"

The guy glanced behind him toward a blond-haired girl waiting patiently beside a red car. "I have a ride."

"Oh . . . yeah, sure. Don't worry, I'll get Michael home."

The guy left with the girl and Jory waited, holding her breath, until Michael wove his way back through the crowd. He dropped a cola in her lap and took a long swallow from a plastic mug. Jory realized that in spite of all he'd had to drink, he hadn't forgotten that she was too young for beer. She was still just a kid to him. She stood and slipped snugly beneath his arm. "So what now?"

Michael scanned the party scene. "I don't know . . ."

"We could dance," she said, deftly sliding her free hand into his pocket and taking the keys to his truck.

"We could."

She slipped the keys into the pocket of her hooded sweatshirt, where she kept her own. She remembered that it was only a week after his surgery and asked, "You are recovered, aren't you? I mean, the last time I saw you, you couldn't even stand up straight."

"See what a few beers can accomplish?" he said. "Naw, I'm all better, Jory. Fit and perfectly healthy."

She thought she detected sarcasm in his voice and didn't want to be the one to bring him back to reality. Not when she knew firsthand how much reality hurt. Michael put his cup on the hood of the car and took the cola from Jory's hand. "Are we gonna dance or not?"

She went to his arms without a word. Slow music pulsed through the woods, throbbing with words of broken promises and lost love. She felt nervous, being so close to him, as if she might wake and discover it was all a dream. He draped his wrists over her shoulders and toyed with the back of her hair. He touched his forehead to hers and she closed her eyes, held her breath, and hoped the music would never stop.

"Let's get out of here," Michael said, his voice low and soft.

Her eyes flew open and her mouth went dry. "All right."

She watched him as he fumbled for his keys, feeling guilty because she knew they were safe inside her pocket. "What's wrong?"

"Can't find my keys. Hell, I just had them . . ."

"No problem." Jory displayed a dazzling smile and hooked her arm through his. "I've got my car."

"But my truck . . . and my buddy . . ."

"Who's going to miss you in this crowd? And so what if your truck sits here all night? You can get it tomorrow." She was glad he couldn't follow her logic because she had none. She had only her smile and bravado.

Michael shook his head, as if to clear it, but didn't protest as she led him to where she'd parked. "Ah, you brought your lean, mean machine," Michael said when he saw her convertible.

"Put the top down," he ordered. "I want to ride with the wind in my face."

She lowered the roof and maneuvered the car through the maze of other vehicles. At the road, she asked, "Why don't we just drive? I know these back roads like the palm of my hand." She didn't want him to decide he had to go home. She just wanted to prolong the night spending time with him.

"Suits me," Michael said, scooting down into the bucket seat and crossing his arms.

Jory drove cautiously. Fields stretched on either side of the two lanes and there wasn't another car in sight.

"Is this the best it can do?" Michael asked.

"What do you mean?"

"Is this as fast as this baby can go? I want to go fast, Jory. Real fast."

She stared over at him. His face was pale in the moonlight, his eyes dark hollows. "Buckle up and hang on," she said, remembering the last time she'd blasted down these roads and a cop had stopped her. She reached out and turned up the radio full blast, gunned the engine, and floored the accelerator. The car responded instantly, and she watched the speedometer needle climb from the fifties through the sixties and into the seventies. The road beckoned like a long white river. The wind stung her face. Fence posts and telephone poles streaked by in a blur. Her exhilaration and sense of recklessness rose until she felt at one with the wind and the moon and the night.

Jory tipped her head back and laughed. The sound seemed to bounce off the stars. She looked toward Michael. Her heart almost stopped. Michael was sitting on the top edge of the front seat, with one arm grasping the seat belt and the other raised above his head. The wind whipped his hair.

"Michael, no!" She pumped the brake, jolting the speeding car, causing it to careen. It took all her skill to keep it on the road. She managed to slow down and coasted along the shoulder of the highway, where the vehicle finally rolled to a halt. The screaming radio shattered the stillness. She turned it off so violently that the knob broke.

Lazily, Michael slid downward into the seat cushion, as if nothing had happened. "Why'd you stop? I was having fun."

"You scared me to death! Are you trying to get killed?"

"I just wanted to feel what it was like . . ."

"Then go to Busch Gardens and take a ride on the roller coaster!" Jory's whole body quivered. "What's the matter with you?"

Michael shrugged his shoulders indifferently. "Don't get so bent out of shape. It was a little like riding in my balloon, only faster."

"But there's no basket to hold you in," she said, gritting her teeth.

He stared at her, his eyes calm in the moonlight. "I know."

The words sent a chill through her, more intense than the fear. She sucked in a long, shuttering breath. "Why don't we try it again," she said. "This time I'll keep the speed down and would you please keep your seat?"

"You don't have to get pushy," Michael said, grinning.

Her hands trembled, but she returned a shaky smile. "I'll try not to act so bossy the next time my passenger almost climbs out of my car when I'm doing seventy." She put the car into gear and inched out onto the highway. She drove more slowly, glancing at Michael every few minutes. He was brooding now, quiet and pensive. She wanted to touch him, chase away the darkness that was engulfing him.

"I know someplace I could show you," Jory said brightly, with an edge of mystery. "It's a great place and I know you'll love it."

He only shrugged, so she drove until she came upon a dirt road, where she turned off and followed the trail that was sheltered by overhanging trees. She came to a clearing where moss hung from trees and a stream gurgled in the woods. Jory cut the engine, and night noises filled up the silence.

Michael looked around. "Where are we?"

"A place Melissa showed me." Jory wondered if she should have told him because he might want to know how Melissa had discovered it.

Instead, he took a deep breath and closed his eyes. The sweet scent of orange blossoms and night-blooming jasmine drifted on an occasional breeze. "I like it," he said and she relaxed. "I wish I had a beer," he told her. "The wind and the ride seem to have sobered me up."

"What's wrong with that? Now you can see the hands on your watch, I'll bet."

"Because sober isn't where I want to be. Because when I'm sober I know the truth."

The look of pain that crossed his face etched a line across Jory's heart. "What truth, Michael?"

"That my sister's dying. And it's all my fault."

Chapter Fourteen

His words stunned her. It took a moment before she found her voice. "Michael, that's not true! How can you even think that?"

"Because it is true. Who'd she get that lousy bone marrow from? Who told her it was 'primo stuff'? It isn't first-rate after all, Jory. It's killing her."

"Michael, it isn't your fault. Melissa would never think that. You were the best donor—" she paused, "the *only* donor. Without you, she had no hope."

"And with me, she got a one-way ticket to doom." A bitter frown formed on his mouth. "She trusted me . . ." Michael opened the car door and walked away. Jory scrambled after him, anxious and fearful.

At the stream, he stooped and gathered a handful of pebbles and began to bounce them into the water. "The first time she was in the hospital, I thought I'd go nuts." A pebble plopped, sent rings through the moonlit water, and sank. "Every day, I'd go in and see what the chemo was doing to her. It invaded her, turned her inside out, and made her hurt so bad. All the doctors said was 'It's normal. It's always this way.' I hated those doctors, and I hated what their 'cure' was doing to her."

He'd said the word *cure* like it was dirty.

"But the chemo did help," Jory told him. "It put her into remission, and she went home and back to school."

Michael depleted his supply of rocks and stared out across the stream. "Yeah, she did. I thought, 'It's over. A nasty business, but all behind us now.' "

"But she relapsed," Jory said, reliving her own reaction to the news.

"It was like a bad joke. Like Lucy holding the football for Charlie Brown. You know, every time she promises to keep it upright for him to kick, and every time he gets suckered in and runs to kick it.'

"And Lucy jerks it away," Jory finished.

"That's the way the doctors were. 'So sorry, Melissa. But we have this other cure. Want to go for it?'" He mimicked Dr. Rowan's voice. "And I said, 'Go for it, Melissa. You can have my bone marrow, and afterward you'll be cured.' "

Jory searched for words of assurance. Anything that would make him stop blaming himself. "Sometimes I feel like I'm responsible too, Michael. I wanted her to have the transplant. I encouraged her too."

"Well we were both wrong, weren't we?" His tone was bitter.

"But the odds were so bad without it," Jory rationalized, not sure she was addressing Michael at all.

"That's the way it is with doctors," he interrupted. "They're always quoting the odds. Makes me wonder why they don't play the horses and leave people alone."

An icy lump settled in Jory's stomach. Hesitantly, she reached out and touched his arm. "It's going to work, Michael. I know it is. Melissa is seventeen years old and she's pretty and smart and she has everything going for her. W-we just have to have h-hope . . ."

Her voice broke and Michael gave her a piercing look. "Come back to the car," he said gently, taking her hand. She followed, fighting for composure. She couldn't lose it in front of Michael. Mature girls don't cry, she reminded herself as they walked.

At the car, Michael climbed into the backseat, nestled into a corner, and pulled Jory next to him. He placed her head against his chest and stroked her hair. She settled into his embrace and listened to his heart, its rhythm calm and soothing.

His mouth pressed against her temple. "It's okay, Jory. Take it easy. I didn't mean to get so morose. I'm sorry." She couldn't move, didn't want to move. "I just feel so helpless," he whispered. "I thought my bone marrow would stop it. I thought that after the operation, she'd wake up the next day and smile and get up out of her hospital bed and be well. Like a miracle would happen and Melissa would be healthy again." His voice sounded thick and she was afraid to look into his eyes in case there were tears in them.

"It might happen yet," Jory said, her voice small and hopeful. "Melissa's a fighter and it's worked for others. Don't give up, Michael. Please." She looked up at him finally. She wanted to make him stop hurting, wanted to make everything all right again. His mouth was but inches away. She stretched upward and kissed him.

This time he was not asleep and his lips moved beneath hers, hesitantly at first, then more urgently. His arms tightened and his hands began to move down the length of her back, urging her against him. She pressed into him, feeling energy and fire along the hardness of his body.

She shifted, brought her arms up around his neck and stroked his hair. His mouth left hers and began to travel, in frantic little trails over her hair, her face, her throat. She gasped, tugging him closer, wishing she could sink into him. He caught his fingers in the sides of her hair and found her mouth again.

For Jory, time stood still and six years of frustrated yearning erupted like a volcano. Her head spun and every nerve in her body tingled. Her blood sizzled. The scent of jasmine drenched the air, and the taste of Michael blotted out reason and doubt. His hands found her bare skin, making her shiver. She poured herself into the kiss, giving, giving . . .

Without warning, Michael broke away. The night air chilled her face and she shifted uneasily. The tilting world slowly righted itself. He was staring at her, his eyes unblinking, his breath coming in gulps. She drew back, confused and disoriented.

"Jory, I . . ." His voice shook.

"Don't," she said, reality rushing over her like cold water. She tugged her clothing into place with numb and clumsy fingers.

"Jory, I'm sorry. My God . . . what almost happened. What I almost did to you."

She covered her embarrassment with nonchalance, trying to sound sophisticated. "What's the big deal? You think some guy's never tried anything with me before?"

"You're my sister's best friend. You're a seventeen-year-old kid."

Blinding anger exploded in her. She seized the front of his jacket and jerked it. "I'm not a kid, Michael," she said through gritted teeth. "Stop treating me like I'm some stupid kid."

Michael gathered her clenched fists in his hands and locked her eyes with his. His gaze stung and she felt naked and hot all over. His voice came low, his words gentle. "You're right, Jory. You're no kid. You're pretty and soft and very much a woman. You don't deserve to have it happen for you this way."

Michael was rejecting her! The realization jolted Jory, and her anger became burning humiliation. She averted her eyes and mumbled, "You were drunk and I was scared because of almost having an accident. We got carried away talking about Melissa and . . . and . . ." She struggled to rise, to get out of the car and run off. "We were just two c-crazy people . . ." Her voice wavered.

Michael hauled her back down. "If this had happened to Melissa and I found out about it, I would have gone after the guy with my bare hands."

He sounded as if he were apologizing to her, but her head was beginning to throb and she couldn't sort things out. "You don't have to make up excuses, Michael. I'm a big girl."

"Jory, listen to me." His tone pleaded and he held her hands so tightly that it hurt. "I can't even help myself. I don't know up from down, right from left. But I do know what's right and wrong, and this, with you, out here in the woods, in the backseat of your car, is wrong. I should never have come here alone with you."

"I'll take you back to the party." Her tone was wooden and she felt as stiff as a tree. "You can get your truck and leave."

"I don't have my keys."

She reached into the pocket of her sweatshirt and pulled out his ring of keys. "I have them." He looked startled. She explained, "You were too drunk to drive. I thought I was doing you a favor."

He took them, letting his fingers linger on hers. "You were right. Thanks."

"My good deed for the night," she retorted and climbed into the front seat, still drowning in shame and unwilling to look Michael in the eye. They drove in silence, and at the party site he got out. He hesitated but she didn't allow him to speak. She threw the car into reverse and the tires spit gravel and dirt as she pulled away.

Jory made it home and quietly let herself into the sprawling, sleeping house. In her room, she undressed quickly and slipped between fresh, cool sheets. She stared into the darkness, numb and empty. She wanted to cry, but now the tears, which had threatened all the way home, refused to come.

Jory shivered and curled herself into a ball. She wished she had someone to talk to. Someone to tell about what had happened between her and Michael and help her understand. She couldn't tell her mother. The notion caused a sardonic smile. She couldn't tell Melissa, because Melissa was sick. And even if she weren't, how could Jory tell her about something so personal between herself and Melissa's own brother?

Lyle. She could tell Lyle. Not really, of course, but somehow she knew that deep down he would understand and help her make sense of it. "You must have a screw loose, Jory," she muttered. She'd been mean and hateful to Lyle and had all but told him to get lost. He'd never want to talk to her again. Michael had been right for years in his assessment of her. She was nothing more than a silly, ditzy girl. A kid.

The phone rudely woke Jory the next morning. At first, she tried to ignore it, burying her head under her pillow, but the thing refused to be quiet.

She gave up, groped for the receiver, and mumbled sleepily, "Hello."

"Jory, it's Michael."

She was instantly awake. "Yes?"

"Melissa's better, Jory. She's done a one hundred and eighty degree turn. Her white blood count is over four thousand, her platelets are up around fifty thousand, and her hemoglobin is ten point six."

"That's good?" Jory asked, trying to clear her head.

"It's terrific. It means that my bone marrow is doing the job, Jory. It's working."

Chapter Fifteen

~~

Since it was a Sunday, the highway wasn't crowded and Jory made it to the hospital in record time. She hurried through the isolation ward and almost flattened Mrs. Austin, who was just leaving Melissa's room. "Isn't it wonderful?" Melissa's mother asked, her eyes shining.

"Fabulous," Jory cried. "Can I see her?"

"She's been asking about you." Mrs. Austin pulled off her sterile gown and stuffed it into a special container by the door.

Jory paused and shifted from foot to foot. "Uh . . . where's Michael?"

"He had to go to work. Evidently, he took last night off and now has to make it up. He looked like the devil this morning too," Mrs. Austin added, almost to herself.

Jory was relieved that she didn't have to face him first thing this morning. Not after what had happened the night before. "How is Melissa feeling?"

"By comparison, like a million dollars. The change is dramatic, Jory. Of course, the doctors say that she's still not out of the woods, but the latest results of her blood work are very encouraging."

Jory made a face. "Oh, those doctors would be pessimistic if we won the state lottery."

Mrs. Austin laughed. "You're right. Go on in, Jory, but don't stay too long. She thinks she's stronger than she actually is."

Jory put on the sterile scrubs, then pulled open a second door to Melissa's room. Her friend was sitting up in bed devouring breakfast, a plate heaped with scrambled eggs, grits, sausage, toast, and jelly. Jory watched, speechless.

Melissa smiled and waved between bites. "What's the matter? You've seen me eat before."

"Not that *fast*," Jory said. "And never anything that fast that wasn't drenched in chocolate."

"It's my blood that's messed up, Jory, not my stomach."

"I guess so."

Melissa shoved the plate aside. "Come here— give me a hug!"

Jory wrapped her arms around her friend. Melissa felt thin and feather light. "I've missed seeing you," Jory said, smiling to disguise her shock.

Melissa patted her bed. "So sit down and tell me all the news from school. What's happening?"

Jory took a chair and pulled in close to the bed. Where should she begin? How could she catch someone up on six weeks of life? "We had a carnival at school for you." She quickly filled Melissa in on the details.

"You mean people came and gave blood and donated money for me?" Melissa asked. "That means so much, Jory. It really does. I didn't realize that so many people really care. I know Mom can use the money too. I think her insurance ran out long ago."

Jory couldn't imagine what it would be like to worry about paying a bill. "We had a good time, and besides—you know me—any excuse for a party."

"Who helped?"

"The whole school. Especially the senior class."

"But you were the instigator?"

"Well, me and Lyle Vargas."

Melissa looked surprised. "Lyle?"

"He . . . um . . . he's been pretty nice . . ."

"But you don't like him? As a boyfriend, I mean."

"No way," Jory said. "We worked together, that's all. There's nothing going on with us, and I'm not looking for anything to be going on either."

"Are you still hung up on Michael?"

Jory suddenly felt extremely warm. "Haven't I always been?" She couldn't deny that she was still attracted to him, regardless of the fact that he'd rejected her the night before. "Some things will never change, Melissa. But I'm trying not to let it cramp my style." Jory didn't ever want Melissa to know how frustrated she felt about Michael.

Melissa plucked at the covers. "Tell me everything about school. And I mean *everything*. I even want to know what they've served in the lunchroom since I've been gone."

Jory began to relate everyday occurrences, silly

gossip, who was dating whom. Even the tiniest, most boring details made Melissa smile, and Jory wished she'd been more observant so she'd have more to tell.

"Any word on National Merit finalists yet?" Melissa asked.

"You told me they won't be announced until April," Jory reminded her.

"I know. I'm just getting antsy now that I feel better. It seems like I've been here a year and life is passing me by. All I want is to go home."

"When do you think they'll let you out?"

Melissa shrugged. "No one answers a direct question like that around here. They keep telling me it's too soon to tell. There's also been some more damage to my heart."

Jory felt her stomach plummet as if she were on an elevator falling too fast. "How much damage?"

"They'll do another EKG in the morning. It should give the cardiac specialist a better idea."

The ordeal isn't over yet, thought Jory. She wondered if Michael knew. "I sure hope this specialist gets you in top shape soon, Melissa. You've got to get out of this place—we've got a zillion plans to make for the prom."

"The prom?" Melissa studied Jory as if she'd suddenly grown another head.

"You know, the senior prom. The once-in-a-lifetime event every senior girl lives and breathes for."

"Jory, who's going to take *me* to the prom?"

"We don't know yet, now do we? But some-body will."

Melissa reached out and took Jory's wrist. "Don't you dare set something up, Jory. Don't you bribe some poor kid and beg him to take me."

"I wouldn't do that," Jory exclaimed, secretly calculating whom she could approach. "I think we should double-date, that's all. Cripes, Melissa, no one's even asked *me* yet."

Melissa interrupted, her voice pleading. "Jory, please listen to me. You can't manage my life this way."

"I don't do that!"

"The heck you don't," Melissa countered. "Maybe the prom is like the Brain Bowl for me this year—something I can't go to. I don't want to even think about the prom right now. Or where I'm sup-posed to get the money for a new dress. Besides, I've seen myself in the mirror and I look like a cir-cus freak . . ."

Jory hadn't meant to upset Melissa. She'd only wanted to give her something to look forward to. "Okay. We won't talk about the prom now. We'll have lots of time for that later." She rose to her feet, patting Melissa's hand and saying, "You get some rest and I'll come back tomorrow. And call me if you want anything."

Tired, Melissa sank slowly down under the covers. "You get too involved, Jory."

"No I don't. I'm just looking to the future. After all, you'll be away at college this time next year and won't be home until summer vacation.

We'd better have all the fun we can before we leave Lincoln High."

Melissa sighed. "I'm sure you won't let me leave without a ticker tape parade either. Did you ever stop to think that I may not want to come back here?"

Jory grinned, dismissing her comment with a wave. "Goodbye doesn't have to mean *forever*, Melissa. I want to make it worth your while to come back, that's all." Jory promised to return later, and she went into the air lock, where she stood for a few minutes against the door, trying to calm her racing pulse and catch her breath.

Jory parked her car at the far back corner of the Steak 'n Shake restaurant after school. She ordered fries and a cola from the curb service waitress and scrunched down in the seat, hoping no one from school would see her. Right now she wanted to be alone.

Her latest run-in with her mother still thundered through her head. Mrs. Delaney had confronted Jory the minute she had gotten home from school, brandishing Jory's most recent grade sheet under her nose.

"What have you got to say about *these*, young lady?"

Jory shrugged and waved the computer printout aside. "I'm not a scholar."

"Look at this!" Her mother continued. "Cs, a D, and even an Incomplete. How do you ever expect to get accepted to the University of Miami with grades like this?"

"You're the one who wants me to go to the U of M, Mother. I never said I wanted to go there."

"Well don't worry. With these grades, you couldn't get into a vocational school! What is the matter with you, Jory? Where is your common sense? *Everybody* goes to college. You can't expect to make it in the world without a degree."

Jory silently counted to ten, then dropped her books on the spotless kitchen counter with a thud. "Stop pushing me. Stop forcing me to decide about college right now. I've got a zillion things on my mind, Mom, and getting into the U of M is at the bottom of the list."

"Jory, I haven't said much about the inordinate amount of time you spend dealing with Melissa . . ."

"She's sick, Mother. I can't abandon her."

"I'm not asking you to, but for heaven's sake, keep it in perspective. You act like you're one of *her* family instead of *ours*. You're not, Jory."

Jory felt as if her mother had slapped her. She was about to say something angry and cutting when the phone rang. Mrs. Delaney grabbed the receiver, listened for a moment, and snapped, "Can't you handle it, Lucille?" Jory leaned back on the counter. "Oh, all right," Mrs. Delaney grumbled. "I'll be there in fifteen minutes." She hung up and turned toward Jory. "I have to go to the office. But don't think that this discussion is finished, young lady. It isn't—not by a long shot."

Jory watched her mother sweep out the door and felt hollow and numb. She picked up the crumbled grade sheet, glanced over it, and was forced to admit that her grades were pretty bad. She really didn't know why she hadn't tried harder. According to her SAT scores, she was smart enough to have done better.

She tossed the paper onto the counter. She glanced around the kitchen at the gleaming appliances and the freshly scrubbed counters and sinks, smelling of disinfectant and lemon wax. Mrs. Garcia had the place sparkling. *As clean and sterile as Melissa's hospital room*, Jory thought.

"Here's your order, honey." The waitress's voice snapped Jory out of her funk. She paid for the food and nibbled halfheartedly on the fries. They weren't greasy enough. Jory gazed out the window. Across the parking lot she recognized a car full of guys from school. She saw Lyle in the front seat, and he was staring straight into her eyes.

Jory almost smiled at him, but she remembered what he'd told her about flashing smiles she really didn't mean. Her face felt frozen. Flustered, Jory looked away.

When she looked up again, the boys had gone inside the restaurant and the car was empty.

Chapter Sixteen

"What do you mean Melissa has another fever? I just saw her two days ago and she was perfectly fine." Jory had met Mrs. Austin at the hospital.

Mrs. Austin rubbed her eyes, and Jory saw the exhaustion in her face. "Well, she's not perfectly fine now. She's spiking a fever and the lab people are running around like mad."

Jory swallowed hard. "Is it . . . I mean, could she be rejecting the transplant?"

"No. They're certain that the transplant is taking hold. Her white blood cell and platelet counts keep climbing. It's something else entirely. Dr. Rowan's called in another specialist."

"Gee, Mrs. Austin, I'm really sorry."

"So am I, Jory. I don't think I can take much more of this. First they give you hope, then it's snatched away. Then hope again, followed by despair. My nerves are shot."

Melissa's mother looked frazzled and Jory wanted to reach out to her, but didn't know if it would be proper. "Maybe I'll come back later," Jory said, not wanting to leave, but not sure she should stay.

"No," Mrs. Austin said, taking Jory's arm.

"Don't go yet. Melissa's asked to see you. The doctors don't want visitors except the immediate family, but Melissa's begged me to let you come in."

"I . . . uh . . . I think of Melissa as my sister," Jory said softly, shifting from foot to foot because the sense of urgency was scaring her.

Mrs. Austin nodded. "So does Melissa, Jory. And so do I."

"Can I go in right now?"

"Michael's in there with her, but go on anyway. If anyone says anything to you, send them to me."

Jory struggled into the sterile gown, finding it difficult to tie the strings on her mask because her fingers were shaking. She took a deep breath, swallowing the lump that had formed in her throat, and went into Melissa's room.

The room was crowded with even more machinery than Jory had seen before. Something ominous, with hoses and an oxygen tank, stood in a corner. Jory ignored it and turned her attention toward the bed, where Michael sat holding his sister's hand. He looked up as Jory entered and from over the top of his mask Jory felt his searing blue eyes burn holes right through her.

Cautiously, Jory approached the bed. Melissa's breathing was light and shallow. Her cheeks were flushed and her skin appeared translucent. "H-How is she?"

"Not so good." Michael's voice was brusque and Jory got the impression that he resented her intrusion.

"Your mother said for me to come in," she explained apologetically.

"The fever's wringing her out. She's in and out, so don't expect too long a social call."

His words were like tiny barbs and Jory winced. What had she done to make him dislike her so? The night in the car had been like a time warp, when the rules of life had been suspended and they'd reached out and joined with one another in some special way. Now, here in Melissa's room, it was as if that night had never happened. "Can I touch her?"

"Sure," Michael said grudgingly.

Jory stroked Melissa's forehead. It was dry and hot. She watched the rapid rise and fall of Melissa's chest through the thin material of her gown and followed the wire leads taped inside the material to the monitor where the green line zipped, fast and ragged. "She doesn't look good."

"Tell me about it."

Jory blushed, feeling stupid for making such inane comments. "What do they think is wrong?"

"They haven't said."

"But it isn't rejection?"

"No. My bone marrow's working just fine. Ironic, huh? The cure works, but the patient's still sick."

"Sh-She'll be all right. They'll find out what's got her and give her medicine, and she'll be all right again."

Melissa's eyelids fluttered open. "Hi, Melissa,"

Jory said gently, managing a smile. "It's only me. I stopped by to see if you'd like me to bring you a chocolate cheesecake or something."

Melissa slowly focused on Jory's face. "Maybe some other time. Are you skipping school?"

"Me? Come on, you know I never skip school. Why, I hear I'm up for the perfect attendance award this year."

"You've got to get serious about your life, Jory. You have so many things to do . . ." Melissa sounded almost pleading, ignoring Jory's attempt at humor. "You've got to go do them. You've got to do *everything*." Melissa realized that Michael was holding her hand and softened her grave expression. "Hi, Big Brother. You look like a doctor."

"No need to insult me, Sis." He squeezed her fingers. "How are you feeling?"

"Like a train ran over me. Do they know what's wrong?"

"Not yet. But you'll probably shrug it off before they figure it out."

Jory added, "Yeah. After all, you've got all that good bone marrow now."

"I'm so tired," Melissa said with a sigh that made Jory's heart skip a beat.

"Would you like us to leave so that you can sleep?" Michael asked.

"Oh no, don't leave. Please. I don't want to be alone. I want you—all of you—with me. Where's Mom?"

"Probably tearing some unsuspecting doctor

apart." Michael stroked Melissa's cheek. "I won't leave you."

Melissa turned toward Jory. "I thought it would hurt, but it doesn't."

Jory wondered what Melissa meant by *it*. She didn't ask, but she didn't like the way Melissa was talking. She sounded weary and resigned. "They'll give you shots for pain if you hurt, won't they?" Jory asked.

"They give me shots. I've had a bunch of shots. But every time I wake up, it's nice to have one of you with me. I like knowing I'm not by myself, and that I'm not facing this alone."

Jory exchanged quick glances with Michael. "Well, here we are," she said brightly.

"I'm acting like a baby, aren't I?" Jory and Michael shook their heads in unison. "Yes, I am," Melissa said. "I don't know why I'm acting so weird. It's just that I'm lonely and so tired. I think I could sleep for a month, but I'm sort of afraid too."

"How so?" Michael asked.

"What if I don't wake up?"

A sudden chill shook Jory. Why was the air-conditioning on? Didn't the hospital realize that Melissa's room felt like a meat locker?

"I'll shake you until you do wake up," Michael said.

"You shouldn't hold on so hard, Michael."

He dropped her hand. "Gosh, I'm sorry. Was I hurting your hand?"

Melissa smiled in a strange way. "I didn't mean my hand," she said.

Jory's teeth began to chatter. She felt her breath growing short and wondered if she might be catching a cold. It wouldn't do to be around Melissa if she was catching something. "Look, maybe I should be going."

Melissa glanced back at her. "I want you to take the journal," she said.

Jory's mouth opened, then closed. She wanted to cry, "No!" Instead she asked, "Really? Right now? What if I lose it? What if I can't think of anything to write? What if . . .?"

Melissa tapped Jory's hand. "You promised."

"But I can bring it back just as soon as you're feeling better, right?"

"Sure."

Michael eyed her stonily as Jory reached into the bedside table drawer and removed the blue leather book. Jory hugged it to her chest, staring only at Melissa and trying desperately not to allow Michael's hostile eyes into her line of vision. "I promised your mother that I wouldn't stay long. I'll track her down and tell her you want to see her. That way Michael won't have to leave."

Melissa managed a half wave. "Come see me again soon, Jory, and don't forget to keep up the journal."

Jory made it out of the room and into the corridor, where she leaned against a wall and struggled to catch her breath. She felt as if she'd run ten miles. She found Mrs. Austin and quickly left the hospital. In the parking lot, she sat in her car with the top down, resting her head on the seat and staring at the brilliant blue sky and white glowing sun until her eyes hurt. She wished the noonday sun would warm her.

The party seemed endless. Franklin Cortez, the last of Mrs. Delaney's prearranged dates for Jory, was trying hard to be charming, but Jory had no interest in him or in the party.

Jory watched her parents dancing. Her father was tall and bronzed by the sun. His silver hair gave him a distinguished look. Her mother was elegant, almost regal-looking in a flowing chiffon gown. They were a perfect couple glowing with good looks and good health. Jory wished she were at the hospital with the Austins.

"Melissa has meningitis." Jory would never forget the sound of Mrs. Austin's words as long as she lived. The diagnosis had come four days before, striking like a hammer blow. Meningitis. The membranes surrounding Melissa's brain and spinal cord were inflamed. She wasn't responding to treatment and her heart was damaged and very weak.

Jory hadn't seen Melissa since the day her friend had insisted she take the journal. The book weighed on Jory's conscience. She hadn't touched it since she'd taken it home and hidden it away in a drawer in her room for safekeeping. It was Melissa's and full of her private thoughts. For Jory to read it or write in it wouldn't be right. It seemed like eavesdropping to her.

Franklin interrupted her thoughts by saying he liked her dress. Jory thanked him. It *was* a beautiful dress, emerald green, strapless, with a flared skirt that came just above her knees. Jory's mother had outdone herself in choosing it, for it complemented her auburn hair perfectly. But right now, Jory couldn't have cared less. She felt an urge to escape. To escape Franklin and the party and an incredible sense of sadness.

She excused herself, smiling gaily at Franklin and promising to be right back. Instead, she went to the front entrance and, without a second thought, left the club and drove off in her car. She wanted to be alone. She needed time to think.

It was after one A.M. when she turned into her driveway. She was surprised to see all the lights still on. She groaned. That meant her mother was waiting for her, and Jory knew she'd be on the warpath. After all, Jory had simply walked out of the country club without telling her parents or Franklin Cortez that she was going. How could she explain herself? How could she make her mother understand that she couldn't have stayed there one more minute without screaming? Jory sighed, squared her shoulders, and walked quickly into the house.

"Where have you been?" Her mother stood alone in the living room, her arms crossed.

"Driving."

"Since nine o'clock?"

"Yes." Jory put her keys in her purse, snapped it shut, and dropped it onto the cherry wood end table. "Listen, Mother, I know I shouldn't have run off, but I was bored stiff. I know you're mad, but I'm really wiped out. Could we have our fight about it in the morning?"

"Jory, I need to tell you something."

Jory's gaze flew to her mother's face. She expected anger and fire. She saw wariness and . . . tears? Jory stiffened and said, "Not tonight, Mother. I'm exhausted. I'll get up early and we can talk then."

Mrs. Delaney stepped in front of Jory as she started to leave. "Mrs. Austin called here about ten tonight, and Mrs. Garcia called us at the club."

Jory felt her heart pounding. "Tell me in the morning," she said, trying to step around her mother.

"Jory, you must listen to me."

"I don't want to listen." Jory fought a rising sense of panic. The walls seemed to be closing in. Why wouldn't her mother get out of her way? Childlike, Jory clamped her hands over her ears. "I can't hear you, Mother. I'm not going to listen."

Mrs. Delaney reached out, took Jory's wrists, and tugged. "Melissa died tonight, honey. Her heart gave out."

Jory felt her throat constrict. She stared wide-eyed because the awful words confirmed what she'd known deep inside, all along. What she'd realized the moment Mrs. Austin had told her about Melissa's meningitis. "I-I'll go to bed now and get some sleep. I'll . . . um . . . call Mrs. Austin tomorrow. She must be hurting. And Michael too. He wasn't prepared for this, you know. He wasn't ready for it . . ."

Mrs. Delaney gently shushed Jory's senseless babbling, smoothing her palm over Jory's hair and down her cheek: "I'm so sorry, baby. So sorry."

"Don't leave me alone."

"I won't, Jory. I'm right here. For as long as you want."

Without warning, a wail started deep within Jory's soul and rose, until it ripped its way out her mouth. Her whole body began to tremble and she would have crumbled, except that her mother wrapped her arms around her and supported her. Mrs. Delaney stroked Jory's hair and crooned nonsensical things, as a mother would to a child, rocking her, comforting her, while Jory wept for hours into the night.

Chapter Seventeen

~~~

Melissa Austin was buried on a glorious day in March that looked like a greeting card colored in bright crayons. The sky gleamed sapphire blue and the sun was a fiery yellow. The breeze smelled of flowers and new grass. Lincoln High School closed at noon and the senior class, and even some juniors and sophomores, came to bury their classmate, who, according to the student newspaper, had "died too young."

The cortege of automobiles wound its way through the streets of Tampa in a slow, steady crawl to the cemetery. Jory inched along in the snaking line, alone in her convertible. Her parents had driven too, and they were somewhere behind in traffic. It meant a lot to her that they had come. But she'd driven by herself because despite her mother's kindness and understanding, today she could not share her grief with anyone.

Jory surmised that grief had an anesthetic quality to it. She had functioned in a normal capacity during the few days following Melissa's death, without remembering exactly how she'd made it through. She'd eaten and slept, and talked to her parents and made phone calls to friends. But she'd

felt numb, detached, as if she were moving through
mist in a dream.

Now she had time to think, and the previous
days came back in bits and pieces. She recalled
weeping with Mrs. Austin in the kitchen, the
friendly yellow kitchen she'd all but grown up in
since fifth grade.

"She doesn't hurt anymore," Mrs. Austin said.
"In some ways, knowing that makes it easier for
me."

Jory wanted to shout, "It's a lousy price to pay
to never hurt again," but instead she plucked at a
tissue in her fist and said, "Melissa was the bravest
person I ever knew."

"It's hard to believe she'll never come through
that door again."

"I know."

"That she'll never call me up and ask, 'Mom,
what do you want me to start for supper?'"

"I know," Jory said, and she and Mrs. Austin
held each other and cried.

Later, Jory had gone to Melissa's bedroom, but
she lost her courage and shut the door quickly, staring at it so long that her knees locked. She had
avoided Michael, who looked to have aged ten
years. He wore dark glasses, even inside the house,
and he never once spoke to her until the day of the
viewing at the funeral home.

Jory had been the first one there aside from the
immediate family, but she couldn't bring herself to
walk over to the open casket. The notion of seeing
Melissa's body terrified her, yet she knew she

couldn't leave without telling her best friend goodbye.

Struggling to keep her composure, Jory
watched Michael approach the coffin and, as he
knelt down her courage returned. Timidly she went
forward and knelt next to him. Her hands were
clammy and her throat ached with unshed tears,
but she forced herself to look at Melissa who rested
on a bed of white satin. "Crazy, isn't it?" Michael
said. "She had to die in order to be beautiful again."

Jory nodded, awestruck. Melissa *was* beautiful, dressed in white eyelet, her hair—the wig
Jory had given her—framing her flawless face. She
was no longer bloated, and the sores and lesions
were smoothed away. Jory said, "Death gave her
back what life took away. She looks like a princess."
Then she asked Michael, "Does your father know?
Was there any way to let him know?"

Michael's eyes never strayed from his sister's
face. "He left years ago and if Mom has an address
for him, she never told me. But I wouldn't want
him here. Why should he share her death, when he
never shared her life?"

Jory allowed herself one final lingering look at
her friend, then she stepped aside and watched
others file past. Ric came. She recognized his sharp
features and shaggy brown hair immediately. He
was with a girl Jory didn't know. Michael's friends
came too. People she recognized from the balloon
club, and the guy who'd asked Jory to drive Michael
home on the night of the party in the woods.

Kids from school came. Jory caught snatches of their conversations.

"It's awful, so awful."

"Poor Melissa. Why did this have to happen to her?"

"She had everything to live for. It's not fair."

"I thought she was getting better, then just after Christmas, bam! Back to the hospital."

"I'm glad I gave blood. It makes me feel I helped in some small way."

Many of the girls wept and for some reason it irritated Jory, for they hadn't known Melissa half as well as she, and she was taking great pride in staying dry-eyed throughout the evening. She refused to cry in front of them. Melissa would have wanted her to keep it together, because Jory had a reputation for smiling, for always having a happy-go-lucky attitude. It was the least she could do for Melissa. The very least.

Lyle came, of course. She saw him across the room, walking past the casket, tall and lean, his amber eyes downcast and serious. He was dressed in a dark brown suit and there were streaks of blond in his hair from being outdoors a lot.

Lyle stepped away and glanced up. Jory tried to look down to avoid meeting his eyes, but she was too late. Lyle nodded, acknowledging her, and their estrangement reared between them like a wall. She had avoided him for weeks, ever since the night of the party when they'd fought. She turned quickly to scan the masses of funeral bouquets. Seeing him had suddenly made her throat tighten and tears threaten. Jory clenched her teeth, dug her nails into her palms. *This is stupid,* she told herself. How could she make it through this terrible evening without shedding a tear, then almost lose it because she'd looked into Lyle Vargas's eyes? It made no sense.

She had slipped away right after seeing Lyle and gone home. Now, as the endless line of cars filed through the gates of the cemetery, Jory remembered how confused she'd felt that night of the viewing. And she couldn't call Melissa and ask, "What's the matter with me? Why am I acting so dopey?"

The graveside area was crowded with people overflowing from under a canvas canopy, where a minister waited and Melissa's few relatives sat stiffly in chairs. Michael wore a black suit and dark glasses. His expression was stony and he held his mother's hand without moving. Jory's heart ached. The minister spoke of heaven and how Melissa was already there. Jory glanced away, toward the section of the cemetery where she'd brought Melissa last winter to see Rachael's grave. She wondered if Melissa was playing with the little girl.

The minister read some Bible verses. Jory tried to concentrate on the words but couldn't. He said, "And I will turn your mourning into joy," and the idea was so ludicrous to Jory that she almost laughed out loud. The minister's voice seemed to be coming from far away and Jory felt a lightness in her head. Her vision blurred and the ground tilted.

She felt an arm around her waist as she sagged.

Her legs collapsed, beyond her control. A guy's voice said, "Come with me. You'd better sit down."

She allowed him to lead her away from the service toward the line of parked cars. Her breath was coming in short gasps and she felt sick to her stomach, cold and clammy. A car door opened and hands guided her into the cool interior of a large gray automobile. "Lean back against the seat," his voice said.

Shakily, she obeyed, but her breathing was erratic. "W-why can't . . . I catch . . . my . . . breath?"

"You're hyperventilating. Put your head between your knees. Your brain needs oxygen. Relax." He dipped her head forward, all the while holding her hand. "You almost fainted. You were as white as a sheet, but your color's better already."

Jory did as she was told. In a few minutes, her head began to clear and her breathing slowed. She sat up and confronted her white knight. *Lyle*. Words of thanks died on her lips as Jory felt extreme embarrassment. "I think I'm all right now," she mumbled. "I need to get back. I'm missing the service."

Lyle held her shoulder gently, restraining her. "Not so fast, or it'll happen all over again."

Jory felt woozy and realized he was right. She dropped back onto the car seat and closed her eyes. The car was cool and quiet, and she welcomed the relief from the sun. She kept her eyes closed, still embarrassed. Finally, she said, "Thanks for the rescue."

Lyle explained, "I happened to glance over and you looked so pale I thought, 'Jory's going down.' So I moved next to you as fast as I could. I don't think too many people noticed."

She hoped not. Jory felt utterly ridiculous and foolish. "I've never fainted in my life."

"You've been under a lot of stress. Sometimes it comes out in odd ways and at inconvenient times."

"You'll make a great doctor, Lyle." It came out sarcastically and she saw him flinch.

He gazed out the car window. "The service is over."

An incredible sadness filled Jory. "I missed the minister's final words." Her tone was flat. "About how happy we'll all be someday."

"Come on," Lyle said. "I'll take you to your car."

She let him help her out because her legs were still wobbly. She leaned on the car door. "I can make it," she told him.

"You shouldn't drive."

"I can drive fine. Stop treating me like an in-valid."

"Are you all right, Jory?" It was Michael.

Instinctively, she leaned toward him. "I'm all right," she said. Lyle's eyes darted between Michael and Jory. He stepped aside.

"Mom saw you almost faint and she was worried."

"Lyle rescued me."

Lyle and Michael exchanged nods. Michael

adjusted his dark glasses. "Mom wants you to come back to the house for the afternoon. Everybody on the block sent food and we have enough for all the relatives and their relatives too."

Jory agreed. She wanted to be with the Austins. It made Melissa seem closer, more tangible. "I'll be there soon. Let me tell my parents."

Michael walked away and Lyle turned his attention to Jory. "If you ever want to talk, Jory, call me."

"I don't want to talk. All I want to do is forget."

"Well, you take care. I'll . . . uh . . . see you next week in school."

Jory looked at him, and a deep, dark despair welled inside her, making her throat ache. "Melissa would have been eighteen years old next month. We were planning to go register to vote."

"Goodbye, Jory," Lyle said.

She watched him, unblinking, as he walked away. She gripped her arms tightly to her chest and allowed her gaze to drift to the canopy and to the coffin waiting to be lowered into the ground. Baskets of flowers and wreaths stood vigil around the pale blue casket and spilled over in lush abundance, reminding Jory more of a garden than of a funeral. Their colorful, velvet petals fluttered in the breeze—jonquils and daffodils, daisies and iris, pansies, black-eyed Susans, tulips, lilies, and exotic birds of paradise. "A thousand pretty petals," Jory said under her breath. "With nothing to do but die."

Chapter Eighteen

~~~

Dear Jory,

If you're reading this, it means you finally picked up my journal and found this letter I stuck in the back for your eyes only. It also means that I have probably died, because that's the only way you would have picked up the book in the first place. Sorry—just a bit of dark humor.

It's three o'clock in the morning here in the hospital and all I have is the beep from my monitor to keep me company. They say the transplant is working, but they still won't let me out of here. If I regret anything, it's that I had to spend my last days trapped in this place, when I'd rather have been at home. Anyway, I wanted to get this written while I'm lucid and sane (no smart aleck cracks, Jory!).

I know they say I'm getting better, but I don't think I believe them. I'm not giving up, but I'm not clinging to false hope either. You know, it's not death that's

149

so hard—it's getting there. Sort of like waiting in the dentist's office, knowing some horrible torture waits, only to think once it's over, "That wasn't so bad."

If I am dead when you read this, I hope that you're not all sad and weepy over me. Oh, I expect you to cry, but please don't get carried away. There's too much for you to see and do instead of crying over me. Go to the prom. Okay? And wear your cap and gown to graduation no matter how dorky you feel in it. I would have graduated, so make sure Mom gets my diploma and my tassel.

Kids don't make out wills, Jory. But I do have a few worldly possessions that I want you to have. Mom knows, because I've written her and Michael letters too. You get the program from the Springsteen concert. You got the autograph—and almost got trampled getting it—but you made me take the program. I want you to have it back. Also, keep the page from the coloring book little Rachael gave to me. I don't know why I've grown so attached to it, but I have. Maybe I understand what Cinderella must have felt like when she was having such a good time at the ball and heard the clock strike. She wasn't ready to leave, but knew she had to.

Of course, if there's any of my clothes you want, take them. And my barrette

and combs collection. I haven't worn any
of them since I lost my hair, but I couldn't
bring myself to throw them away. Oh,
take that stupid vase I made in seventh
grade crafts, the one I accidentally re-
corded my thumbprint on before it was
fired in the kiln.

Now to the serious stuff. Everyone's
going to say, "How sad that Melissa died
so young." I agree. There's a thousand
things I'll never get to do. I'll never graduate from college, have a career, get married, have a baby (back up! I forgot "have
sex"), watch my kids grow up, sit on the
Supreme Court bench, and grow old with
my husband. I was really mad about all
that for a long time. I wanted all those
things, and it stinks—really stinks—that
I have terminal cancer instead.

But Jory, I've had lots of time to lie
here and think this out. There were plenty
of things I did get to do. I saw the sun rise
and set over six thousand times, I petted
fuzzy little kittens and puppies, tasted
chocolate, smelled roses and gardenias,
and heard the ocean in a seashell. I kissed
Brad Kessing, and Ric kissed me and
made me feel all gooey inside and at least
invited me to go to bed with him—which I
was real tempted to do. Sometimes I wish
I had, but other times I'm glad I didn't.
This way, they can bury me in virginal

white with a clear conscience. Sorry, Jory, that's that black humor again. Keep remembering as you're reading this, it's three A.M. and Melissa is bored and alone, and trying to cram everything that's inside her into a few pages of a letter.

I want to clear another thing up with you too. I'm not mad at God anymore, like I was that night on the beach. I've had some heart-to-heart talks with Him and I've come to believe that He loves me enough to want me with Him in heaven. And that once I'm in heaven, I'll never have to die again. (Just think. I get to do something before you do, Jory Delaney!) We all didn't come into the world at the same time, so it makes sense that we all won't leave it at the same time.

You once told me, "Goodbye doesn't mean forever." You're absolutely right. I know I'll see you and Mom and Michael again someday. I know I will. But knowing still doesn't make leaving any easier. All of you will miss me. And you'll feel sad and that makes me sad.

Jory, I know you love Michael and have for years. I don't know how it will work out between you, but I hope that whatever the outcome is, you're happy. Don't forget to go do something with your life, no matter what happens between you and Michael. I've never known anybody like you, Jory. You have a million, zillion things going for you. You light up a room just by walking through the door, and people like you, really like you. And no matter what, you've always been my very best friend.

I guess I'm starting to ramble now and get mushy, so I'd better cut it off before my heart monitor sends out an alarm and the nurses come running. I think you know what I mean by all this stuff I've written.

Also, you don't really have to write anything in my journal, Jory. It's mine and it should start and stop in my handwriting. But please make sure to give it to Mom. I've written down a lot of things about my illness and my feelings about my illness in the book. Maybe the doctors can use it to help some other girl my age who gets cancer. Who knows?

Be good and have a wonderful life. Name one of your kids for me. And never forget me. Because as long as one person remembers you, you're never really gone. (Doesn't that sound deep?) One day, you'll be happy again, and so will Mom and Michael. Always keep in touch with each other. I'll be watching you! And when you least expect it, you'll hear me call you in the wind. I promise.

Love, your friend, your sister,
Melissa

Jory didn't know how long it took her to read Melissa's letter because tears kept filling her eyes. After she read it, she cried for a long time, then tucked it back inside the envelope and put it safely away in her drawer.

Jory stood before Lyle's front door, trying to muster the courage to ring the bell. "This is dumb," she told herself. "Why did you come?" She could have seen Lyle at school, but instead she'd gotten up early on Saturday morning, looked up his address in the phone directory, and driven over to his house. She couldn't even explain why.

His neighborhood was nice, with large ranch-style homes and clipped, manicured lawns. From the porch, Jory saw a wheelbarrow full of mulch and a lawn mower in one corner of the yard. It amazed her that everything around her could appear so tidy and neat, while inside she was feeling such turmoil.

"It's now or never, Jory," she muttered. She took a deep breath and pushed the bell. No one answered and she almost turned away when the door flew open. Lyle stood in the doorway wearing cutoffs and a tank top and a sweatband around his forehead. "Jory!"

"Is this a bad time?"

"No, it's not a bad time at all. It's a good time. I was just about to start on the lawn. Come in."

She followed him inside, glancing about rooms that were casual and homey, with a lived-in look of scattered pillows and a newspaper on the floor and a few coffee cups perched on end tables. He led her into a big, friendly kitchen painted yellow. Jory felt a sense of déjà vu.

"Sit down," Lyle said, pulling out a bar stool and shoving aside breakfast dishes on the counter. "Sorry the place is a mess, but Dad's out playing a few rounds of golf and Mom took my sisters to ballet class."

"I didn't know you had sisters." Jory realized there was a lot she didn't know about Lyle, and a lot she suddenly wanted to know about him.

"Yeah, eleven-year-old twins." He flashed a grin. "I call them Tweedledum and Tweedledee. It drives them crazy."

She looked around. The walls were covered with pictures and plaques and sprays of flowers. Papers, obviously schoolwork, were stuck to the refrigerator with tiny magnets. "Mom never throws anything away," Lyle said. "If I didn't hide my term papers, they'd be plastered all over the fridge too."

"I like it," Jory told him. "It looks like real people live here."

"Yeah. Well, after Mom was diagnosed, our whole family began to rethink its priorities. At the bottom of her list was kitchen floors you could eat off of. We do more as a family now too. We learned the hard way about what's really important, and the time we spend together tops the list."

An unexpected lump stuck in Jory's throat. "Could I have a drink?"

Lyle hit his forehead with his palm. "What's the matter with me? Sure. How about some root beer?"

"Sounds good." She watched him find a glass in the cupboard, fill it with ice, and pour a frothy head of root beer.

He set it in front of her and leaned forward on the counter, bracing himself on his elbows. "I'm really surprised to see you. I mean, you didn't say you might drop by at school. But I'm glad you came." Jory nodded, still unable to clear her throat enough to speak. "Uh . . . why did you come, Jory?"

A hundred things raced through her brain, and nothing made sense. She wanted to run out the door and drive off. She wanted to throw herself on the kitchen floor, kicking and screaming. She wanted to crawl out of her skin because she hurt inside so bad. She gripped the glass until her knuckles hurt, almost pasted a silly smile on her face, and slid off the stool saying, "No reason. Just thought I'd stop by and visit. It's been a while since I've visited friends, that's all."

Jory's face felt stiff and frozen, and she wanted to cry. "You said if I ever wanted to talk . . ." Her voice was so low that Lyle had to stand directly in front of her to hear her. She fell silent.

Lyle reached out and placed his hand on the nape of her neck and drew her gently to his chest. With her forehead on his chest, and his hand warm and soothing on her skin, she slowly relaxed and took a long, deep breath. He smelled of clean, fresh soap. She squeezed her eyes shut. "I . . . well, if you're not too busy . . . maybe we could talk right now. I'll understand if you're too busy. I know I stopped by uninvited . . ."

"Hey, it's okay. I've got time." His fingers played with her hair. "Believe me, Jory, I've got all the time in the world for you."

Chapter Nineteen

"Are you sure you're awake?" Michael asked Jory.

She stifled a yawn and wiggled into the corner of the cab of his truck. "I just forgot how early four o'clock in the morning comes. Want some coffee?"

He nodded and Jory poured him some from a thermos, being careful not to spill any as the truck moved along the dark, empty highway. She handed him the cup and cranked down the window. A muggy breeze flooded the cab. "It's going to be a long, hot summer," Jory observed. "It's only the middle of June and already I can feel the heat building for the day."

"You nervous?"

"About my first balloon ride?" She offered a wide smile. "Scared to death. What if I throw up?" The words evoked the memory of Melissa. Jory wished Melissa could have been with them. "You never told me why you wanted to take me up."

Michael sipped from the Styrofoam cup. "Melissa asked me to in a letter she left for me. It's just taken a while for me to get around to it. Do you mind?"

Jory understood. Michael would have done

158

anything for his sister. "It's been a busy time for all of us. What with graduation and all."

"It was nice of you to stop by dressed in your cap and gown. It meant a lot to Mom. Oh, and thanks for getting Melissa's diploma for us."

"No problem. She was a straight A student and made the dean's list—even if it was posthumously. She would have been pleased about the National Merit Scholarship too. I know how much she wanted it."

A line formed on Michael's mouth, as if the coffee had gone bitter. "I guess they gave it to someone else instead."

"A boy from Lincoln named Lyle Vargas. He's the guy who helped me on the day of the funeral when I almost fainted—do you remember him? Lyle wants to be a doctor." Jory smiled secretly. She'd been dating Lyle steadily since April. She remembered the night of the prom, when some of the gang had gone to the beach to watch the sun rise. Lyle had led her off alone. He'd rolled up the cuffs of his tuxedo, and they'd stood together in the moist sand with the cool water lapping over their bare feet, looking out over the dark, glassy sea. As dawn broke, Lyle had taken her in his arms, kissed her, and told her he loved her.

"So what are you going to do in the fall, Jory?"

She snapped back to reality. "Believe it or not, I'm going to college."

"I assumed you were," Michael said, puzzled.

"For a long time, I wasn't sure I even wanted to go. But after—you know—the funeral and all, well, I buckled down in school and suddenly I really wanted to work hard and go to college." She fidgeted with her hands. "Of course, I got a late start and my grades were pretty sorry, but I've been accepted at USF on academic probation. If I do well as a freshman, my parents said I could transfer to wherever I want to go."

Michael glanced over at her. "Any ideas where that might be?"

She thought of Lyle and how he'd been accepted at Duke. "Maybe someplace in North Carolina."

Michael turned the truck into a pasture and the ride turned bumpy. In the middle of the dark field, he stopped. Jory climbed out. A small group from the balloon club were already waiting, laying out their balloons and filling them with propane. "You want to help?" Michael asked.

"If I remember how," she said, scrambling to help him haul his balloon from the truck bed. They worked side by side without speaking. Jory stood back when the tank of propane was turned on for Michael's balloon. The nylon filled and rose lazily. Overhead, stars still twinkled although the horizon was turning gray.

When the balloon was filled and straining against its ropes, Michael offered Jory his hand. "Ready?"

Her heart thudded as she remembered all the times she'd longed to climb into the basket with him and sail off into the heavens. "Let's go," she said, taking his hand.

The basket rocked, and Jory gripped its edges as she found her footing. Michael adjusted the gas jets of the propane tank on board and called to the people holding the ropes, "Let her up!"

The ropes slackened and the balloon wobbled as they drifted upward. Jory watched the ground fall away, her heart in her throat. As the people and vehicles grew smaller, she felt a delightful floating sensation. "Oh, Michael! This is fabulous!"

She leaned out over the edge and Michael caught her arm. "Whoa! Not so far."

The balloon continued to rise, and Jory peered up at the sphere looming above. She wondered if she could reach out and pluck a star from the sky. "How high will we go?"

"Not too high. Things only get smaller the higher you go, and that's not half as interesting as just going up about a thousand feet and watching the world drift by."

She spotted the chase vehicle on the road below and it looked like a toy. Michael released a valve, and the balloon dipped toward a clump of trees. "What are you doing?"

"When we pass over the top of the trees, grab a leaf. It's good luck if you can snag one right off the top."

The basket skimmed the uppermost part of the trees. "This must be how a bird feels," she cried. How different a tree looked from the top. For the first time she was seeing the world from a unique perspective.

The basket brushed the treetops again. "Grab one!" Michael yelled.

Jory leaned out and the leaves fluttered, turning their soft undersides toward her. She felt as if they were clapping and she should take a bow. She snatched one from the very tip-top of the tallest tree and, laughing, clutched the fragile piece of green to her breast. "That was wonderful! Thank you, Michael."

He grinned boyishly, turned the jets higher, and the balloon once again soared upward. They floated, suspended between heaven and earth as the sky faded from indigo to gray-blue. "How long before the sun rises?"

"It's hard to say. You'll be drifting along and then suddenly, it's there. It's best if you can actually watch it pop over the horizon. But that's rare. Usually, it just turns from dawn into daylight."

Jory faced him across the compact basket, braced herself on the side of the gondola, and studied him. Wind ruffled his black hair and something stirred within her heart. When the blast from the gas died and only the soft hiss remained, she asked, "How have you been, Michael? How's it been going for you?"

He stared off to the horizon. "Some days are better than others. Sometimes I still can't believe she's really gone. It's like she's going to come through the door from school and throw her books on the table and yell at me for leaving the milk out or something." He dipped his head. "God, I miss her."

"I miss her too. Sometimes I think of something I want to tell her and I pick up the phone and get your number half dialed before I remember that she's not there."

"I'm still pretty mad about it," Michael confessed. "Why Melissa? Why her?"

Jory thought of what Melissa had written in the letter. *People will ask, Why Melissa?* She thought back to what Mrs. Austin had once told her, *"The rain falls on the just and the unjust."* Jory rubbed her palm along the rim of the basket. "We may never know the answer to that, but I think Melissa found some answers for herself. I have a friend, Michael, a guy whose mother had cancer. She beat the odds and recovered, but he had the same sorts of questions. His whole family went through counseling and I've talked with him a lot over the past months, and he's helped me understand some things."

Michael glanced at her, but said nothing.

"I was angry about Melissa's being sick for a long time. I even denied it and told myself that she'd be all right. When she came out of remission and had to go back to the hospital, I got depressed—so depressed, in fact, that I had symptoms myself. My heart beat faster. My palms sweated. Whenever I even *thought* about Melissa's dying, I actually lost control of my own breathing. That's what happened to me on the day of the funeral. I stressed out." Jory shifted and the basket tilted with her. "And I felt guilty, Michael. I felt so bad because I was perfectly healthy, and she wasn't.

Yet I didn't want to take her place. And that made me feel more guilty. Maybe that's why I worked so hard on the blood drive. I was trying to make it up to her."

A small knowing smile crossed Michael's mouth. He folded his arms over his chest. "I know all about guilt. It was my bone marrow, remember? But then when it started working, I thought, 'All right! This is it. She's home free.' But she wasn't, was she?"

Jory heard the pain in his voice and wanted so much to touch him. She clung to the basket. Michael Michael tipped his head and asked, "Do you know that when she was sick the last time, I was actually mad at her for not getting well? I'd done my share. Why wasn't she doing hers? I thought she was giving up."

"I don't think she gave up. I think she just came to accept death. There's a difference between giving up and accepting. If we're going to get over Melissa's death, we have to accept it, too, the same way she did."

Michael sighed heavily. "I'm not there yet, Jory. I've still got a lot to work through."

Jory nodded. "Me too. But every day it's better for me," she added.

"I'm glad you've found some answers for yourself. In her letter to me, Melissa said that you 'loved life and people too much to let either get you down for long.'"

The way he quoted it brought a lump to Jory's throat. "She wrote me a great letter too, Michael. I'll treasure it for as long as I live."

"I told you in the truck, Jory, that I brought you up here because Melissa asked me to. But I also brought you for a reason of my own."

Her heart tripped and she smiled shyly. "To throw me over the side?"

He returned her smile. "I guess it must seem that way to you at times. I was never very nice and I've wanted to say I'm sorry for a long time."

Surprised, Jory straightened. "I know I've always been Melissa's pesky little rich friend to you, Michael. It's no secret."

"You shared things with her, Jory, that I couldn't share. I was only her brother, but you well, you were her buddy. You two always seemed to have secrets, especially during her last visit to the hospital."

The notion that Michael had been jealous of their friendship stunned her. "Cripes, Michael, we were best friends and girls! Girls are like that. They just"—she hunted for the right words—"share things. But you were her brother and she worshipped the ground you walked on."

"You won't hold it against me?"

"I could never hold anything against you, Michael."

They stood staring at each other across the basket as it bobbed in the gathering morning light. Michael's face was awash in pink and gold, and his eyes had trapped the gold. Jory felt warm and content. She remembered the night she'd almost shared her body with him. Her feelings for Michael remained, but they had changed. She loved

Michael Austin, and a part of her would always love him. But Michael belonged to the sky, and to her childhood dreams.

Lyle, on the other hand, was like the earth— firm and solid and constant. Best of all, Lyle loved her, and she knew then, with the dawn inches from her fingertips, that she loved him too.

A gentle breeze blew, filling the basket and caressing Jory and Michael. It felt like silk against Jory's skin. "I feel like Melissa's here with us, Michael," she whispered.

"I know. I often feel like I'm in a cathedral when I'm up here. Like the earth's too small. Maybe that's why I came today and why I wanted you to come too. Maybe I thought the two of us together could touch her one more time."

Jory stepped next to him, and shoulder to shoulder they looked across the glowing heavens to where the curve of the horizon met the curve of the earth. The last clouds of night clung to the sky, then suddenly, the brilliant red-gold rim of the sun punched through them. Jory's breath caught at the sight and she felt an overwhelming sense of joy. She said, "We're going to make it, Michael. All of us are going to make it just fine."